Belonging

By

Teresa LaBella

This is a imprint of 4Wurdz Press
Caledonia, NS, Canada

Author's Web site www.storyteller30.com
4Wurdz Press www.4wurdz.com

Alistair buried his troubles in finishing the workday's required chores.

In the moments before twilight, he climbed to the highest point on his property, listened and tried to imitate Robbie's expert whistles directing the black and white fur flash of border collies herding livestock. He searched the horizon over rolling hills of spring green and imagined her there, running toward him ahead of the advancing fog blanket. He spread his arms, tilted his handsome face to heaven, and let the anguish flow from his soul in a mournful cry.

"Where are you lassie?"

The whispered reply, carried on a rare puff of warm wispy breeze, echoed in his ear.

"I'm here. I'll find you."

Reader reviews

"A terrific book with marvelous characters and just the right amount of steam and humor."

"Marisa has the talent to be a top-rate chef like her father but isn't able to follow her dreams to go to New York and conquer a place in her father's former restaurant. In fact, her dreams lead her further afield. Her adventures in Scotland reveal a different path for her to find healing and love." Mary Davidsaver, author,

Clouds Over Bishop Hill

Books by Teresa LaBella

Romance
Reservations
Heartland
Belonging
Tales from Heartland

Romantic Suspense
The UnMatchables Case #1: Danger Noted

Acknowledgements

To my husband John, the wearer of many hats and bearer of several titles – photographer, designer, cover artist, publicist, research assistant, head cheerleader and best friend.

My heartfelt thanks goes out again to Linda Cook, Lucinda Resnick and Nancy Senn, colleagues and friends who devoted time and talent to the editing process that made these books possible.

Most of all, to my readers who told me they needed "Belonging." This book and every story that I write is for you.

Dedication

To Indie Authors everywhere pushing pens and chasing cursors to realize a dream.

FIFTEEN

Chapter 1

Marisa McKenna stood inside the doorway to her mother's home studio, long fingers clenched into fists planted firmly on her hips. Steel grey eyes the mirror image of her father's smoldered. Midnight black hair as Darien McKenna's had once been brushed her squared shoulders.

"What are you doing?" Marisa scolded her sister seated cross-legged on the hardwood floor. The door to the room's seldom-used closet stood open. A banker's box marked 'Brooklyn' was missing its lid.

Rachel McKenna didn't look up from the photo album in her lap. "That's Dad. But who's this?" Rachel pointed a polished pink fingernail at the smiling woman wearing a wedding dress. "She's a lot shorter than Mom and she's got brown hair." Rachel flicked a honey blonde ponytail over her shoulder and squinted blue eyes at the digital image on the page. "Her eyes are brown, too."

Marisa covered her curiosity with a threat. "You are in so much trouble. Don't think I won't tell Mom you were snooping in her stuff."

"This isn't her stuff," Rachel shot back.

"No, it isn't." Both girls jumped at the unexpected sound of their mother's voice.

Rachel slammed close the photo album and put it back in the box. "I'm sorry, Mom."

Miranda McKenna's emerald green eyes flashed. "Don't apologize to me. Everything in that box belongs to your father. Apologize to him."

When her husband called to tell her he'd be late getting home after his last class at the community college, Miranda locked the door to her art studio and gallery in Harmony an hour earlier than the usual closing time. She'd hoped peace and quiet in the family's Iowa farmhouse meant her daughters were busy studying for end-of-school-year exams. The scene witnessed from the second floor hallway caught Miranda off guard. She counted to ten twice to regain her composure before entering her violated space.

Miranda's long strides on ballet flats slapped the hardwood floor. She took the lid from her daughter's hand, put it back where it belonged and lifted the box to the shelf where Darien had stored it fifteen years ago, three months before Marisa was born.

She closed the closet door, turned and glared at her daughters. "Don't you both have something better to do? Like homework?"

"Yes, ma'am."

The girls walked, head down, shoulder-to-shoulder, out of the room and into the hallway. Marisa shoved Rachel toward her bedroom at the opposite end of the hallway, stuck out her tongue, and rounded the corner into her own open bedroom door on the right. "I can't wait until Daddy gets home," she muttered and threw herself across the width of her queen-sized bed.

Darien breathed in the sweet, familiar scent of his wife and stroked her copper-colored hair. His fingers followed the luscious length of it over the soft mound of her breast under cool white cotton. He traced the contour of her, curved in all the right places, deliciously damp between her thighs through the sheet that covered her. He sealed his lips over hers, parted them with his tongue, and moaned when she teased his erection with her soft fingertips.

Darien loved and desired Miranda more than he'd imagined possible. Sixteen years and a shaky start to love and marriage nearly a year after a night of unleashed passion between friends conceived Marisa, he still couldn't get enough of her.

He peeled back the sheet to reveal and revel in her naked body next to his in the bright early morning sunlight. He caressed her soft breasts and raised nipples, opened her legs wide and tasted her, slid the length of him inside her, and joined her in the pure pleasure of mutual climax. He held her, breathed with her, shared the warmth of intimate afterglow.

"Darien. I've got something to tell you."

He nuzzled and kissed her soft neck. "You're not pregnant, are you?"

"Of course not."

"Is Sam?" Samantha "Sam" Grady, his veterinarian sister-in-law and mother of three, had threatened to castrate her wide-eyed husband Trevor during the labor and delivery of their now seven-year-old twin sons.

Miranda laughed. "I think Trevor wants to keep his balls." She rolled on her side and propped her head on plumped pillows. "The girls got into the box you brought from Brooklyn. I caught them red handed when I got home. Rachel recognized you in the photo album. I overheard her ask Marisa about the woman in the wedding dress."

Darien exhaled an audible breath and lay back on his pillow. "What did you say?"

"Nothing. I put the box away and told Rachel she needed to apologize to you."

3

Darien sat up, swung long legs over the side of the bed and ran his hands through thick black hair salted white. The spring breeze through the open windows carried the scent of lilacs, Ali's favorite fragrance, blooming in the garden below. "What should I tell them?"

"That's up to you." Miranda got out of bed and crossed the floor to the walk-in closet. She slipped into and tied her robe around her. "Pandora is literally out of the box." She sat beside him on the bed, kneaded and rubbed the knotted muscles in his shoulders and neck with her fingers and palms. "You can't avoid it any longer. You'll have to tell them something, love."

The routine drive along the highway to Harmony from the community college where he spent three afternoons each week teaching culinary skills to future chefs gave Darien time to consider how much he would tell his young daughters about his life before Iowa. The SUV took him down Main Street, past Harmony Drug, Doc Sam's veterinary office and Hank's Longhorn Café where lunch at the counter on a stool next to Miranda started the improbable chain of events that had changed his life.

Rows of newly-planted corn and soybeans lined up along the last stretch of road to his driveway. Darien parked the car and grumbled at the uneven shrubs along the front porch that needed his attention. He pulled mail from the box and turned the key in the lock. Scooter's gleeful butt wiggle greeted him on the other side of the door.

"Hey, old boy." He scratched the senior schnauzer behind the ears, closed the door and walked through the entryway, past the staircase and into the kitchen.

The box marked Brooklyn was on the table with a note from his wife taped to the side. "Good luck. I love you," it read. He dropped the mail and removed the lid on memories lovely, poignant and painful. He lifted the book with images of love vowed on a long ago evening in August and remembered the last time he'd opened its pages.

He felt good at the start of the day before. The former executive chef at Chez Nous in Manhattan's upper west side couldn't explain or admit to himself at the time why he had made an offer and bought the farm. Months of massive renovations brought the century-old homestead back from the crumbling brink. All skilled trades involved with finishing jobs well done had been paid in full with money to spare. Darien's inflated feelings of accomplishment abruptly collapsed in a torrent of tears and emotional agony he'd held at bay for a full calendar year since Ali's death.

Alison Clarke McKenna, the lovely love of his life, the sophisticated, sexy, successful older woman whose chocolate-brown eyes distracted his days and haunted his nights until he found her weeks after a love-at-first-sight charity gala encounter. The love they'd made that first night together ignited a blazing passion that doubts fueled by age difference reservations could not extinguish. The couple in the wedding pictures loved and lived their happily-ever-after until the dreadful afternoon a drunk driver swerved his speeding vehicle over a Long Island highway's center line and took her from him.

Darien spent that night paralyzed in pent up grief, huddled on the front room floor of the farmhouse with the white Husky he'd rescued from imminent euthanasia and named "Ivory." He tore into and through every unpacked box the next morning in a frantic search to find photos of her. He'd turned the pages of the wedding album, reliving every detail of that day and the eight years after with Ali. Weeks later, Miranda announced their one night of sexual inhibitions released by wine and his ragged emotions and burning physical need to be with a woman again had impregnated her. He'd emptied his wallet, promised her future financial support and taken the box and all his East Coast possessions back home to Brooklyn.

But he wasn't at home there anymore. He belonged in Iowa, on the farmstead he'd purchased for the woman whose beauty, love and strength of spirit sparked the hope he'd lost to love again.

He sat at the head of the table in the same ladder-back chair he'd dropped into when Miranda shared the reality that eventually brought him back to her. Now he had to find the words to tell his story to his teen-aged daughters. Help them understand. Let them know he loved them and their mother more than life itself. He closed his eyes, composed his thoughts, and waited for his girls to come home from school.

Chapter 2

Sam brushed sweat-soaked blonde bangs from her damp forehead. "Thank God for air conditioning." She popped the top from a can of store-bought frosting and dipped a pastry knife into the buttery confection tinted pink, her niece's favorite color. She glanced out the McKenna kitchen window overlooking the backyard and apple orchard beyond and began to decorate Rachel's birthday cake with swirls of icing and 14 candles.

Miranda closed the refrigerator door with her hip and nodded in agreement. "I could have cried when the game went into extra innings. At least Rachel's team won."

"She sure can turn the double plays," Sam remarked. "Wasn't this her first season at shortstop?"

"Yup. She was in the outfield last year." Miranda set bowls of potato salad and cole slaw on the long kitchen table covered by a red and white checkered tablecloth topped with nine plates, cups, forks, spoons and napkins. She peeled off the cling wrap that had protected the food stored in the fridge and stuck a wooden serving spoon in the mounds of sliced, diced and seasoned potatoes and cabbage.

Sam stepped back from the counter away from the cake and admired her work. "What do you think?" she asked her sister.

Miranda walked around the end of the table, studied the cake for any fixable imperfections, and nodded her approval. "Looks good." She leaned her elbows on the counter, looked out the kitchen window and smiled at the late summer afternoon scene in progress and play. Sam's husband Trevor tossed a baseball back to his oldest son over the heads, outstretched arms and hands of his bouncing twin boys and squatted catcher-style to take another pitch. The tall brawny boy with the buzz cut under his cap thumped the ball in his leather glove, stepped off an imaginary pitcher's mound and fired the ball into the mitt his father wore. The force of ball hitting glove could be heard through the closed pane of glass.

"My Jacob has a good arm, too," Sam observed and signaled a 'thumbs-up' to her 12-year-old son. "He pitched an impressive game Thursday night. Only allowed two hits in nine innings."

"Our Dad would have been so proud of his grandbabies." Miranda's attention turned to her husband supervising their daughter flipping burgers on the grill. Marisa followed her father's instructions in wrist-snapping maneuvers from plate to grill and back again, testing the meat in between for table readiness with stabs from a thermometer's probe. "Who knew we'd raise ballplayers and a chef."

Sam squeezed her sister's forearm. "Are you sure this trip to New York is such a good idea?"

"Yes, I am." Miranda's green eyes communicated confidence in the decision she and Darien made regarding Marisa's apparent need to know more about the big city life he'd left behind. "It's what Marisa wants."

"Why isn't Rachel going? Her softball season is over and school doesn't start for weeks."

"She doesn't want to go. She couldn't wait to get back home after her Grandpa Stewart's funeral. She complained the whole time we were gone, said she hated the big city."

Sam's blue eyes narrowed in concern. "Mira, what do you and Darien hope this will do for Marisa? I mean, exactly what will being where he lived and meeting the people from his old life accomplish?"

Miranda watched her husband and daughter move in unison preparing the family dinner together. "Closure, Sam. That's what I want for both of them."

The back porch screen door slammed shut and the door to the

kitchen opened to admit a pair of pint-sized red-haired tornadoes. Sam intercepted and stopped their spinning advance toward the table. "Keith! Kevin! Wash your hands first!" she commanded and steered them to the kitchen sink.

Trevor kissed his wife, reached for the soap, rinsed off his and two sets of smaller hands and grabbed paper towels from the roll on the counter's wood dispenser spool. "OK, guys dry your hands and take a seat."

"But no eating until everyone sits down," Sam ordered.

"Yes ma'am." Darien placed a heaping plate of burgers in the center of the table between a bread basket filled with wheat buns and a lined-up regiment of condiments in plastic squeeze bottles.

"I'm starving." Jacob dropped in his chair and stared at the plate of burgers in front of him. "Are they all cooked the same?" he asked his cousin.

"The ones on this side are well done." Marisa pulled out her chair and sat next to Jacob. "The ones on the other side are medium well. The medium rare burgers are on top."

"Ooo, can I have a redder one?" Keith asked his mom seated between him and his twin.

"No, you cannot," Sam answered and opened burger buns on her young sons' plates.

Trevor plopped potato salad on the plate of the twin to his left and did the same for himself before sitting down. "Where's the birthday girl?" he asked.

Miranda sat in her usual place at the end of the long table and spread a napkin across her lap. "She went upstairs to take a shower."

Darien carried pitchers of lemonade from fridge to table and called up the stairs to his daughter. "Rachel!"

"Coming!" The slap of flip-flops on the hardwood steps preceded her appearance. Darien pulled out the chair at the head of the table for her. "But this is your place, Dad," she protested.

"It's your day, honey," he said, kissed her cheek and took the last vacant chair at the table beside Marisa.

Hunger conquered all but necessary conversation until the plates were cleared and the candles lit on Rachel's birthday cake. She grimaced, pretended to cover her ears during the off-key group Happy Birthday chorus and blew out the candles with one big breath.

"Great game today, Rach," Jacob complimented her between forkfuls of his second piece of cake.

"Thanks," she said. "I'm kinda glad the season is over."

"Well, it ended with a big win," Trevor remarked.

"Yeah, I guess." Rachel poked her fork at a glob of scraped off icing. "Good luck at state, Jake. Maybe one of us will take home a trophy this year."

"Are you coming to the game?" Jake asked her.

"Wouldn't miss it," she said, grinned at Miranda then frowned at her sister. "We'll be there, won't we Mom?"

Marisa frowned back. "I am not going to punch your guilt trip ticket."

Trevor took his turn to frown. "Excuse me, but did I miss something?"

"Darien and Marisa are leaving for New York City tomorrow," Miranda explained.

"We'll be gone for a whole glorious month," Marisa crowed. "Dad's promised to take me shopping for school clothes in Manhattan!"

"That takes a month?" Trevor teased.

Darien grinned. "I hope not. My wallet couldn't take it. We'll be spending some time with my Mom. She moved to a senior community near my brother and sister-in-law in New Jersey after Dad died. Jack wants me to help him go through stuff in storage that came from my folks' brownstone in Hoboken."

Rachel snorted. "That sounds boring."

"Not as boring as spending the rest of the summer in Iowa," Marisa shot back.

"OK, that's enough," Darien warned. "It's your sister's birthday."

Rachel pushed away from the table and stretched her arms over her head. "I'm going to stay in bed until noon and have the house to myself."

"Oh no, you won't," Miranda said. "You'll be at the studio with me."

Marisa chortled in triumph at her sister's shocked expression. "What? Why?" Rachel whined. "I'm 14! I'm old enough to stay home alone!"

"Because I'm your mother and I said so," Miranda began.

Sam interrupted her sister's scold and Rachel's retort. "You could help us out, Rachel. We need to hire a sitter for the rest of the summer."

Jacob bristled and his blue eyes opened wide. "I do NOT need a babysitter!"

"You want to look after your brothers?" Trevor asked his oldest son. The twins giggled and squirmed. Jacob looked down and shook his head. "I didn't think so."

"You'd earn your own spending money," Sam continued. "You and your mom and I could make a day of it in Des Moines before school starts. Get our hair done, a manicure and a pedicure. What do you say? Is it a deal?"

Rachel glared at her sister in a gesture of mini-triumph and nodded. "Sure," she said.

Chapter 3

Darien closed the front door on his daily walk and scratched behind the ears of his hiking companion.

Three winters past, he'd opened the door to the shaggy grey schnauzer mix huddled on their front porch, shivering beneath layers of matted and frozen fur. Darien wasn't surprised that no one claimed the malnourished mutt with no microchip. He tried to find the dog a home. Darien wasn't ready for another pet so soon after he'd buried the ashes of his white Husky under a tree in the orchard they'd patrolled together for thirteen years. But he gave in to his daughters' tears and pleas. Rachel christened the dog "Scooter" due to the dog's need to find relief from what ailed him by scooting on his backside. Under Sam's expert care, Scooter recovered, grew strong, flourished in the love of his new family and took his place at Darien's side pacing out the family's fourteen-acre farmstead.

He turned and nearly tripped over the lineup of luggage. Only one of the six bags packed to travel in the belly of eastbound jets to Newark belonged to him.

He glanced at the mantle clock over the fireplace along the far wall of the spacious front room and groaned. "Get a move on, ladies!" he bellowed up the staircase. Footsteps overhead scattered in patterns from bedrooms to hallway and converged at the top of the stairs.

Flush-faced Marisa bounced down the steps ahead of Miranda and Rachel. The shifting contents of her backpack unbalanced her when she bent to grab the first suitcase. Marisa tumbled to the hardwood floor to the howling delight of her sister and clucks of concern from her mother.

Darien helped his oldest daughter regain her dignity. He gestured over the line of luggage. "Is all of this really necessary?" he asked her.

"Dad, we're going to be gone a whole month!" she protested.

13

Darien scratched his head. "Did you leave anything behind?"

Rachel snorted. "Only the stuff she doesn't care about."

Marisa whirled around and pointed an accusatory finger at her younger sister. "Well, if you weren't so nosy."

Miranda stood between and towered over her daughters. Her stiff body language and warning stare commanded attention. "Rachel, promise your sister you will not go into her bedroom while she's gone."

"I promise," Rachel mumbled.

"Marisa, I want you to take what you think you need with you. But what stays here will be safe at home until you get back."

Darien put his arm around Marisa's shoulders. "Can you lighten the load a little, honey?" he asked.

"I guess." Marisa dropped and unzipped the bloated backpack, pulled out two pair of shoes and a wad of magazines, slung the backpack over her shoulder and picked up a large suitcase. "OK. I'm ready to go."

Bags were checked and tickets stamped at the terminal two hours later. Marisa hugged her sister and held back tears as she held on tight to her mother. Rachel clung to her dad and turned her back to him at the last boarding call so he wouldn't see her cry.

Miranda touched her husband's cheek and her eyes filled with tears. "I'll be sleeping alone tonight for the first time since I moved in with you."

Darien cradled her face in his hands, brushed the tears from her cheeks, and pressed his lips to hers until the last moment. "I'll be back," he told her.

"I know." She took his hands in hers and backed away from him. "Now go," she said, "before I change my mind and beg you to stay."

Chapter 4

Marisa amazed Darien. He'd anticipated high anxiety during his daughter's first flight and fear at every jolt of turbulence. Instead, he marveled at her delight when the climbing aircraft broke through heavy gray overcast to crystal blue sky and grinned at her preoccupation with the array of beverage choices from the attendant's rolling stainless steel cart.

Darien dozed off somewhere over Indiana. The pressure and squeeze of Marisa's fingers on his forearm woke him in mid-descent. "Dad, we're here!" She strained against her seat belt for a better view of New Jersey and skyline of the great city beyond.

The last McKenna family residents of the Garden State and a uniformed sky cap employee of Newark International Airport greeted Darien and Marisa at the eastbound flight terminal destination. Darien hugged his older brother Jack, kissed his sister-in-law Beth, told her she hadn't aged a day and meant it, and fretted over the frail appearance of his mother in a wheelchair. He bent and kissed her hollow cheek.

Donna cradled Darien's face in her aged hands. "I can walk, just not as fast or as far as I used to," she assured him, winked and tilted her head toward the sky cap behind her. "Besides, this young man looked like he needed some exercise."

The middle-aged man smiled, touched and tipped his cap. His round face and double chin hovered above the elderly woman's shoulder. "If I get tired, we'll change places and you can push me, ma'am," he said.

Donna grinned and reached out to her granddaughter. She grasped Marisa's hands as tightly as she could. "You're so beautiful, child. So much like your father."

Jack groaned. "Yeah, I've always been D's ugly brother."

Darien laughed and mussed the thinning equal parts gray and sandy hair on his brother's head. "Yeah, but we had to keep you."

Their mother sighed and clucked her tongue. "Oh, you two," she muttered and commanded the sky cap forward toward the baggage reclaim carousel.

An uneventful drive to Montclair and family chatter preceded dinner at the dining room table in the home Jack and Beth moved into the day after their wedding. Photos of passage featuring daughter Hannah and son Nathan in childhood poses, graduation caps and gowns, wedding dress and tuxedo hung alongside a portrait of Hannah's family on the wall opposite the kitchen.

Darien marveled at the memories and passage of time. He whistled through his teeth when his gaze focused on the family photo. "I remember the New Year's Eve when you told me you were going to be a grandpa."

"Yeah," Jack said, "the same night Miranda told you she was pregnant with Rachel."

Darien smiled. "That's right, it was. So Hannah and Evan have five kids now?"

"Yup. Beth just got back from the land down under. She was there for Katrina's christening. Hannah swears this baby is her last. While we're on that topic, have you talked to Nathan lately, D?"

"I called him last week to congratulate him on his latest bestseller. I think he said this spy thriller is his twelfth novel."

Jack nodded. "It is. He's got me beat by eleven. Apparently my son the university professor is a writer, not a lover. His mother is afraid that we've celebrated the birth of our last grandchild."

Beth nudged Jack with her hip and set a steaming side dish of green beans on the dinner table. "He just hasn't found the one." She sat at her usual place near the kitchen and spread a checkered celery green and white cloth napkin across her lap. "I haven't given up hope."

Conversation flowed through wine with the main course and coffee with dessert. Donna's lips pursed when her granddaughter sampled both beverages.

"Dad says a good chef tastes everything," Marisa explained.

Donna grinned. "Oh, I see."

Jack's eyebrows arched to his receding hairline. "So you couldn't talk her out of following in your footsteps?" he asked Darien.

He shook his head and smiled at his daughter. "Not yet."

"Dad promised to take me to Chez Nous and show me the kitchen where he was chef." Marisa's flushed cheeks framed a spreading grin. "Then we're going to the markets and delis and Little Italy and Chinatown and …"

"Whoa, that itinerary is wearing me out!" Jack turned to his brother. "When are the two of you planning to do all this? Need I remind you there are a couple storage units full of boxes and most of that stuff belongs to you."

"I know. I didn't forget. We'll tackle that first," he said to Jack and nodded at Marisa, "and then we'll go to the city, sweetheart."

Marisa's smile dropped to a frown and her shoulders slumped. Donna folded her hands in her lap and leaned over her empty pie plate. "Marisa, I need help putting the rest of my things away in my apartment. Would you like to spend a day or two with me?" She winked at Darien. "I've hardly used that new kitchen."

Darien dropped his daughter off at his mother's front door in the gated senior community at mid-morning the next day. Donna welcomed her granddaughter with a pot of green tea and a recipe for gingerbread muffins. Marisa gathered the ingredients from her grandmother's pantry and combined all that was called for in a brown ceramic bowl with thick edges trimmed gold. Stirred batter

17

dropped into the paper-lined cupcake pan baked to sweet-smelling perfection in the 375 degree oven. Marisa squeezed the juice from a lemon into a small mound of powdered sugar and added a splash of half-and-half from the fridge for a tangy glaze to spread and drizzle over the spicy muffins.

"My goodness," Donna crooned and reached for seconds. "I've been making gingerbread muffins since I was a wee girl in my gram's kitchen. Neither hers nor mine ever tasted this good."

"I followed the same recipe. Dad says you have to in baking. I get to experiment with the icing."

"So did your Dad. He begged me to let him make his own birthday cake when he was only eight years old. I stayed with him in the kitchen, of course. I knew when he ignored the canned frosting and started tossing sticks of butter in a mixing bowl that he would work in a kitchen." Donna poured them each another cup of tea. "Sweetheart, you can be whatever you want to be. Why do you want to be a chef?"

Marisa shrugged and sipped her tea. "I've watched and learned from Dad since he caught me whisking dirt in one of Mom's flower pots."

"You like cooking with your Dad."

Marisa nodded. "Yeah."

"It's your special time together. Just the two of you."

"Mom helps sometimes."

"What about Rachel?"

Marisa snorted. "Rachel would rather hang out on a dusty old ball diamond than be in a kitchen."

Donna settled in the ladder-back chair she'd brought with her from her home in Hoboken and fingered the ivory lace tablecloth covering the matching wood table. "Will you still want to be a chef in another kitchen?"

Marisa stared at her grandmother. "What do you mean?"

"Is it the work you like? Or do you like the work because you're with your Dad?"

Marisa blinked. "I-I don't know. I hadn't thought about that."

Donna smiled into steel-grey eyes identical in color with the son she'd adored since his birth. "You will and you'll know." She flattened her palms against the table for balance and pushed off to rise on arthritic knees. Marisa moved to clear the table. "Leave that for now, dear. Come with me. I've something to show you."

Marisa followed Donna across newly-installed flat tan carpet suitable for walkers and wheelchairs, past upholstered arm chairs and the living room television to the apartment's only bedroom. Donna sighed on her way down to settle on the sunny yellow comforter of her double bed and search through the contents of the open drawer of her night table.

"Ah, here it is." Donna opened a hinged black box and reverently lifted a piece of jewelry from its white satin resting place. "Your grandfather gave this to me on our wedding night." She raised the piece to her lips, whispered "I miss you, Stewart," and handed the brooch to Marisa.

Three lions' heads with glittering emerald eyes adorned a green shield divided by silver fess swirls. Marisa turned the brooch over in her hands, feeling its weight and a curious vibration. "It's beautiful. What is it?"

"That is the McKenna family crest," Donna explained. "Stewart's grandfather Gavin McKenna brought it from Glasgow. It's been in the family for generations. And now it's yours."

Marisa gasped. "Why me? Why not Uncle Jack or Dad? Or Nathan?"

Donna curled her fingers around Marisa's and the brooch she held. "The brooch passes from father to daughter, mother to son. Gavin gave it to Stewart's mother. She gave it to Stewart. We didn't have a daughter. Hannah married and left for Australia before we could give it to her. When you were born, we decided that the brooch belonged to you." Donna hugged her granddaughter and held her close. "Take it, my special one. Keep it safe and close to your heart. It will help you find your way."

Chapter 5

Darien guided his daughter through an urban world he'd cherished in another lifetime. The thump and grind of city rhythms pulsed and wheezed around them in the subway and on the streets of New York City. Marisa's eyes squinted in the glare of Times Square and widened at the glamorous temptations that beckoned her in to Manhattan's myriad fashion centers. He shrugged and smiled as the choices she pulled from store racks grew to small mountains, nodded approval at the swirling image of her in coordinated and accessorized layers, amazed at the lovely young woman his child had become.

Hours later, surrounded by several bags and parcels of purchases, Darien dropped into a chair outside another dressing room and tapped a Brooklyn number into his cell phone. David Dupuis answered. "Well, hello, stranger!"

Darien laughed at the genuine delight in his longtime friend's voice. "Please tell me there's room at the inn for a tired dad, his daughter and a butt-load of stuff."

David laughed in response. "Been shopping, have we?"

Darien groaned. "You better believe it. We may need two taxis, one for us and another for the bags."

"The two-bedroom apartment on the second floor is ready and Wong's is waiting for me to call in the takeaway order."

"Man that sounds great. I'm hungry enough to eat Peking Duck."

"I'll sound the three course alarm," David replied.

The shimmering reflection of Brooklyn Bridge lights danced in the taxi's backseat window. Marisa pressed her forehead against the cool glass. "Where are we going?" she asked her father.

Darien took a deep breath, closed his eyes, and let the memories wash over him. "Where I used to live."

Marisa sat back and crossed her arms over her chest in an outward sign of inner pout. "I figured we weren't going back to Uncle Jack and Aunt Beth's when you made me put underwear and PJs in my backpack. And I saw you buy boxers, socks and a shirt. But I thought we were staying in New York."

"Brooklyn is in New York. I told you it's one of the five boroughs, remember?"

Marisa snorted in disgust. "But it's not Manhattan." Her frown deepened with Darien's laugh.

"Relax," he said. "We'll go back to Manhattan tomorrow. I want you to meet some old friends." The cab rolled to a stop at the curb in front of the four-story brick-front building on Water Street. Darien paid the fare, emptied the trunk of its cargo, and opened the door for his daughter. Marisa stepped onto the sidewalk, slung her backpack over her shoulder and scooped up an armload of packages. "It looks like an office building," she said.

"It is at street level," Darien explained. "The other floors are apartments." He turned a key on a chain with a silver heart-shaped charm in the lock. The door opened to a hardwood staircase. Marisa followed her father up two flights and down a well-lit hallway to another door opened by a second key on the chain. Her jaw dropped at what was on the other side.

The sprawling living space with high-end furnishings and finishes flowed to a kitchen equipped to satisfy a chef's demands. Marisa kicked off her shoes and sank her toes into the plush area rugs cushioning the walk across polished hardwood floors. She ran her fingers along the kitchen's massive quartz-topped island and peeked past an open bedroom door on her left. She flopped and rolled in the comfort of the California king sized bed, and propped on her elbows to see what wonders lay beyond the open door on the opposite side of the large room.

"My very own bathroom!" She bounced off the bed and tested the taps in the double sink vanity and jetted tub with shower. Her Dad's voice and another she didn't recognize drew her back toward the apartment's front door.

"Darien! It's been too long!" The other voice belonged to a middle-aged man almost half her Dad's well above average height bearing bags of takeaway from a place called Wong's.

"It's good to see you, Kenny." Darien motioned Kenny toward the kitchen and bear-hugged him once the bags were stowed on the island. "How's business?"

"Business is good both at the firm and at the restaurant. Can't complain." Kenny turned toward Marisa. "Life goes on." He glanced at Darien and winked. "Who is this beautiful young lady?"

"This is my daughter, Marisa."

"She sure is." Kenny smiled and nodded at the pile of shopping bags. "Welcome to New York."

Marisa giggled. "Thank you."

"Well, you're probably both pretty hungry and I've got to get back to the restaurant. See you tomorrow?" he asked Darien.

"Plan on it," he said and walked Kenny to the door.

Marisa set places at the island with plates and silverware from cupboards and drawers and filled glasses with ice water from the fridge. Darien pushed the knife and fork aside for the preferred chopsticks his daughter was too hungry to try. They devoured the contents of containers from the takeaway bags, dumped the remnants into the trash and loaded the dishwasher.

"I see you've already claimed the biggest bedroom." Darien tried to hold the scold but his smile gave him away. "I'm teasing you. Both bedrooms are the same size."

"But do they both have bathrooms?" Marisa teased back.

"As a matter of fact, they do."

Marisa sank into the brown leather sofa cushion next to her father and sighed. "I wish we could stay here forever."

He curved his arm around her shoulders. "Here in New York or here in this apartment?"

"Either. Both."

"I doubt if your mother and sister would agree. We're a family. We belong on our farm in Iowa."

"Dad, you said you used to live here. Did you mean in this apartment?"

"I lived in this building in the top floor apartment," Darien hesitated and summoned the strength to continue, "with Ali. The woman you and Rachel saw in the wedding pictures. My wife."

"Dad, you told us about her. You said that you met Mom after your wife died in a car accident."

Darien nodded. "That is true." He looked into his daughter's eyes, so much like his own. "Honey, what else do you want to know about my life here and with Ali? Before I met your mother?"

Questions she'd held in poured out. "Why did you leave New York? And why did you go to Iowa? How long was it after Ali died that you met Mom? I mean, I know I was born before you got married and I'm OK with that. But how long were you and Mom together before, well, you know ..." Marisa stifled a sudden yawn. Her father did the same.

24

"Look, we're both tired. Let's talk about this tomorrow."

"OK." She picked up her backpack and kissed his cheek. "Goodnight, Dad."

"Sweet dreams, sweetheart." He waited until the door to her bedroom door closed, turned out the lights, got ready for and into bed. Her questions ricocheted behind the burn in his closed eyes.

Images of the women in his life consumed brief pockets of fitful sleep. His mother in a fuzzy pink robe and slippers spooned steaming oatmeal into his favorite blue china bowl on a frosty winter morning. Beth careened with clipboard in hand between reception area tables decorated to identical perfection at the botanical garden where he'd married the love of his life. Hannah, grown up and radiant in white lace, walked down the aisle on Jack's arm. Rachel turned another double play on a dusty ball diamond beneath the blazing Iowa sun. Miranda, heavy with Marisa, coaxed peaks of whipped egg white finishing touches on a lemon meringue pie. His arms circled her and he felt their child move under palms he pressed to her belly. "I don't know what to tell her," he whispered in Miranda's ear.

Miranda's long copper hair turned chocolate brown and he breathed in the scent of lilacs. The petite woman he held wore a red dress. She turned in his arms and looked at him through eyes the color of her hair. "You'll find the right words, my love," she said. "She's stronger than you think. She's part of you."

"Ali! Oh my beautiful love. I've missed you so much!" She disappeared when his lips touched hers. The hard slap of waking reality and the smell of bacon dragged him back to twisted sheets and damp pillows in the here and now.

Glasses filled with orange juice, knives, forks and napkins waited on placemats expecting plates. Darien sat on a stool at the kitchen island, rubbed his eyes fully open and smiled at his atypical teenager who rarely slept in. Marisa grabbed a spatula to turn bacon sizzling in a pan on the stovetop. "Careful of the grease splatter," he warned.

"I know how to cook bacon, Dad," she replied without looking up or over her shoulder. She covered her hands in mitts to reach into the oven for a pair of symmetrical folded omelets on plates. Bacon and biscuits, browned and warm, complemented the egg dish served.

Darien tasted the omelet and nodded approval. "How long have you been up?" he asked.

She poured coffee brewed by the hissing espresso machine on the counter and set the cup in front of him. "An hour, maybe two." She sat on the stool next to him and picked up her fork.

He sipped coffee for courage to clear and center his thoughts. "Marisa, I .."

"So what are we doing today?" she interrupted him.

"Well, I thought we'd catch lunch here in Brooklyn, check out the markets in Little Italy and Chinatown and then I'll take you to dinner in mid-town Manhattan. How does that sound?"

Marisa grinned and her eyes sparkled. "I'd like that!"

After breakfast clean up and a long luxurious soak in the jetted tub, Marisa made her wardrobe choice from the bags of clothes bought in New York. Satisfied, she walked down the hall to her father's closed bedroom door. His voice within stopped her knock on wood.

"We haven't talked about it yet. I know we agreed. That's the whole point of this trip. I miss you both. Give Rachel a hug. I love you, too." A second conversation began seconds later. "Eric Lanahan, please. Eric? Darien. How's it going? Yeah, I'm in the city. I'm bringing my daughter Marisa to dinner at Chez Nous tonight. We'd like a table with a view. Seven o'clock? Thanks, man. See you then."

Chapter 6

David stood on the other side when Darien opened the apartment door for Marisa. The thin man wearing jeans and a rolled-up sleeve work shirt held a screwdriver in his hand from the tool belt around his waist like an exclamation point behind the big grin on his face. "Handy man."

Darien laughed. "Nothing needs repair here."

"High praise from the absentee landlord." David stowed the tool in his belt and the men hugged in a back-slapping embrace.

Marisa's almond-shaped eyes widened to round. "Who's this, Dad?" she asked, "and what does he mean by absentee landlord?"

"Oh my God! Is this Marisa?" David stepped back and grabbed his chest. "What a beauty!"

Darien nodded. His hands rested on his daughter's shoulders. "Marisa, meet my good friend and the building manager, David Dupuis. He and his family own the top floor apartment."

"Correction, you own the building. Jayson and I pay the mortgage. Josh and Alicia are our much loved and privileged tenants."

Marisa's mouth dropped open. "You own this building, Daddy?"

Darien sighed. "Well, yes, your mother and I do. I sold the apartment upstairs to David and Jayson and the main floor office to the owners of the business before you were born."

"Sorry," David apologized. "I didn't mean to …"

"It's OK, man," Darien assured him. "Are all of you going to be there at lunch?"

David smiled. "Wouldn't miss it." He stuck out his hand and kissed the hand she offered. "Pleasure meeting you, Marisa." The hardware in his belt jangled with his spirited walk down the hallway and jog up the stairs on electric pink sneakers.

Marisa looked at her hand and back at Darien. "Why did he do that?"

"That's David." Darien locked their apartment door. "C'mon, sweetheart. I've got a few more old friends for you to meet."

Marisa followed her father downstairs to street level. After taking a few steps to his right, Darien opened the glass office door for her. "First stop in Brooklyn," he said. Kenny Wong greeted them on the other side.

"Didn't you bring our dinner last night?" Marisa asked him.

Kenny laughed. "Yeah, the restaurant is my night and weekend job. This is my day job," he explained. He ushered them past the front desk and called through the open door of the inner office. "Hey, Mimi! Look who's here."

A slender well-dressed woman of color rose from her place of managerial power behind a sleek executive desk of glass and stainless steel. She stepped around the desk and into Darien's outstretched arms. "Darien! It's so good to see you!" Her cheek rested against his chest despite her four-inch high heels. She stepped back and looked him up and down. "You're as handsome as ever!"

He laughed. "The years have been good to you, too, Mimi." He reached out and touched Marisa's elbow. "Marisa, this is Mimi Teague."

"Mimi Morales since last summer," she corrected him.

"Congratulations!" he said and hugged her again.

The large oil portrait on the wall behind Mimi caught and held Marisa's attention. The artist's detail in the painting nearly brought the beautiful woman to life. "That's Ali," she said and turned to Mimi. "Was this her office?"

Mimi nodded. "Yes. She was my boss and my friend."

Marisa moved closer to the painting. "What was she like?"

Mimi stood beside Marisa, raised her gaze to the image, and smiled. "She was the kindest person I ever met. Strong and tough in business. Caring and giving to her friends and the people she loved. She gave me a job and a chance when nobody else would. She paid my son's way through college." Mimi sighed. "I would have moved heaven and earth for her. But I would have had to wait in line with all the other people whose lives she touched."

Darien cleared the lump in his throat. "Wong's at noon, Kenny?"

"The back room is reserved, my friend."

Darien guided their walk along the East River past the fenced dog park to a bench with a panoramic view of the Manhattan skyline. Darien pointed to the plaque of dedication on the bench backrest, worn but still shiny and legible.

"From your brown-eyed girl, all my love, Ali," Marisa read. She looked down at the engraved paver near her feet. "Who's Max?"

Darien sat on the bench and patted the place next to his with his palm. Marisa sat and waited for a response.

"Max was our dog or rather he was Ali's dog when I met her. She rescued him from a shelter." Darien smiled at the memory of the shepherd-mix mutt meeting him at the door after midnight on New Year's Eve with a leash in his mouth and a gaudy party hat on his head. "He was a good dog."

"Dad, why did you leave New York after Ali died?"

"I had no reason to stay."

"What about your job?"

"Ali and I had given up our careers to be together for the rest of our lives. We were going on a long second honeymoon, travel the world, revisit all the places we'd been and everywhere we hadn't but wanted to see together. She was killed on her last day of work, the day before we'd planned to leave."

"Oh, Daddy, that's so sad." Marisa choked back a sob and hugged her father.

"Yes, it was, baby." He kissed the top of her head and held her tight. "But if I hadn't lost Ali I wouldn't have found your mother and we wouldn't have you and Rachel."

"Why did you go to Iowa?"

"I didn't plan on it. I had time on my hands, too much time. I just started driving west with no destination. Then I met your mother and Harmony seemed like a good place to start over." He checked his watch and squeezed his daughter's shoulder. "One more stop in Brooklyn."

"Then we go back to Manhattan?"

He smiled, stood, took her hand. "I promise."

Early afternoon passed in a flurry of introductions and faces new to Marisa. Kenny's family welcomed, served, and reminisced with guests gathered to honor Darien and meet his daughter. Chef Yoshi Wong blushed at the long and loud round of applause in appreciation for the opulent spread they enjoyed.

Mutual protests and groans of embarrassment from their children didn't deter proud parents David and his husband Jayson Denning from sharing photo galleries of the toddler brother and his infant sister they'd adopted. Alicia posed in her princess costume at Halloween. Josh clutched a Spider Man backpack on his first day of school. Family vacations through the years on the Jersey shore. Josh clad in cap and gown stood proud and tall at his recent high school graduation.

Mimi more than matched them with photos of her Yale-educated son Alex, pediatrician daughter-in-law and her three grandbabies living in Boston.

Marisa answered questions about her family and life in Iowa in neutral brushstrokes of candid conversation. Alicia and Josh spoke freely of their struggle to be accepted as children of color adopted by a Caucasian couple and the joy of being loved by parents who just happen to be gay.

"I hate to break this up," Darien said, "but Marisa and I have got just enough time to check out the Manhattan markets before we meet another good friend for dinner." After hugs all around, a walk back to the subway station and a rapid ride in the metal car on squealing rails landed Marisa in the middle of sensory overload on crowded streets and in shops and delis rich with aromas of ethnic food and gastronomic curiosities. Another subway connection to Columbus Circle ended at the convergence of Central Park and the gleaming glass retail and restaurant hub of Darien's distant past.

Chef stepped through Chez Nous' door into a world he'd left behind, recognizable yet completely changed.

"Welcome to Chez Nous, sir." Darien thought the gangly host looked too young to legally work. "Do you have a reservation with us this evening?"

"Darien!" Eric's red hair had grayed a bit at the temples and the creases were deeper around his eyes. But to Darien, the owner appeared much as he had when he'd hired him as sous chef thirty years before.

"Hey, Eric, business looks good." Darien hugged the man who'd traded chef whites for a suit and tie.

"Yeah, but the best table in the house will always be reserved for you." Eric nodded toward Marisa. "Looks like you've lost your dinner date."

The stunning view of Central Park pulled Marisa toward the restaurant's bank of full length windows. Bustling kitchen activity behind the panes of glass to her left changed her course. Her eyes followed line cooks preparing orders in assembly-line fashion, pastry chefs dodging the vigilant sous chef while the executive chef conducted the players in his culinary orchestra.

"Can I help you, miss?" The mustached sommelier held a bottle of rare vintage in one hand and a corkscrew in the other.

"She's with me." Darien stood beside his daughter.

The flustered sommelier snapped to attention. "Chef Darien! Je vous demande pardon!"

"Il n'est pas un problème," Darien replied. "This way, mademoiselle." Darien directed his wide-eyed child to her seat and table above the teeming traffic below.

"You were executive chef here?" she squeaked.

He nodded, scanned the menu and ordered for them both. "The guy you ignored when we came in is the owner. Eric was my sous chef."

"I'm sorry, Daddy," Marisa mumbled.

"Apology accepted." Eric appeared at their table. He grinned at Marisa. "May I?" he asked and pulled out the chair next to hers.

"I guess so. I mean, sure. It's your restaurant," Marisa grinned back.

"Indeed it is. And from what I've seen, you're impressed and impressionable."

"I want to be a chef in a restaurant like this one."

Eric's eyebrows arched up. "Really? No talking her out of this, Chef?"

Darien shrugged. "I've tried. Give it a shot. Maybe you can."

Eric leaned back in his chair. His gaze swept the establishment where he'd sharpened the skills of his chosen career and invested every dollar he'd saved on a razor-thin profit margin gamble. "It's a hard life. Low pay for long hours and a lot of grief."

"Dad says you were his sous chef."

"That's right."

"And then an executive chef?"

Eric glanced at Darien before responding. "Yes."

"Now you own this restaurant."

Eric sighed. "I think I know where this is headed. But what's your point?"

Marisa folded her hands on the table and stared him down through eyes set in a determined expression wiser than her fifteen years. "If it's such a hard life then why didn't you do something else?"

He studied Darien's daughter, contemplated his response. "Good question. The answer is I couldn't see myself doing anything else. When you can honestly say the same about yourself, come see me." He stood when the appetizers were served. "Always good to see you, Chef," he said to Darien. "Bon appétit, mon ami. Belle demoiselle."

COMING OF AGE

Chapter 7

Marisa forced her shaking fingers to rip open the envelope. She held her breath and unfolded the letter, both afraid and anxious to read the words on the page.

"Well?" Rachel stood in front of her sister, fists folded on her hips. "Did you get in or not?"

Miranda wiped her damp hands on a tea towel and stepped away from dinner preparations in the kitchen. Darien set his briefcase beside the front door he'd closed. Marisa read the letter a second time and gave it to her father.

"You're such a drama queen!" Rachel whined and whirled toward Darien. "What does it say?"

Darien scanned the message printed on Culinary Institute of America letterhead, nodded to his wife and smiled at Marisa. "Congratulations, honey. You've been accepted to a place where I've never been."

"I wouldn't be going there if it wasn't for you, Dad," she said. "You've taught me so much."

"You've got so much more to learn, more than I can ever teach you," Darien replied. He handed Miranda the letter that opened the door to their daughter's future.

She tapped a sentence on the page with her fingernail. "It says you must complete an externship before you can enroll on campus."

Marisa nodded. "I have to work in a non-fast food restaurant kitchen before I can take classes," she explained. "I knew that when I applied."

Rachel snorted. "I guess Hank's Longhorn Café doesn't qualify."

Darien laughed. "No, but Chez Nous certainly does."

Marisa backed away from Darien, her eyes open wide. "Daddy, you didn't!"

He shook his head. "I did not. Eric called me and asked if you were still serious about being a chef. I told him you'd applied and he said he'd do what he could to help you get in."

"So what should I do? Call Eric now?"

"You've only just got the letter. You can't take a job in New York until after high school graduation," Miranda reminded her daughter.

Marisa's chin dropped to her chest in realized disappointment. "I know."

"Enjoy the rest of your senior year, sweetheart," her father said. "This time will never come again."

Later that night, long after dinner's leftovers had been safely stored, Miranda heard the refrigerator door open. She stuffed a bookmark at the opening page of chapter seven and left the world of cozy mystery, cushy sofa and radiated warmth from the fireplace to catch the late night kitchen culprit.

Darien closed the fridge and opened a cupboard. "Having a late night snack, my love?" she asked him.

"Doing inventory." He counted spoons in drawers and pots on the overhead rack. "OK. We're good to go."

"Do you mind telling me what you're doing?" Miranda asked.

"Mise en place. I'm prepping for Marisa's reality check."

Miranda pursed her lips and shook her head. "I still don't follow." Worry surfaced at the sadness she noticed in his eyes and the dark half circles underneath.

"She needs to know what she's getting into. I'm going to show her."
He put his arm around his wife's waist and walked with her to the
stairs. "It won't be pretty and I won't enjoy it." He turned out the
kitchen lights. "But it has to be done."

Darien searched his closet for a set of chef whites rarely worn
since he'd ruled a Michelin star kitchen in Manhattan. He slipped
into the persona with the uniform, flipped on every overhead and
recessed pot light to chase away the dreary gloom of January and
rechecked his kitchen for the ingredients and culinary tools necessary to prepare hollandaise sauce. Chef Darien stood at the island
where he'd prepped and served countless family meals and waited
for Marisa to come home from school.

She blew through the front door with the winter wind, hung up her
coat and stomped snow from her shoes. "Hey, Dad," she greeted
him. Marisa crossed hardwood into the kitchen, dropped her backpack onto the seat of the nearest ladder-back chair at the kitchen
table, and frowned at his stern expression. "What's up?" she asked.

Shivers spiked down Marisa's spine at the deep hard edge timbre
in his voice. "Tonight's featured entrée is roasted salmon with fresh
asparagus." His steel-grey gaze shifted to the saucepan on the six
burner stove. "Hollandaise."

A nervous giggle escaped her. "You're kidding, right?"

Her Daddy was gone. The ogre that had replaced him growled
again. "In the kitchen the appropriate response when you speak to
me is 'Yes, Chef.' Darien checked his watch. "I expect perfection in
fifteen minutes." She didn't move. The intense cold conveyed by his
eyes chilled her to the bone. "You're wasting time."

Marisa swallowed against the lump in her throat. She tied an apron
around her waist and opened the refrigerator door.

"Wash. Your. Hands." Darien commanded.

Marisa scrubbed her hands clean under warm tap water and ignited a gas flame beneath a burner on the stove. She melted butter in a saucepan and lowered the flame to keep the butter warm. She set the bottom half of a double boiler on a separate burner, dumped in enough water to heat without touching the top half of the pan, and lit the flame. A small pan of lemon juice warmed over a third burner. Marisa's trembling hand above the double boiler whisked water and lemon juice into yolks separated from whites. Lumps of scrambled eggs quickly ruined the sauce.

Darien dumped the overcooked eggs into the sink. "Again," he barked over the grinding sound of the garbage disposal.

Eggs broke, water and juice splashed and the whisk churned through four more attempts. Each time Marisa got close to the desired smooth result, the eggs congealed again and Darien tossed her imperfect sauce in the sink. Marisa cracked another trio of eggs from the carton and whisked the mixture frothy to thick. Liquid butter fell from the spoon and fizzled on the burner's heat.

Darien extinguished the gas flame with a flick of his wrist and glared at his flustered apprentice. "Clean up. We're done here."

Marisa fought against the rising threat of tears as she filled the dishwasher and wiped down counters and stove under Darien's silent critical inspection. When she thought she couldn't bear another indignant minute, she scooped up her backpack from the chair where she'd dropped it and slung it over her shoulder. "You are so mean!" she shouted at her father. Her stomping footsteps echoed up the stairs and down the hall to solitude behind a slammed bedroom door.

Miranda abandoned her painting in mid-brushstroke at the sound of muffled sobs in the room next door. She knocked on the door and called out to her distressed daughter. "Marisa, sweetheart, what's wrong?" She turned the knob, slowly opened the door and stepped over the discarded backpack on the other side. Marisa lay on the bed hugging the pillow she'd burrowed into. Miranda sat next to her, smoothed strands of silky black hair, and softly rubbed her daughter's heaving back and shoulders.

"He didn't even try to help me!" Marisa wailed.

"Who didn't try to help you?"

"That .. that horrible man you married!"

Miranda ceased her comforting touch in mid-stroke. "What did you say?"

"You heard me!" Marisa rolled over, sat up and crossed her arms over her chest. "I know how to make hollandaise sauce! But he made me so nervous. I screwed up so many times I lost count! He just kept throwing it down the sink and made me start over! He was so ... mean!" Her lower lip quivered and a fresh flow of tears streamed from puffy blood-shot eyes.

In his office and retreat below the drama being played out overhead, Darien slumped in the worn wingback chair of his long-ago mentor and friend. He sighed and braced for angry backlash when he heard the slap of his wife's footsteps in the hallway and down the stairs. Miranda stormed into her husband's sanctuary. Her green eyes blazed above cheeks flushed fire engine red. "And just what was that all about?" she demanded.

He spoke without looking at her. "If she can't take it from me, she'll never make it in a New York kitchen. She has to learn to stand up for herself when she's right and admit when she's wrong."

Miranda circled around him and dropped into the closest cushion on the black leather sofa. "Did you have to make her cry? Was that really necessary?"

Darien reached for her hand. She started to pull away from him. But the dark shadows under his eyes, deeper than the night before, stopped her. Her fingertips caressed smooth skin covered by the cuff of his chef's coat.

"I'm not sure this is what she really wants." She strained to hear and understand his barely audible words weighted with raw mixed emotions. "I want Marisa to find her own way, not just follow mine. I love her too much to let her make that mistake."

Miranda searched for words she hoped would reassure him. "She's always been a foodie. Buck says she's a natural. And she loves preparing our meals with you."

Darien groaned. "You don't understand because you haven't lived that life. I have. And I won't be there with her. Slinging hash in Harmony is nothing like working the line in mid-town Manhattan. It's grueling, brutal." He leaned back, let the chair enfold him, and closed his eyes. "I'm afraid the pressure will break her."

Miranda felt his fear and loved him all the more for it. She snuggled into his lap, kissed his eyelids, traced the line of his handsome face with her fingertips and savored the joy of a tender kiss. "I can't even think about her leaving us. But I know we have to let her go. We're strong. We have to believe she shares our strength. She's a part of us. We made love and made her."

Darien grinned. "Yes, we did." He nuzzled his wife's neck and slid his hands beneath her sweater. The clasps of her bra separated at his easy touch and freed what he desired. He cradled her breast in his right hand and rolled a raised nipple between wandering fingers. His left hand unzipped her jeans, parted and fondled her inner thighs. Miranda moaned and sighed ragged breaths. She wriggled out of his embrace, stood and held her arms out to him. A curled finger beckoned him. Her sultry femininity aroused him. "Come with me to our bed, my love," she purred. "I want what's cooking under those chef whites."

Chapter 8

Marisa excused herself from dinner because of an upset stomach caused by a severe headache. She lay in bed on her back and stared at the ceiling of her dark bedroom until the house was quiet. Glowing digits of the alarm clock perched on her bedside table marked three minutes into a new day. She got up, crossed round shaggy rugs tossed on hardwood, and pressed her ear against the closed door.

Silence.

The knob turned easily in her hand. The door hinges made no sound. Marisa knew that nothing short of blaring bagpipes would wake her sister. The door to her parents' bedroom at the top of the stairs was closed. Marisa tiptoed down the hallway and stairs and across the great room floor.

"Shhh, Scooter. It's me." Marisa scratched the senior mutt behind the ears. Scooter grunted, circled, and flopped back into orthopedic canine bed comfort beside the fireplace. Marisa side-stepped through the semi-open pocket doors leading to the room her father had designed for his personal space.

Moonlight sifted by enclosed porch screens filtered through dark wood slatted blinds that concealed a long row of thermal windows set in the east wall of the farmhouse. The massive mahogany desk housed a laptop computer and files of papers for Darien's eyes only. All were welcome to curl up on the black leather sectional's cushions. No one but her father sat in the ancient wingback chair. Custom built cupboards and shelves covered walls opposite and behind his desk. Marisa coaxed recessed lights over the shelves behind the desk to low setting illumination and began the search for a title among the cooking texts and cookbooks.

"Yes!" She hissed in triumph mid-way through the second shelf. "Le Guide Culinaire" slid from its place of honor into her hands. She hoped her father wouldn't notice her attempt to fill the gap with another title or worse yet need Escoffier to teach class the next day. Marisa adjusted the lights from dim to darkness. Her bare feet barely touched the stairs and wool rug runner down the hallway. Back in her room behind her closed door, she snapped on the bedside light, opened the revered culinary bible and studied ingredients and technique needed to replicate the five mother sauces of French cooking.

"Feel up to going to school today sleepyhead?" Darien stood over his daughter prone in her bed buried under a blanket, her head sandwiched between pillows.

Marisa came up for air and yawned. She squinted at the bedside clock. "What time is it?"

"Quarter past eight. I can drop you off on my way to the college." He brushed back long damp strands of hair from her cheeks and gently flattened the palm of his hand against her forehead. "Or I can call you in sick."

Marisa rubbed her eyes for sympathetic affect. "Would you please, Daddy?"

Darien smiled and kissed her cheek. "Sure thing, sweetheart. I'll see you later." He covered her with the rumpled blanket and closed her bedroom door behind him. Marisa waited for the sound of car tires on gravel. She did a happy dance at her bedroom window when the tail lights of her father's SUV disappeared down the main road. She showered, dressed and retrieved Escoffier's guide from its hiding place beneath her bed. "You and I have work to do," she said aloud to the book tucked under her arm. She skipped down the stairs leading to the kitchen that she prepped for a day of culinary conquest beginning with béchamel.

Darien opened the farmhouse front door at quarter past four. He set his briefcase against the wall, shook off the cold with his coat and glanced toward the kitchen. "Marisa?" He made his way to the island where his daughter stood, hands folded at her waist over her apron. "Looks like you've recovered." He scanned the residual disarray of pans, pots, bowls and utensils piled on counters, stovetop and stacked in the sink. Five glass bowls lined up like soldiers on the quartz surface. A companion silver teaspoon rested next to each bowl. His eyes narrowed. "What have you been up to?"

"The five mother sauces of French cuisine presented for your critique, Chef." She stepped aside and handed him the first spoon. "Velouté." Darien dipped the spoon and raised blended flour, butter and chicken stock past his lips. "Béchamel." Identical perfection prepared with milk instead of stock rolled from the spoon to his tongue. "Hollandaise." Marisa had conquered the recipe she'd struggled with just 24 hours before. "Tomato." Peeled tomatoes, butter, onions and salt balanced simply with a subtle hint of basil. "Espagnole." Rich meat stock, butter and flour browned to roux with vegetables, tomato paste and herbs merged strong and ready for any red meat entrée.

Darien stifled a groan with each spoonful. Feelings of delight, pride, envy and fear bubbled like a caldron in his belly. "Nice work," he acknowledged. He retraced his steps to the front door and grabbed his briefcase. "Oh, Marisa." He turned back and grinned at her body language change from fist pump and happy dance to rigid good soldier stance.

"Yes, Dad? I mean, yes Chef?"

"When you're finished with Escoffier, put it back please." He strode through the great room and into his sanctuary. The pocket doors slid closed.

"Damn it!" Marisa pounded her fist on the island. The bowls and spoons clattered across the quartz.

Miranda sensed another confrontation had taken place between Darien and Marisa. Dirty dishes rattled in the dishwasher racks. Peels and egg shells spilled from the garbage pail. Marisa's cheeks were redder than the sauce she'd dumped in the sink.

"Are you feeling better, honey?" Miranda asked.

"I'm fine!" Marisa snapped. Hot water steamed from the gushing tap stream.

"Where is your Dad?"

Marisa pointed a soapy whisk toward his office.

Miranda pushed a single pocket door partly open to gain entry. "Darien?" Her husband stood with his back to her silhouetted against natural light and shadows dodging through the window panes and blinds. She went to him, wrapped her arms around him and felt a deep sigh escape his lungs.

"I've known chefs that studied with the best, tried for years to do what Marisa taught herself in our kitchen in one day." He shook his head. "I fucked up those sauces more times than I could count before I even came close to getting them right."

She pressed her cheek to his shirt. "You want to bring me up to speed on what happened?"

Darien turned around in her arms and her knees went soft. After almost eighteen years of marriage, her indescribably handsome 62-years-young husband still took her breath away. "Our daughter conned me so she could stay home and make the five French mother sauces to prove she could do it. And she did. They were perfect. First time scary perfect."

"We both know doing it right once is all well and good. The challenge comes with doing it again."

He rested his hands on her shoulders. "Let me explain it to you in terms you'll understand. What Marisa did would be like an art student sitting down at a canvas for the first time and replicating Van Gogh's "Starry Night" to the brushstroke."

Miranda's eyes opened wide. Her jaw dropped.

"Yeah. Like that," he said.

"What did you say to her?"

"Not much. Good job or nice work." He dropped his arms to his sides and slumped into the wingback chair nearby, his head in his hands. "I'm still not convinced this is what she wants. But I know now that she can do it. She doesn't need me anymore."

"That is pure bullshit!" Miranda glared down at him, hands balled to tight fists on her hips. "I was only a year older than Marisa is now when my dad died. I worked three jobs to keep a roof over our heads and made sure Sam went to university. I miss my Dad every day. I still need him. Marisa will always need her Dad. Now cancel this pity party and go tell her how proud you are of her."

Darien looked up at her, pushed up from the chair and kissed away his wife's pout. "Yes ma'am."

"Excuse me." Marisa stood on the other side of the open pocket door. "Here's your book." She stepped through, set Escoffier on the edge of the massive desk and turned to leave.

Miranda blocked her exit. "I'll go make dinner." She nodded to Darien, winked at Marisa and left them alone behind the closed pocket doors.

Darien sat in his wingback chair, feet flat on the floor, arms at rest. "Sit with me, sweetheart. Let's talk."

Marisa perched on the edge of the sofa's leather cushion nearest her father, hands folded in her lap.

"Did I ever tell you how and why I became a chef?" Darien asked.

His daughter shook her head.

"The kitchen is my comfort zone." He rubbed his jaw and laughed low. "Crazy, isn't it? The stress, the drama, the pressure to be perfect fed my soul. I knew it from my first day as a dishwasher at a diner in Hoboken to my first sous chef job in Manhattan." He patted the arms of the wingback with his palms. "That's when I went to work for the man who owned this chair. He taught me to respect the food, to follow the science exactly when I baked and experiment when I cooked. He gave me the direction, the tools and the confidence I needed to take over my own kitchen and earn that Michelin star. Getting there was worth every sixteen-hour day on aching knees and swollen feet, late nights working out a recipe until the sauce was just right, going in to work on a couple hours sleep and doing it all over again. Chef was all I ever wanted to do, everything I wanted to be."

He leaned back in the chair. "Yesterday I showed you the dark side of who I am, or rather who I was. Because I accepted nothing less than perfection from myself, I expected it of everyone in my kitchen. Turnover was high. Those who stayed, like Eric, toughed it out and learned from me because they wanted to be me. They were like me." Darien's grey eyes searched hers. "I don't want you to be like me, Marisa. I want you to be who you are, do what you want to do. You've got the talent to be a chef. But that's not enough. You've got to have the desire, the passion, the grit to get there or the stress, the drama, and the pressure to be perfect will eat you alive."

Marisa didn't flinch or turn away. She stared into her father's eyes and spoke from the heart. "I don't know what else to be. I can't be anything else but a chef."

Conflicting pride and fear mirrored in his eyes and smile. "Then be the best, sweetheart. You've learned from me. I know you can."

Chapter 9

Darien piloted the SUV through rush hour traffic across the Brooklyn Bridge down once familiar streets to park behind the building where he'd lived a lifetime ago. "We're here." He reached over and patted Miranda's white-knuckle clenched fist. "You can relax now, love."

Miranda exhaled and opened her eyes. "I'd never get used to that."

"That's why the city has subways and trains. I didn't own a car when I lived here."

"Ugh!" Rachel grunted from the backseat behind her mother. "I don't see why anybody would want to live here. I can't wait to get back home!"

Marisa unsnapped the seat belt, opened the back door and bounded into the sunlit mid-summer steam. Savory smells of meals grilled, fried and taken away, shouts from players in a pick-up basketball game on a court across the street and the whirr of an activated freight elevator heightened her excitement.

David cranked open the elevator's mighty steel doors. "Howdy neighbor!" He kissed Marisa's cheek and hugged Darien. "How was the trip?"

"Awful!" Rachel muttered. "I don't know why I had to come along."

"To help your sister settle in," Miranda reminded. "I apologize for my daughter's rude behavior,"
she told David.

"Sweet Maureen O'Hara!" David lifted her hand to his lips and kissed each blushing cheek. "You're even more beautiful than Darien described."

"Gross!" Rachel rolled her eyes and locked crossed arms over her chest.

Marisa scolded her younger sibling before her father could. "Rachel, what is your problem. Stop being an ass!"

47

"That's enough from both of you!" Darien demanded.

David laughed. "Ah, the joys of parenting. Jayson and I have been playing good dad, bad dad to Josh and Alicia since they've been out of diapers." He winked at Rachel. "And we wouldn't change a minute of it." He clapped his hands together. "OK, let's grab some boxes and get this vehicle unloaded!"

Rachel held her sister back from the unpacking and dropped her voice to a hoarse whisper. "Is Jayson another man?"

"Yes, Iowa child." Marisa snapped. "David and Jayson are married."

"And Josh and Alicia are ..."

"Their family."

Boxes and luggage travelled from ground level to the third floor apartment Darien and Marisa had shared during their visit three years before. David invited the family to have dinner with his family one flight up in their top floor home. Marisa helped Alicia put finishing touches on salads and side dishes in the well-appointed open-concept kitchen. Rachel followed Josh carrying a heaping plate of Jamaican jerk chicken to sear and sizzle on the rooftop garden grill.

David guided Darien and Miranda through rooms divided to accommodate their children. "We took the front bedroom but kept the ensuite bath and walk-in closet for us," David explained. "The master bedroom was so big. We put up walls and gave Josh and Alicia their own rooms."

"You moved the French doors to the walk-in closet," Darien observed.

David nodded. "Yes, we were a bit selfish there, too. Besides, the kids needed separate doors for privacy."

"Is this where you and Ali lived?" Miranda asked Darien.

He nodded. "That was a long time ago."

She forced a smile. "It's lovely."

"Something smells good." Jayson's arrival ended a semi-awkward silence.

"Well it certainly isn't you," David teased his partner.

"Give me a break. I've been shuttling bolts of fabric around a hot city all day long." Jayson shook Darien's hand and kissed Miranda's cheek. "Excuse me," he said and headed for the shower.

Rachel bounced into the room ahead of Josh and the plate of chicken wings, breasts and drumsticks he carried. "Mom, you've got to go up on the rooftop! It is way cool up there!"

"Maybe after dinner, sweetheart." Darien pulled out a chair for his wife from the long dining room table and joined Marisa and Alicia in the final preparations.

David sat across from Miranda. "Go ahead, lovely lady. Ask away."

"Oh, was I that obvious?"

David squinted blue eyes and grinned. "Very."

Miranda glanced down at the laced fingers in her lap. "Darien told me he met you through Ali."

"Yes and no. Ali was the dearest friend I ever had. She lived and worked here and was a chronic workaholic. I got her to go with me to an event where Darien was one of the celebrity chefs then tricked her into dinner at Chez Nous. So I guess you could say I introduced them."

"How long have you lived in New York?"

"A long time. I was a starving couch surfing food stylist when Ali hired me to help her renovate this building even though she knew I knew nothing about construction project management." David leaned his elbows on the table. "But that's not what you really want to talk about is it, Mom?"

The apprehension and sadness behind Miranda's smile had given her away. "I'm worried about Marisa. She's a small town girl with big city dreams. We're dropping her off on your doorstep, two thousand miles away from home, and leaving her here with strangers."

David reached across the table and opened his hand palm up. Miranda grasped it. "I'm a parent, too. I'm not going to insult you by saying I know exactly how you feel. But I do have a pretty good idea. Marisa won't be with strangers. She's with friends. We're her extended family and we'll look out for her as if she were our own. I promise."

Miranda brushed away a tear and squeezed David's hand. "Thank you."

Darien brought a bowl of tossed greens to the table. He glanced between his wife and friend. "Everything OK?"

"Yes, love, everything is fine." Miranda took the bowl from her husband and set it in front of her. Main dishes arrived on oval serving plates and in bowls passed after Jayson joined them at the table.

"How was your day, Dad Jay?" Josh forked a second helping of chicken legs and thighs onto his plate.

Jayson wiped his mouth with his napkin. "Good, very good in fact. I picked up two new clients today."

"No bridezillas, I hope," Darien teased.

Jayson laughed. "No, I rarely design wedding gowns anymore.

Mostly executive's wardrobes, celebrities walking the red carpet, that sort of thing." Jayson's look of palpable pride acknowledged his daughter. "I couldn't get all the work done without Alicia. She is so talented."

Alicia's long eye lashes fluttered over dazzling green eyes set above chiseled cheekbones. Her smooth milk chocolate skin flushed from the neckline of the tan tee she wore to the black curls that swirled around her face. "I do my best," she said.

"She's in the top of her class at Pratt Institute," David bragged, "and Josh has been accepted into the MSW program at NYU."

"Tell my Mom and Dad what you told me about why you want to be a social worker," Rachel prodded him.

A gentle smile spread across the fine-featured face of the handsome young man of color. "I want to help other children find a home where they are loved and belong like my sister and I."

"Good for you, wanting to do good," Miranda said to Josh, "and what an impressive accomplishment Alicia. Congratulations."

"So Marisa, when do you start class at the culinary institute?" David asked.

"Next semester. I have to work in a real restaurant first," she explained. "I start at Chez Nous on Friday."

David's blue eyes twinkled. "Second generation at the old stomping grounds, eh Darien?"

Darien shook his head. "I had very little to do with that. Marisa impressed Chez Nous' owner. Eric offered to help her become a chef. The rest was and is up to her."

"That calls for a toast." David raised his water glass. "To the future Chef Marisa!"

Chapter 10

Miranda spent the next day unpacking boxes in Marisa's apartment. She fussed over clothing hung in her closet and folded in drawers, the placement of family photos on her dresser and nightstand and the need for a more colorful shower curtain.

"Mom, I'm only going to be sleeping here. I'll be at the restaurant most of the time. Tell her, Dad," she pleaded.

"She's right, Miranda." His arm around her shoulder guided his wife to the front door. "Why don't we go down to the market and stock her shelves and fridge?"

"Thank you." Marisa silently mouthed words of gratitude.

Rachel wheeled her packed suitcase from the bedroom she temporarily shared with her sister. Marisa eyed the suitcase. "You're not leaving until tomorrow morning."

"I left out what I need. I can't wait to go home."

"You're just jealous because I am home."

"Hah! There's no way I'd stay here."

"Not even to be with Josh?" Marisa delighted in her sister's visible squirm. "I knew it! You've got a crush on him."

"I admit he's cute." Rachel's freckles disappeared with the wrinkle of her nose. "But not that cute."

Marisa grabbed her keys. "Then you won't mind if we ask him to go out with us for ice cream."

Rachel shrugged her shoulders. "If you want to." She changed her mind when Marisa scampered through the open apartment door. "No! Wait!"

"Too late!" Marisa shouted over her shoulder from the top floor landing. She knocked on the door. Sounds of footsteps and deadbolts sliding signaled someone was at home.

Josh stood on the other side of the open door. "Marisa." Rachel trotted up the last step. "And Rachel." His dazzling smile showed white teeth, dimples and genuine delight.

Marisa nudged her sister forward. "Go ahead and ask him."

Rachel nudged back. "It was your idea! You ask him!"

Josh looked amused. "Ask me what?"

"Rachel wants to get to know my neighbor."

"I never said that!" Rachel glared at her sister.

His level of amusement increased with Rachel's discomfort. "So you don't want to get to know me?"

Rachel frowned and shifted her weight between sandaled feet. "I didn't say that, either!"

The door opened wider. "Well, we'd like to get to know you." Alicia stood in near equal average height beside her brother. Their smiles were identical to the depth of the dimples.

"Would you like to go get some ice cream?" Rachel blurted out her invitation.

"Let me grab my purse," Alicia replied.

Josh pulled keys from his jeans pocket and stepped back to lock the door behind his sister. "Ladies first," he said and followed the trio to the shop across the street where candies and cold creamy snacks were ordered and served across a glass fronted and topped counter.

Alicia and Josh relayed their preferences from the extensive list of flavors and options posted on the menu replicated in large letters along the back wall. "What's your pleasure?" Josh asked. Rachel fidgeted and blushed at his innocent question.

Marisa rolled her eyes in mock disgust. "She looks at everything and always gets French vanilla."

"Maybe I'd like to try something different this time," Rachel snapped.

"How about I order for you?" The earnest look in Josh's deep brown eyes earned her trust.

"OK," she agreed.

The questions and answers that begin friendships were exchanged over bowls of heaping double-dips. Favorite subjects in school, sports teams, films, actors, singers and songs, and plans for a limitless future passed between them during lively getting-to-know-you conversation.

Later, in the dark of that last night under the same roof, the sisters lay side-by-side, comforting each other as they had when wicked lightning split the rural Iowa darkness and thunder rattled the old farmhouse.

Rachel picked at tufts of cotton blanket fluff with her fingernails. "They're really nice."

"What do you mean 'they're nice'," Marisa teased. "You hardly talked to Alicia. But you hung on every word Josh had to say."

"That is not true." The sisters turned heads to face each other on plump pillows. Rachel giggled. "OK, I admit. He's cute. But I think maybe he's interested in you."

"He's not my type," Marisa disagreed.

"What is your type?"

"I'll know when I see him and fall madly in love."

Rachel snorted. "It sure wasn't Tim, that guy Mom set you up with for prom."

"Mom only wanted me to go the prom so she could dress me up and take pictures."

Rachel giggled again. "I felt sorry for him, poor skinny guy in a tux with baggy pants and jacket sleeves down to his knuckles, standing there with that stupid corsage in one hand and the other one on the doorknob."

Marisa laughed. "He was so scared of Dad."

"I can't believe that was only a month ago."

"Me either."

"You're going to miss us," Rachel whispered.

Marisa reached across the blanket and squeezed her sister's hand. "I know," she whispered back. "I kinda already do."

"It's going to be weird being an only child." Rachel sniffed and turned her head away.

"Take care of Mom and Dad. And Scooter. OK?"

"I will."

"Take care of yourself." Marisa squeezed Rachel's hand again. "Promise?"

They turned to each other again and exchanged a silent message of goodbye with their eyes. "I will if you will."

"I promise."

The sisters snuggled together and slept on pillows damp with tears.

Chapter 11

Marisa plopped into the lone open seat on the last train leaving mid-town Manhattan for Brooklyn before Sunday turned into Monday morning. After only one month in Chez Nous' kitchen, she was beginning to question and regret her choice of career. The shift scheduled to end after brunch stretched through dinner and close to cover call-ins and no-shows in the already short-handed kitchen. Marisa dozed off and nearly missed her stop.

She trudged over pavement and up stairs that her pain-numbed feet refused to feel. She grabbed a bottle of soda from her near-empty fridge, peeled down to her panties and fell across the unmade bed. The soda quenched her raging thirst but the buzz in her head would not let her sleep. She phoned home without checking the clock on her bedside table.

"Hello?" Her father's sleep-heavy voice made her look at the digital time displayed. One a.m. Midnight in Harmony.

"Oh Daddy, I'm so sorry I woke you up."

"That's alright, baby." She heard her mother ask the identity of the late night caller. "It's Marisa," he told her. "Are you OK, sweet-heart?"

Homesickness overwhelmed her. Marisa bit her trembling lip. "I'm OK. I'm just so tired."

"So tired you can't sleep. I know how that feels."

"I was only supposed to work seven hours today and I worked seventeen!"

"That's a normal work day for a chef. I usually did the paperwork during my break." Darien sighed. "So what do you want to do?"

"I don't know. I guess I should suck it up and stick it out."

"Honey, your mother and I will support any decision you make. Stick it out, do something else or come back home. It's up to you. Just do your best and enjoy what you do. That's all we ask."

Marisa yawned, pulled up the blanket and stretched underneath. "I love you, Dad."

"I love you, too. Try to get some sleep, sweetheart."

She fell asleep with the cell phone in her palm.

Darien couldn't take his own advice. Worry and the gnawing return of persistent heartburn kept him awake hours after he'd severed the open cell phone link to Brooklyn. He waited until Miranda's steady breathing signaled her return to sleep. He slipped quietly out of bed and into yesterday's jeans and tee shirt that littered the floor, a messy bedtime habit Miranda had given up on nagging him about years ago. Full moonlight filtered through sheer curtains over screened window, creating beams and shadows across the curves of her body. Her long copper hair tumbled like rivulets of precious glowing metal onto a foaming sea of white linen sheets. "I love you," he whispered and thought he saw her lovely lips curve into a smile.

He padded down the hallway and stared out the window overlooking the barn, orchard and cornfields beyond. Memories made on this small patch of the heartland paraded past his mind's eye; the ceremony that pronounced him and Miranda husband and wife and the celebration that followed, attended by friends he knew and Harmony neighbors he would come to know. Marisa's first wide-eyed ride on the back of Miranda's gentle paint pony named Sunny. Rachel's tomboy tumble out of the apple tree and the panic at his little girl's cries over cuts, bruises and a minor bump on the head. He peeked in at her, sprawled on her back, asleep on a mound of twisted blanket and puffy pillows. He whispered the nickname he'd given his six-pound squeaking, wrinkled daughter at her birth. "I love you, Peanut." He retraced his steps past Marisa's unoccupied bedroom, cursed the creak in the top step near the master bedroom door, and vowed to fix it sometime today.

Songbirds announced the impending arrival of a new day as the first fingers of deep pink dawn painted the eastern sky. Darien slipped bare feet into flip-flops at the back screen door and scratched a grumbling Scooter curled up in his summer spot for slumber. "It's too early for your old bones boy. You can pass on this walkabout." Darien opened the screen door and descended steps into dew damp grass he'd tread countless times with Scooter and Ivory, the white angel he'd rescued from a shelter's death row along his way from despair in New York to new life and love in Iowa.

Darien paused beneath the orchard tree where he'd buried Ivory's ashes and tried to shake the ache and tingle from his arms. The tightness in his chest was definitely getting worse. He made a mental note to call Dr. Gregson after breakfast.

Darien never got the chance.

The sudden death hammer of excruciating pain dropped him to his hands and knees.

"Miranda!" The breath he needed left him. He couldn't push the cry for help past the constricted muscles in his throat. He clawed the ground and dragged his legs in a desperate futile crawl toward the farmhouse.

He clamped his jaw and ground his teeth against the final fatal hammer blow that claimed him.

His stricken heart fluttered, quivered and stopped. His arms collapsed. Damp grass cushioned his chest and cheek. Muscles stiffened, fell slack and moved no more. Tears of sorrow for his wife and daughter who would find him there fell from eyes that turned lifeless, staring into the cloudless blue sky horizon.

Other-worldly white light descended, enfolded, swirled around him. The familiar shape of a canine head with thick fur crowned by erect alert ears nudged his hand. Ivory's marble blue eyes sparkled. She howled in delight and licked his face as she had long ago when grief and longing for his lost love had pierced his soul.

He reached out for and beyond her to embrace the departed forever living.

His grey-haired mentor, the stooped shoulders he remembered now straight and strong under a white chef coat.

Regal and wise Stewart, no longer crippled and silenced by the cruel ravages of stroke, called him son.

His brown-eyed girl patted the smiling shaggy shepherd dog at her side.

"My beautiful love," he said without speaking. "I've missed you so much."

Darien's spirit soared in joyful reunion with them all.

Chapter 12

A car horn blast woke her at quarter past ten. Marisa fought the urge to sandwich her head between the pillows and sleep away her day off.

"What else is Monday good for?" she grumbled. Then remembered. "Oh shit! I told Chef I'd cover lunch!" She threw off the blanket and sheet, ran for the shower, and toweled off as she searched for a clean set of chef pants and coat. Her dash for the subway got her a seat on the train to Columbus Circle scheduled to arrive at eleven.

She dodged shoppers and tourists clogging the escalator's snail-pace ascent and ran through Chez Nous' employee entrance spewing apologies over the din of kitchen chaos. Eric stopped her before she could tie her apron. "Marisa. Can I see you in Chef's office, please?"

Her heart sank to her rumbling, empty stomach. Her chin dropped to her chest. "Yes, sir," she mumbled and followed him to the reprimand or worse that she was sure awaited her behind the closed office door.

"Have a seat." She did as she was told and folded her shaking hands in her lap. Eric crossed around the desk that had once been her father's and sat in the exec's chair. He laced his fingers on the desktop before he spoke. "I tried several times to call you."

"I know. I'm sorry. My cell phone needs charging. I called home last night and fell asleep and left it on and ..." Eric's pained expression halted her explanation.

"Your uncle Jack called. He's on his way to pick you up."

"Why?"

"Your mother and sister need you at home."

Shock waves rippled down her spine with the cold wave of dread that chilled her. Sweaty palms gripped the arms of the chair. "What h-h-happened?" she stammered.

Eric looked down at his laced fingers. "I think it's best if Jack tells you."

The office door opened as if on cue. Jack's slumped shoulders erased inches from his tall stance. His bloodshot blue eyes stood out against puffy blotches on unshaven cheeks. The tails of his wrinkled sport shirt hung over the band of his belted khakis.

She looked up at him through gathering pools of tears and spoke the impossible. "My Daddy is dead, isn't he, Uncle Jack."

Jack's lower lip quivered. He nodded his head.

She hugged her ribs and folded against raging inner turmoil and pain caused by confirmation of the unimaginable. Jack's strength helped her to her feet. "C'mon, sweetheart. The cab is waiting."

"Jack, please let me know when … the details … of services …" Eric's voice trailed off.

"I'll call you," Jack promised.

Marisa stared out at the relentless ribbon of traffic along the city streets and New Jersey turnpike to the Newark International Airport terminals. "Heart attack," she heard her uncle say. "Happened early this morning, I think. No time to go back to your apartment for your things. Beth is waiting for us at the airport." Jack checked the signs along the roadway and his watch for an estimated time of arrival. "She'll take care of getting whatever you need."

"I just talked to Dad last night." Marisa delivered her tale of painful protest in a low steady voice. "I called home after my shift and woke him up. I told him I was tired and whined about working seventeen hours. He tried to warn me. I didn't want to listen. He kept asking me if I really wanted to be a chef. He said he'd support any decision I made as long as whatever I did made me happy." She hugged her ribs and sobbed. "Maybe if I hadn't called him so late and upset him he'd still be alive!"

Jack held her against his chest. He stroked her hair, thick and black like that of the brother he'd loved and lost. "Marisa, please don't blame yourself. Don't take that on. Your Dad wouldn't want it. He is so proud of you. He loves you so much." He held her tight. "So very much," he whispered.

The heart of the home Marisa knew had stopped beating with her father's. Nothing about the once familiar felt right to her. She went through the motions, cooking meals, thanking neighbors offering covered hot dish casseroles, accepting plants and flowers sent in condolence, taking Scooter on short walks around the orchard.

Miranda sat in her place at the kitchen table and stared at the empty chair opposite hers as though waiting for Darien to pick up his fork. Samantha had been at her sister's side since she'd persuaded Miranda to let the medics take her brother-in-law's body away. Rachel chose to cope by helping her Uncle Trevor care for his young sons and home in Sam's absence. While she was grateful, Sam fretted about the long term effects of delayed grief on her family as she struggled with her own.

Beth and Jack did all they could to spare Miranda the tasks related to the memorial service. They asked Marisa to join Sam and her mother at the table Miranda rarely left to make a decision on the last detail.

"Mira," Sam began. "The funeral is at ten o'clock Friday morning."

"At the church?" Miranda's glassy-eyed stare shifted from Darien's empty place at the table to her sister seated in the chair next to hers. "I want Pastor Chad. He married us."

"Pastor Chad moved to Omaha. But we called him. He'll be here, Miranda," Jack assured her.

"Are Buck and Shayla doing the luncheon after the service?" Miranda smiled. "Darien loved Buck's barbecue sauce. He didn't ask for the recipe or try to replicate it. He thought it was too perfect." Miranda turned to her daughter. "Did you learn how to make that barbecue sauce when you were working at Hank's, honey?"

Marisa shook her head. "No, Mom. He wouldn't show me."

"Of course he wouldn't." Miranda's gaze returned to the empty chair.

"Mira." Sam took her sister's hand. "We need to talk about what happens after the services. Did you and Darien ever talk about where or if he wanted to be … buried or … what?"

"We didn't discuss it." Miranda's face contorted. She pulled her hand away from her sister's grasp. "Maybe he'd want to go back to New York. Be sealed up in that crypt next to Ali. She was the love of his life. Not me." Unleashed anger flashed in her eyes. She aimed and fired the heat of it at her firstborn. "He never would have come back here if I hadn't been pregnant with you!"

Marisa gasped.

Jack groaned. "For God sakes, Miranda! Don't go there! Not now!"

"What are you saying, Mom?" Marisa searched for answers from three stunned faces. "What does she mean?" she demanded.

"Marisa, honey, your Mom is upset. She didn't mean to upset you," Sam pleaded.

"She needs to know the truth!" Miranda bolted upright with a force that toppled the ladder back of the chair to the hardwood floor. She slapped her palms on the table. "Your father got me drunk and I got pregnant!"

Marisa caught a sob in her trembling hands. The legs of her chair scraped hardwood. She rose, pivoted, and ran from the kitchen. The back screen door slammed.

Miranda rocked from side to side, dropped her head in her hands, her distress intense and intolerable. "I broke our promise! We said we'd never tell her!" she wailed. "Oh, Darien, what have I done!"

Beth tugged at her husband's sleeve. "Go after her, Jack," she implored him.

"What do I say to her?" he asked his wife.

"Tell her the truth."

The hum of crickets and cicadas called to their mates in the orchard's sultry darkness. In a brief yet endless while, after his eyes adjusted to the pale glow of early evening, Jack spotted Marisa, silhouetted in the mist. She sat with her back against the apple tree near the spot where her father died.

He trod a straight line in the dewy grass between them. "Is this seat taken?" he asked. She didn't look up. He used the trunk of the tree for hand-over-hand leverage and grunted when he touched ground. "That's a long way down for this old man."

She didn't smile. "All of you knew and none of you told me. Not even my Dad."

"Life gets complicated sometimes."

"Was I a complication?" she shot back.

"Marisa, my brother came back to Iowa because he wanted to be your Dad." He filled his lungs with misty night air and collected his thoughts before telling her the back story as he knew it. "Are you willing to listen to what I have to say?"

She nodded, hugged her shins and wedged her chin between her bent knees.

"We all loved Darien. The role he played in our lives defined what his life meant to us. His death left a hole that no one else can fill. Your Mom has lost her life partner. I've seen what that kind of pain can do to a person. I was with Darien in the ER when he had to say goodbye to Ali. She couldn't hear him. The shock, the finality, the reality of time's up. It tore him up. He hid in that top floor apartment for two months after she died. When he finally came out he ran away. He got as far as Iowa and met Miranda. He believed his feelings for her betrayed Ali. Guilt drove him to New York. Love brought him back to your mother and you."

Marisa shivered. Jack draped his arm around her slumped shoulders. "He invited me over for dinner the night before he left Brooklyn. We went up on the rooftop in January to grill burgers. It was freezing cold, snowing even. We were sitting around the fire pit having a beer. That's when he told me he realized why he'd bought this farm and fixed up this old farmhouse. He'd done it for Miranda. He wanted to be with her, have a home, a family. He bought this place months before she told him that she was pregnant with you."

He squeezed her shoulder. She leaned against him. He tossed a fallen apple at the spot where Darien fell. "Your Dad was gone before your mother could tell him goodbye. I hope for their sake and yours you can find it in your heart to forgive them."

Chapter 13

The population of Harmony swelled and nearly doubled the day of Darien's funeral.

Culinary students and graduates of the community college program that would or had helped launch their careers travelled miles across states and the Canadian border to pay their respects to Chef. Colleagues from coast to coast joined the well-represented New York contingent in filling the pews at Our Savior Lutheran Church. Kenny, Mimi and members of the Wong and Teague families of Brooklyn mourned their mutual loss. Miranda thanked David and Jayson for attending without appearing to connect the sad faces with recent happy memories.

Rachel leaned against Josh and cried into the handkerchief he offered. Alicia kept Marisa supplied with tissues from the eulogy written and delivered by her cousin Nathan, the University of Iowa professor of English and Creative Writing, to the closing words of gratitude and respect from Eric, Chez Nous' owner.

The tall, handsome duplicate of Jack delivered an eloquent speech of admiration and love for his uncle on behalf of himself and his sister Hannah, who was unable to make the trip from Australia with her husband Evan and their five young children. Eric credited Darien's role model example and mentoring advice for his success in the restaurant business.

"Your Mom and sister need you more than Chez Nous does right now." Eric sat in the metal folding chair next to Marisa as the last of the post-service luncheon plates were cleared from tables. "Your job will be waiting for you when you're ready to come back."

Marisa handed her full plate of untouched food to the scurrying clean-up crew. "Thanks for being here and for what you said about my Dad."

"I meant every word of it." He stood to go, hesitated, searched for the highest yet simplest compliment to summarize a relationship that had transformed his life. "He was my friend."

Marisa's stay in Harmony stretched past ten days of surreal pain and paperwork. Death certificates, insurance claim forms, and the choice of headstone marking the fresh mound of earth on her father's grave required family member attention only she seemed capable of giving. Rachel stayed away working overtime hours behind the counter at Harmony Drug or helping their Aunt Sam at the veterinary clinic. The rest of her days were spent coaching and playing softball. Miranda nodded her head, signed at the X, and went up to bed after pushing food around her dinner plate. Marisa buried her head between the pillows on the bed in the private room of her childhood to muffle the sound of her mother's sobs.

Clutching her one-way ticket to get on with living, Marisa hugged her housebound mother goodbye and climbed in the passenger seat of her father's SUV with her sister behind the wheel. Sporadic, strained idle chatter passed the time on the road to the Cedar Rapids airport.

"Well, this is it." Marisa hauled three suitcases stuffed with all she owned and cared to keep from the car to the curb, certain that Iowa was firmly in her past.

"Yeah, well, you know the way from here. I guess I'll leave then." Rachel jangled the keys on the chain in her left hand and nibbled at her right thumbnail.

"Stop that," Marisa scolded.

"Stop what?"

"You always chew on your nails when you've got something to say but don't want to say it. So just say it."

Words tumbled and fell with the stream of Rachel's tears. "I didn't keep our promise. I couldn't take care of Dad and I don't know how to help Mom."

Marisa pulled her sister into her arms and hugged her heaving shoulders against her own. "Rachel, listen to me. Don't blame yourself for what happened. You did what you could. You can't help Mom. She has to want help, accept the fact that she needs help." Marisa softly squeezed her sister's elbows, allowing distance between them. Eye-to-eye, she asked a favor. "There is something you can do for me."

Rachel whimpered. "What's that?"

"Keep your other promise. Take care of yourself."

Rachel nodded and wiped her nose on her sleeve. "OK." The sisters parted at the final boarding call for New York.

Chapter 14

Eric read the text message from his chef. "We have to talk about Marisa." He rubbed at the worry lines creasing his forehead and placed the call to confrontation that he'd tried to avoid.

He knew this was coming. Marisa's job performance slide began within a week after her return to Chez Nous. She punched in late. Her impaired attention to mise en place sent her scrambling from the line to the walk-in cooler for common menu ingredients, forcing her co-workers to cover for her. Rejected sloppy plating delayed orders. Complaints filtered up the chain of command from dish dogs to sous chef and on to Chef. Spinach discovered in prepped and trashed Caesar salad finally raised Chef's angry, red-flagged text to Eric.

"She's so far in the weeds we have to send a search party after her." Chef's deep voice rumbled through Eric's cell phone. "I've cut her enough slack. If she were anyone else, she'd already be out of here. Frankly, I don't see a future for her in my kitchen or any kitchen."

Chez Nous' owner closed his eyes and kneaded the muscle knot in his neck. "Thank you for bringing this to my attention. I'll take care of it."

Eric played out the consequences of his options. He decided to meet with Marisa on neutral ground at an East Village coffee shop.

She was late.

"I'm so sorry." She skidded into the booth between the stationary hard seat and moveable table. "I took a wrong turn and had to backtrack and …"

"Save it." Eric sighed. She looked as tired as he felt. "Chef brought a laundry list of problems to my attention."

Marisa swallowed hard. "My name is at the top of the list."

"I'm afraid so." Eric stirred cream into his cup of black coffee. "Do you know why?"

Marisa fidgeted with the zipper on her purse. "I know I've been late a lot."

"And?"

"I messed up a few orders."

"You've screwed up on the no-brainers. Your mis en place is nonexistent. Do you know what that does to the line?"

Marisa looked away. "I'm sorry."

"Another apology." Eric's fingers drummed the tabletop. "Chez Nous' patrons expect, no, they demand that we deliver a superior dining experience. Every employee in the kitchen and on the floor has to work together to make that happen." He turned down the waitress' offer of a refill. Marisa shook her head when asked for her order.

Eric stirred more cream into his coffee, grateful for the interruption that he hoped would give him time to find the words to let her down easy. It was the least and most he could do for Darien's daughter.

"Marisa, you've had a helluva shock. Take a couple of days off. Get your head together before you come back. Ask yourself if you're ready to go forward. Are you committed to working your ass off, do what you know it takes to be a chef?" He gulped coffee cooled by cream and adjourned the meeting with money pulled from his wallet and tossed on the table. "Think about what you want to do with your life. Then tell me what you decide."

Stone-faced Marisa held on tight to emotions roiling from her gut to her pounding head. The subway screamed louder, moved faster and shuddered to more violent stops along the line from the East Village to Brooklyn. Habit steered her to the front door of the apartment she now shared with Alicia. Marisa's confidence had caved in to apprehension at being alone in the city following her return from the trauma in Harmony. Alicia accepted the invitation to move one floor down. She appreciated having a living space exclusively her own during Marisa's long work days.

Marisa breezed past the sofa where Alicia huddled, a bowl of popcorn perched on her knees, intently watching the flickering big screen image of Bradley Cooper dancing with Amy Adams under a 1970s era disco ball.

"How'd it go?" Alicia asked.

"Swell." Marisa slammed her bedroom door, punted her purse across the room, belly-flopped on her bed. And cried.

Alicia paused her afternoon matinee to go to the aid of her room-mate. "Marisa?" She tapped her knuckles against the closed door. "Are you OK?"

Marisa grabbed the box of tissues from her bedside table and blew. "Do I sound OK?"

"Can I come in?"

"This is MY pity party."

Alicia turned the knob and peeked in. "Am I invited?"

"I guess." Marisa rolled on her back and scooted across the tangled sheets to rest against the pillows.

Alicia sat next to her, long legs stretched over lumps in the comfort-er. "I take it the meeting didn't go so well."

 Marisa dabbed at tears collecting in the corners of her eyes before more could fall. "It's my own fault. I've been getting to work late and screwing up big time when I am there."

"Screwing up how?"

"Not prepping my station. Forgetting to slice tomatoes. Pulling spinach instead of romaine lettuce." She shook her head and wiped her nose. "Stupid stuff."

Alicia shrugged. "You've got other stuff on your mind."

"That's a piss poor excuse."

"Maybe so. But it is a good reason."

"I've got two days to get over myself, do what Iowans call fish or cut bait." Marisa sank back against the pillows. "You and Josh are so lucky."

"We know we are. But why do you think so?"

"You're where you want to be doing exactly what you want to do."

"Are you saying you're not?"

"I guess maybe I am. I thought I did. I just don't know anymore."

"Know what?" Josh's unexpected appearance at the open bedroom door startled them.

"Did you even think to knock?" his sister demanded.

"How did you get in?" Marisa asked.

"The front door was unlocked. I came in to see if I should call 9-1-1."

Marisa blushed. "Sorry. My fault." She sighed. "I've been saying that a lot lately."

"You apologize to intruders?" Josh's teasing smile made Marisa giggle.

"Not usually," she retorted. "But, thanks, I needed that."

73

"Can I hang with you or should I let myself out?" he asked.

"Please stay," Marisa implored. "I need you both to answer a question for me."

Brother and sister looked at each other then back to Marisa. "And that would be?" Josh asked.

"When and how did you know who you are and where you belong?"

"Whoa! That's a big question to answer on an empty stomach," Josh joked.

"I'll order pizza," Alicia offered.

The summit between friends resumed on stools around the kitchen island topped with open boxes of delivered pepperoni and mushroom on thin crusts. Marisa shared details of her difficulties at work and the decision she had to make in forty-eight hours. "Dad told me all the horror stories. The long hours, high stress, the power plays, the drama. I was so pumped to get out of Iowa, live in the city, work in the same kitchen he had. I wanted to prove myself, show everybody I could do it. I'd be the rock star executive chef, get a Michelin star, maybe two." Marisa squelched a sob with a gulp of soda. "Then Dad was gone ..."

"And that's when you started to doubt yourself." Alicia finished the sentence for Marisa.

"I could use his death as an easy way out. But that's not the whole story. I called home and talked to him the night before he died because I was tired and scared and totally miserable." She swirled the sparkling liquid and imagined the soda bubbles were dreams about to burst in a half-empty glass. "Dad was right. I can never be what he was."

Josh pointed the tip of his fourth piece of pizza at Marisa. "You have to be who you are," he said.

"That brings us back to my question," she reminded them.

"It may look like I chose to be like my Dad, like you did when you wanted to be a chef," Alicia said. "I mean, New York is the place to be for fashion design, right? But it was more than that for me. I'd do my other homework as fast as I could so I could sit with my sketch pads and draw for hours. I spent as much time as I could in his studio watching him work with the fabrics and the colors. I'd beg him to let me go with him when he called on his clients. I can't explain it. I just knew."

Marisa nodded. "What about you, Josh? Did you always want to be a social worker?"

He shook his head. "Not at first. I kinda wanted to be a firefighter or a police officer."

"Get out!" Alicia punched his arm and laughed.

"No, really! I knew I wanted to help people."

"What changed your mind?" Marisa asked.

"I job shadowed. Toured a fire station. The equipment was really heavy. Then I spent an afternoon at the forty-seventh precinct in the Bronx." He gritted his teeth at the memory. "Scared the shit out of me!"

The friends laughed.

Marisa sobered first. "So what do I do now?"

"Well, whenever I'm having a tough time trying to figure something out, I go talk to Grandma," Josh said. "She makes a batch of chocolate chip cookies and brews a pot of coffee. Never fails to clear my head."

"Why don't you talk to Grandpa? He's always given me the best advice," Alicia commented.

"That's because you prime him with apple crumble," Josh accused. "He'll talk to you for hours if you satisfy that massive sweet tooth."

"That's a good idea." Marisa snapped her fingers. "Now, where's my cell phone?" She scanned the likely surfaces, found what she was looking for on the table next to her bed, and punched in a New Jersey number.

"Hey, Uncle Jack. What's Grandma Donna's favorite dessert?"

"Almond cookies with powdered sugar. Why?"

"I'll bake a batch and take them to her tomorrow."

Jack frowned against the phone in his hand. "I don't think that's a good idea."

"What! Why not?"

"We had to move Mom into memory care last week." Jack tried to rub the sting and burn from his bloodshot eyes. "She's not adjusting well to the change. The meds they've got her on seem to help." His deep sigh transitioned to a drawn out yawn. "She knows Beth but she gets confused sometimes and thinks I'm her brother John."

"Who?" Marisa asked.

"The uncle I was named after. You never met him. I barely remember him. He went into the Marines right out of ROTC and was killed in Desert Storm." Jack sighed again. "I'm not sure she'd remember you, honey."

"But I look like Dad. She'll see me and know who I am," Marisa insisted.

"Yeah, that's another problem. She doesn't know Darien is dead."

"You didn't tell her?"

"No, I didn't. I couldn't. She's so frail and her link to reality is so fragile. Beth and I talked it over and decided to let her live out the rest of her days with good memories as long as she can."

Marisa paced from the door to the open bedroom window and turned her head to look toward Water Street. A petite silver-haired woman stood close to the curb clutching a green shopping bag with one hand and the tiny hand of a bouncing dark-haired toddler in the other. That could have been me and Grandma Donna, she thought. "I want to see her, Uncle Jack," she said. The prolonged response stretched too long. "Uncle Jack? Are you still there?"

"Yeah. I'm here. OK, if that's what you want. Call me when you get to the Montclair station."

Marisa rode the subway to Hoboken and took the train to Montclair. Beth and Jack were waiting for her. She climbed into the seat behind her uncle and buckled up. Jack shifted the idling four door sedan into gear and drove the familiar route to the nursing home.

"I called ahead this morning to let the nurses know we'd be visiting Donna this afternoon." Beth glanced between the headrests and smiled at Marisa. "I spoke with Amanda. She's a social worker in the memory care unit. She told me your grandmother seemed very responsive this morning."

Marisa nodded. "That's good." Embarrassed at the lack of what else to say, she stared out the window at the nondescript New Jersey landscape.

Amanda met them at the nurses' station. Marisa's first impression dispelled her mental image stereotype. The young woman in the stylish salmon pink suit wore her natural platinum blonde hair in an attractive upsweep. The powder blue cowl-neck top that matched her eyes dipped in soft folds just low enough to accentuate her long neck. Pumps the color of her suit slightly elevated her tall, slender stature. Her smile revealed straight teeth between lips glossed petal pink. "So nice to meet you, Marisa," she said and extended her hand in warm greeting. "Good to see you again." She nodded to Jack and Beth and walked with them down the hallway of open doors. Marisa focused straight ahead to avoid unwanted observation and invasion of residents' privacy.

"I told Donna you were coming. She's waiting for you in the Home 1 sunroom. Natural light and the view of the green space are calming to her." Amanda waved to a resident who called out her name. "I'll be right there, Eloise." They continued on to the end of the brightly lit hallway lined with wheelchairs, walkers and rolling metal carts dispensing medication and transporting plastic water pitchers.

Donna sat in a wheelchair, hands folded in her lap covered by a red crocheted shawl. She gazed out into the sunlight and the splashing pattern of shadows cast by leaves dancing in puffs of breeze through sturdy branches of mature trees.

Jack bent to kiss his mother's cheek. "Hi, Mom." Marisa stifled a gasp as Donna turned her head toward them. The animated elderly woman she remembered from the afternoon in her assisted living apartment three years before had withered and aged. Gnarled hands reached out to her son. "Jack. My darling boy."

He smiled and gently patted her hand. "You know who I am today."

The gathering light of recognition glinted in her eyes. "Of course I know who you are." She tilted her head. "Is Beth with you?"

"I'm here, Donna." Beth stepped forward and touched her palm between Marisa's shoulders. "We've brought you a visitor."

Donna squinted through framed trifocal lenses. Her eyes flew open and her thin lips formed an O. "Marisa! My beautiful child!" She lifted her arms, welcoming her granddaughter's embrace. "So much like your father."

Jack moved a chair from a nearby round dining table and placed it

78

in front of his mother's wheelchair.

Beth took her husband's hand. "We'll leave you two alone to chat."

"Alright, dear." Donna watched her son and daughter-in-law walk hand-in-hand down the hall. "So much in love, they are. Just like Stewart and I." She smiled at Marisa. "Do you have a young man, my dear?"

"No, Grandma. Not yet."

Donna nodded. "There's plenty of time." She wagged a crooked finger under her granddaughter's nose. "But don't wait too long. Time passes so fast." She sat back in her chair. "So. Tell me why you came all the way from Iowa to spend this lovely day talking to an old lady in a nursing home."

Marisa smiled. "I live in Brooklyn now, Grandma."

"In that building where your father lived with Ali?"

"Yes. I share an apartment with Alicia, a friend of mine. She's studying fashion design."

"That's nice," Donna replied. "And what are you studying?"

Marisa shrugged. "Nothing at the moment. I thought I wanted to be a chef like Dad. I applied and got accepted at the Culinary Art Institute. I was supposed to start class in a few weeks. I had to get experience working the line in a kitchen first. Dad's friend Eric owns Chez Nous. He asked chef to hire me." Marisa looked away.

"You don't want to be a chef." Donna's bang-on observation startled Marisa.

"I don't know what I want to be, Grandma. I'm just so confused. And I don't know how to get un-confused."

"That's why you came to see me. Darien told me you would."

Marisa's jaw dropped. "What do you mean? When did you talk to Dad?"

"He came to me last night. Stood at the foot of my bed as plain as day." Donna reached out and patted Marisa's now pale cheek. "Sweetheart, I know my beautiful boy is gone. I felt him leave this life. If you're ever blessed to be a mother, and I hope someday you will be, you'll understand." Donna folded her hands in her lap. "Do you still have the brooch I gave you?" Marisa nodded. "Remember what I said? It will help you find your way if you use its power wisely." Donna's aged eyes shone through gathering tears. "Whatever path you choose, be happy, child. That's all your father ever wanted for you."

Chapter 15

Light from the hallway through the opening door split Marisa's darkened apartment cocoon.

Alicia hummed notes from a favorite tune on her way in. Her long fingers slid the dimmer switch on the wall between living and kitchen space. She nudged the door closed with her hip and settled a bag of groceries on the granite countertop.

Marisa unfolded from her fetal position on the sofa. "I hope you brought dinner," she said.

Startled, Alicia jumped. Her purse and keys tumbled to the floor.

"Sorry." Marisa picked up her roommate's belongings. "That was rude."

"Yes, it was. But you're forgiven." Alicia unpacked and refrigerated perishables from her recyclable cloth bag. "Why were you sitting in the dark?"

"To be honest I hadn't noticed." Marisa rubbed her legs. "I've got a lot on my mind. Like what I'm going to tell my boss tomorrow."

Alicia opened the first item pulled from her bag, grabbed a handful of chips and offered the addictive salty obsession to her grateful roommate. "I thought you were going to see your grandma today."

"I did."

"And?"

Marisa chewed and swallowed a mouthful of chips. "She looked so much older than I remembered. The last time I saw Grandma Donna was three years ago when I was here with Dad." Marisa leaned forward and lowered her voice to just above a whisper. "She told me she saw Dad in her room at the nursing home last night."

Alicia frowned in sympathy. "Oh, Marisa, I'm sorry she's slipped that far away. Dementia is so cruel."

81

"She may have her bad days. But today wasn't one of them. She knew us and she knew what she was saying. She asked if I still had the brooch she gave me and said it would help me decide what to do."

"What brooch?" Alicia asked.

Marisa opened the hinged black box on her lap. The heavy adornment covered her hand from knuckles to wrist. She trembled at the curious contradiction of sizzle and cold burn she felt whenever the ancient symbol of family touched her skin.

Alicia gasped at the three lions' emerald eyes inlaid and glittering against silver. "Wow!" Her long fingers curled around the McKenna crest. She laid the brooch in her palm and traced the fess swirls in the green shield with her fingertips. "Do you know what it means?"

Marisa shook her head. "I only know the brooch has been in my Dad's family for a long time. Maybe centuries. Grandma said my great-great-grandfather brought it to America when the McKenna family immigrated from Glasgow."

Alicia handed the brooch back to Marisa. "Maybe that's where you should go."

"To Glasgow?"

"Why not?"

"What would I do when I get there?"

"Walk the same streets your great-great-grandfather did. Breathe the air. Look up some long lost cousins you didn't know you had."

"I don't know." Marisa stroked the brooch and wondered at the startling sensation of sizzle and cold. "Alicia, did you feel anything when you held the brooch?"

"Like what?"

"A snap. Like static when you rub your shoes on the carpet and touch something or someone?"

"No. Why? Do you?"

Marisa looked away. "Kinda," she said. "Maybe it's just my imagination." She returned the brooch to its box and closed the lid.

Insomnia fueled by indecision interrupted Marisa's vivid dreams that night. Veiled faces appeared against brilliant backdrops of places known and unknown. Hank's Longhorn Café. Chez Nous. The apple orchard back home. Quaint cottages and a pristine village nestled around a coved port dotted by fishing boats and floating craft with unfurled sails. Jagged peaks painted emerald green as her mother's eyes. Distorted sounds sharpened to crystal clear demands. "What are you going to do, Marisa?" the faces asked.

"I don't know!" she moaned. She buried her head beneath the pillows to shut the voices out.

One voice persisted. She heard the anguish, felt his loneliness and longing pulling her to him, to an ancient land that owned their hearts, spawned their souls, claimed their blood.

"Where are you, lassie?" the voice cried out.

She awoke, her arms outstretched, reaching for a man she knew but had never met in a place unseen but where she belonged. "I'm here," she whispered. "I'll find you."

NEW LIFE IN LOVE
Chapter 16

Low midday clouds shrouded Alistair McKenzie's home in the Scottish Highlands. He shook the mist from his coat, stomped hay-caked mud from his boots, and left both on the back porch.

Thick woolen socks covered feet accustomed to more gentile fabric befitting a barrister. Alistair padded through the kitchen and down the hallway over wide planks of wood original to the modest dwelling on his late uncle's livestock farm. He rounded the corner and crossed into his study sanctuary, the only room in the house furnished with remnants of the life he'd planned and abandoned for the duty of family.

The heavy wooden chair rolled easily away from the roll top desk he'd had transported from his office in the heart of Glasgow two weeks shy of a year hence. Alistair rubbed the ache from muscular thighs with hands calloused from daily labor, then grimaced at the familiar-sized envelope on top of the mini-mountain of unopened mail.

He recited aloud what he knew would be printed on the milky white invitation. "The honour of your presence is requested at the wedding of," Alistair picked up and read the return address on the envelope. "McGowan?" He groaned. "Ah, Danny lad. You coulda done better." He reached for the letter opener once used exclusively on court documents and cut a neat line above the adhesive fold. "Formal attire for afternoon tea? Wear my kilt for biscuits and a spot of? Old man McGowan is so cheap he makes the rest of us look like spendthrifts." He tossed the invitation in the trash can beside his desk. "Well, I'm not going."

"Yes, you are."

Alistair jumped and whirled around in his chair. "Christ, woman!

It's not polite, sneaking up on a man and his thoughts!"

"You were thinking out loud, McKenzie." Brenda Murray retrieved the invitation from the waste basket. "I'm in your house at this time everyday but Sunday fixing a meal for you and me and my Robbie. There's no sneaking up intended." She handed the discarded envelope and its contents back to her boss. "When and where is this wedding?"

Alistair's face flushed deep red as the highlights in the auburn waves and tufts of curls that covered his head. His piercing blue eyes narrowed above prominent cheekbones and a scruffy growth of beard. "You could wait until I see my own mail before you go snooping through it." He took the invitation from her and stuffed it in one of the roll top's many cubby holes. "It's the last Saturday in June in Glasgow."

"How long have you known this groom?"

Alistair sighed and rubbed the furrows above his brows. "Danny was a striker on my football team in secondary school."

Brenda leaned her round hip against the desk and crossed her arms. "Then you've got to go. He wants you to be there, have his flank."

Alistair reacted with a sad half-smile. "Sure. While he scores the goal."

The scold in Brenda's hazel eyes softened and her grin deepened the dimples in her plump cheeks. She tapped his shoulder. "Someday soon, he'll be there when you score the goal."

A low whistle and rattle of a lid lifted and dropped on a cast iron pot announced Robbie Murray's arrival in the kitchen. "Brenny!" he called to his wife of thirty-five years. "Where are ye? The stew's boiled over and the bread smells burnt!"

Alistair grinned at Brenda's irritated tongue-clucking reaction.

85

"Feeding time."

"Aye, that it is." Brenda turned and marched down the hall to her station at the aging stove. Its white porcelain edges had been nicked and gouged over decades of use. But the burners and oven were still in solid working order. She turned off the source of the oven's heat and, with thick gloved potholders protecting each hand, slid baked bread from the oven and removed the lid from a bubbling pot of beef stew. She frowned at her husband already seated at the table. "Go wash up!" she ordered.

"I did already!"

"Well your face didn't feel the soap." Robbie grumbled, pushed away from the wooden rectangular table large enough for six set for three, and shuffled to the single-well sink to do what he was told. "You should wait for McKenzie before sitting down at his table."

Alistair walked in, stood beside his much shorter hired hand, and reached for the soap. What Robbie lacked in height, he more than made up for in brawn. Standing six foot tall, Alistair often felt as though he were the smaller man. Robbie could toss twice the hay, shear three times the sheep and fix a broken fence faster than Alistair reasoned he ever would or could.

"After you, McKenzie." Robbie stepped back and gestured his boss toward the table.

"You've eaten more meals at this table than I have," Alistair said and pulled out a chair for Robbie. "You've earned the right to sit here whenever you've a mind to."

Robbie nodded his appreciation and sat. "Aye, but my Brenny has a point. We wouldn't be here still if you hadn't taken over when McKenzie the elder left this earth. Your kin wanted to sell." He shook his head and sighed. "That would've been a shame, this being one of the few bits of owned land saved from the Clearances."

86

Alistair sat across from Robbie and dug his spoon into the heaping bowl of stew Brenda had set in front of him. "The history of my family's ownership of the property did influence my decision," Alistair said. "But it was the memories I couldn't walk away from. The summers I spent here as a lad, helping Uncle Fergus. The Christmas dinners my Mum prepared in this kitchen for her bachelor brother. All of us seated around this table thanking God for our blessings." Alistair dipped a hunk of bread into the stew's salty sauce. "The pull was too strong."

"Your uncle so looked forward to those visits," Brenda said. "He didn't want to say anything, put any pressure on you or your brothers. But he hoped and prayed that one of you would come here to live after he passed." She smiled. "And here you are."

Alistair shrugged. "Drew and Charlie had no interest in tending sheep," Alistair answered.

Robbie wiped his napkin over chapped lips and the stubble on his chin. "I expect Charlie's Wife didn't fancy the life, either."

"Not so much, no," Alistair agreed.

"Well, that's a shame, too. Don't get me wrong. I'm sure Glasgow and Edinburgh are fine places to raise a family. But their bairns won't know Scotland as you did, McKenzie." Robbie leaned forward, his elbows on the table. "Yours will."

Alistair's face fell. His shoulders sagged.

Robbie yelped when the toe of Brenda's boot connected with his shin. "What did you do that for?" He rubbed at his pain and glared at his wife.

"McKenzie's personal life is none of our business." Brenda began to clear the table. "Getting on with the work at hand is."

Robbie scratched his head. "Did I say something wrong?" he asked Alistair. "I apologize if I did."

Alistair shook his head. "No, Robbie, you didn't. Brenda knows I got invited to another wedding in Glasgow." He sat back in his chair. "The third one this year and it's not even half over."

"Oh." Robbie stood and stacked dirty dishes to wash. "Well, you know Brenny and I will take care of things here while you're gone. Stay in the city a few extra days. Have some pints and toss back a dram or two with the lads." He stopped stacking and winked. "Give the lassies a look over."

Brenda's soapy hands on her husband's shoulders pivoted and pushed him toward the door. "Go back to work, Robbie!" she commanded.

Alistair buried his troubles in finishing the workday's required chores. In the moments before twilight, he climbed to the highest point on his property, listened and tried to imitate Robbie's expert whistles directing the black and white fur flash of border collies herding livestock. He searched the horizon over rolling hills of spring green and imagined her there, running toward him ahead of the advancing fog blanket. He spread his arms, tilted his handsome face to heaven, and let the anguish flow from his soul in a mournful cry.

"Where are you, lassie?"

The whispered reply, carried on a rare puff of warm wispy breeze, echoed in his ear.

"I'm here. I'll find you."

Chapter 17

Marisa woke at dawn to another dreary day of grey dampness.

"Does the sun never shine in Scotland?" she mumbled and covered her head with the lumpy down-filled pillow.

Five months into her life living abroad, Marisa was beginning to regret her destination. Glasgow's near constant cool overcast made her long for a warmer and drier location. Tedious days draining hot oil from fish and chips and serving slices of pizza New Yorkers would laugh at followed by nights pouring pints in a pub paid the rent on her one room flat. But it did nothing to kindle the spark of adventure she craved.

Marisa sat up and cocooned herself in the blanket from the single bed. She pushed her feet into the snuggly pink slippers she'd packed in the single soft-sided bag-on-wheels stuffed with her most valuable possessions. She trudged across naked floor to the tiny bath with toilet and tub but no shower. A young woman older than her nineteen years stared back from the filmy mirror over the sink.

She'd been so certain of her decision when she called Eric to tell him she would not return to Chez Nous. She poured every ounce of waking energy into her plan to live on her own terms in the country of her ancestors. Marisa's joyful whoop and skip down Water Street waving the visa she'd thought would never come drew the attention of every tenant, tourist and pedestrian in the Brooklyn neighborhood. She'd smiled through tears and hugs shared with family and friends at the final boarding call for the international flight and blown one last kiss at the great city vanishing beneath the clouds.

January rain had pelted the shuttle bus Marisa rode between Glasgow Airport and the third floor walk-up she'd rented on the city's west side. Streets bracketed by ancient structures coated with grit stood as the shabby backdrop for a daily monotonous routine.

"What's bothering you, lass?" The fish and chips shop owner glanced up and over the counter at the pretty ex-pat he'd hired on the spot. Marisa wiped clean the last table of four served before her shift ended and untied the apron around her trim waist. "Nothing." She sighed. "Everything." She crossed behind the counter and dropped the dirty apron and towel in the laundry. "I guess I'm just tired."

"It was a busy Saturday." Jim Duffy opened the cash register and emptied excess paper and pound sterling into the unzipped bank bag for later deposit. Thick fingers on wrinkled hands shook slightly with early onset Parkinson's disease. Waves of salt-and-pepper strands swept wiry grey arched eyebrows over heavy lids and clear blue eyes. "It's bound to get busier now that the summer tourist season's come on."

Marisa leaned against the counter. Her gaze wandered to the storefront windows. "What's it like here in the summer? Besides busy," she asked her boss.

The stocky middle-aged man laughed. "You're asking if it ever gets warm. Summer has been a wee bit late this year, I'll give ya that," he replied. "But it's June, nearly July." He winked. "That's when the odd sunny day can really heat things up."

Marisa spent the time between serving food and drink washing the smell of cooking oil from her near elbow-length straight black hair. She wrapped the oversized white terrycloth bath towel under her arms, combed out the few tangles, and picked through her sparse wardrobe on hangers in the closet miniscule by American standards. She reached for and put back the uniform long-sleeved white cotton shirt worn at the pub and selected instead a bright pink gauzy top with ruffles at the elbows and neckline, revealing just enough cleavage to suggest ample breasts.

She smoothed and secured her hair in a ponytail held back by a matching pink ruffled band. "What the hell, it's Saturday night," she muttered at her reflection in the bathroom mirror. Marisa carefully applied eyeliner and shadow to make the steel grey in her eyes pop and ruby red gloss to her full lips. She slipped her sleek figure into tight-fitting black jeans and stepped into boots that added more inches to her five-foot-eight-inch natural height.

"Let's heat things up," she said aloud, grabbed a black leather waist-length jacket, and headed out for a night of bar tending at a west end Glasgow pub.

Chapter 18

Alistair lifted the fluted glass of bubbly in a toast to the bride and groom and politely sipped the champagne he hated. He grinned at the grimace on the face of the man at his right, checked the time and pointed to his wristwatch. "Dougie." Alistair low-tone spoke to one of his few remaining bachelor friends.

"Aye." Dougie MacLeod gratefully took the hint. He smiled and set the nearly full champagne glass on the waitress' passing tray. "Time for something real," he called after Alistair who was already half way to the reception hall exit.

They stepped out into an evening that had suddenly gone sunny. Alistair took off the black waistcoat over his kilt, opened his vest and undid the buttons of his white dress shirt to mid-chest. "Now that's the Glasgow I remember. Cool one minute and steamy the next."

"A few pints and you won't feel the heat." They rounded a corner and passed storefronts to an establishment they'd frequented often prior to Alistair's move from the Lowlands. Dougie grasped the handle tarnished by decades of oil from countless hands and opened the pub's rugged dark wood door. "After you, sir," he said.

Alistair parted the crowd of full tables and standing patrons. He wedged his chest and broad shoulders between men not so formally dressed, turned and scanned the smoky scene in search of his friend diverted somewhere in the crowd.

"What can I get for you?"

"American," he thought without looking. "Single malt," he ordered. "Glenlivet if you've got it." He spotted Dougie and waved.

"Of course I've got it," she said.

Alistair turned toward the voice and nearly knocked over a dram of whisky.

"That was close." Sensual red lips over perfect white teeth smiled at him. The long black ponytail flung over her shoulder fanned between perfectly round breasts under a hot pink ruffle. Sparkling almond-shaped grey eyes sparked a primal reaction under his kilt.

"I'll have whatever he's having." Dougie tapped his fingernail on the bar alongside Alistair's drink.

"You got it." Marisa poured a second shot from the bottle. "Start a tab?"

Dougie chuckled at Alistair's frozen expression of wonderment and lust. "Might as well. I think he'll be here awhile," he said.

Marisa flashed Alistair a second stunning smile and walked away to wait on another customer.

Dougie drank his dram and snapped his fingers under Alistair's nose. "Hello in there. Still with me, lad?"

Alistair blinked. "What? Sorry." He swallowed a mouthful of whisky. "She's a beautiful woman."

Dougie licked droplets of whisky from his lips. "She is that. If I weren't so sweet on my Molly, I'd stay right here and drink that in 'til closing time."

Alistair looked at his friend as though hearing his voice for the first time that day. "Who's Molly?"

"Only the woman I've been seeing for nearly a year now. I've asked her to marry me."

Alistair groaned. "Och, no. Not you, too."

"We're not getting any younger." Dougie downed his whisky and lifted the empty glass to get Marisa's attention. "How 'bout one more for the road." He nudged Alistair in the ribs with his elbow.

"I promised Molly I'd meet her for dinner after she got off work. I suggest you stay right here and ask that lovely lass to do the same." Dougie tossed his share of the tab and a tip on the bar, patted Alistair's shoulder and cut through the crowd to the constant swing of the opening front door.

"Did your friend leave?" Marisa stood in front of Alistair again, the bottle of Glenlivet posed to pour.

"He had a previous engagement." Alistair pushed his empty glass under the lip of the open bottle and smiled at her. "He paid for it. It's a shame to let good whisky go to waste."

Marisa laughed. "I wouldn't know. I've never touched the stuff." She poured the glass full.

"What do you drink?" Alistair asked.

"The occasional glass of wine."

"Red or white?"

"Either. It depends on what I'm pairing it with."

"Ah, a connoisseur. So you cook, then?"

"I know my way around a kitchen."

"So do I. As long as the table is set and someone else has prepared the food."

"So you'd know where to go for a good steak."

"In Glasgow? Aye. The best steak place in the city is a ten minute walk from here. You haven't been?"

She shook her head. "I've lived here almost six months now. My flat, work, the market and a Laundromat are the only places I've seen."

"When do you get off work tonight?"

"At ten."

Alistair drank his dram, set the empty glass on the bar, stood and added coins to Dougie's pile of currency. "I'll be back at ten to take you out for a steak dinner." He stretched his arm across the bar to shake her hand. "Deal?"

She smiled and shook on it. "Deal."

Marisa admired the view and savored her sensual ripple of reaction as he moved to and through the pub's front door. She dismissed the urges when the door closed behind him and went back to work, certain that she'd seen the last of the gorgeous Scot, his sexy bared chest, and his kilt.

Two hours passed as usual on a Glasgow Saturday night. Marisa exchanged the pub apron for her leather coat and slung her purse over her shoulder. She knocked on the night manager's office door. The grunt of acknowledgement within gave her permission to open the door beyond a crack. "I'm heading out, Ryan," she said.

The big forty-something man hunched over a computer on a gouged wooden desk from another era nodded his shaggy mop of dark wavy hair and equally unkempt full shaggy beard. "Guinness goes best with steak. But I'm Irish, so I'm biased."

Marisa's mouth dropped open. "How did you know …?"

He cut her off with a wave of his hand. "Nothing is said or done in my pub that I don't know about."

She laughed. "He probably won't show up anyway."

Ryan Murphy leaned back in his chair. "Oh, he'll show up alright. Alistair McKenzie is a man of his word." Ryan motioned her toward the open door. "But he's not a patient man. He doesn't like to be

kept waiting. Enjoy." He returned his full attention to the unfinished work on the flickering screen.

Marisa hesitated, wanting to know more about the stranger she'd
agreed to blind date. She pivoted on her boot heels instead, stepped
back toward the throng and scanned the scene for a man she knew
she'd never forget.

Breath caught in her throat at the sight of him leaning against the
bar. Fashionably faded denim jeans, a black t-shirt and jeans jacket
hugged near-perfect contours of lean muscle. A lock of stray auburn
curl swiped his forehead. His clean-shaven firm jaw supported an
easy smile. Stunning blue eyes drew her to him. The parting crowd
blurred in her periphery.

"Ready?" he asked.

"As ready at I'll ever be," she replied.

He opened the pub door for her and took her hand in a natural
physical bond of endearment that felt totally right. He guided her
along streets he knew in shared comfortable silence filled with the
promise of words yet to be spoken. She stepped through another
door he opened. Congenial banter between customers and wait staff
at tables and the smell of steak grilled to order welcomed them in.

"Ali!" The round man wrapped thin arms around Alistair, his pale
puffy cheek pressed against the much taller man's chest. Fabric and
thread strained to hold together over the roundness of his midsec-
tion and behind. Marisa stifled a giggle at the mental recall of an
Iowa snowman.

"Good to see you well, Jim. Do you have a table for me and the
lady?"

"Aye! Don't you know I do." The round man released Alistair and
led them through the maze of four-top tables with chairs to the
restaurant's most secluded corner. He grinned and pulled out a

chair for Marisa. "This one is always reserved for you." He winked at Marisa and held up two fingers. "Two steak dinners for you, then? One medium rare," he nodded to Alistair, "and the other, miss?"

"The same, thank you," Marisa answered.

"And to drink?"

"My boss at the pub suggested I order a Guinness," Marisa said.

Alistair grimaced. "Murphy would." He grinned at the waiter. "Give us your best Scottish ale."

The waiter smiled and patted Alistair's shoulder. "How's life in the Highlands treating you?"

"I can't complain."

"Well, we sure miss you here, Ali." He tipped his head to Marisa. "Miss." The waiter scurried on short legs toward the kitchen.

"Ali? Ryan told me your name is Alistair."

He nodded. "It is. Jim Morgan has been a friend of my family for a long time. Only my closest friends have permission to call me Ali." He grinned. "Now you know more about me than I do about you." He reached for her hand. "What is your name, beautiful lady? And where did you come from?"

She grinned back and squeezed his hand. "Marisa McKenna from Iowa via New York City."

His eyebrows arched. "McKenna clan from Lanarkshire?"

"That would be the one. I'm told my great-grandfather immigrated to New York from somewhere near Glasgow."

"So your family settled in Iowa." Alistair drank ale from the pint

97

glass Jim placed on a coaster in front of him. "Forgive me, but where is Iowa?"

Marisa laughed. "Iowa is in the Midwest about halfway between the coasts. The McKenna family lived in New Jersey. Dad met Mom in Iowa. That's where I was born. I moved to New York to work in a restaurant and study to be a chef, like my Dad."

Alistair's intense blue eyes met and searched hers. "Why did you come to Scotland?"

Marisa shrugged. "I changed my mind." She met his gaze with an intensity of her own. "OK," she said, "now it's your turn to tell me more about you."

Alistair downed half his ale and sat back in his chair. "I've lived in Scotland all my life as did generations of McKenzies before me. I was born here in Glasgow. Most of my mother's clan relocated from the Highlands to find work. My great-great Uncle Alistair managed to hang on to property owned by the family about 20 kilometers from the west coast. That's some 12 or so of your U.S. miles. I took over the farm when my Uncle Fergus died a little over a year ago."

"What did you do when you lived in Glasgow?"

"I was a barrister."

"That's like a lawyer, right?"

Alistair nodded. "I spent my days either in court or behind a desk."

She grinned. "What did you know about working a farm, city boy?"

Alistair shrugged. "Not much. Spent a few summers chasing the cattle and sheep with my uncle's dogs. I'm very grateful to Robbie and Brenda Murray. They stayed on to help me as they had my uncle."

Marisa searched Alistair's eyes with hers. "Couldn't your family have just sold the farm?"

"Aye, we could have. My brothers wanted to and so did I at first. Mum would have gone along with whatever we three decided."

"So why did you give up your life in the city? Why didn't you sell?"

He smiled. "I changed my mind," he said.

"Dinner is served!" Jim arrived with steaks, fried onions, mushrooms and potatoes sizzling on hot plates.

Marisa breathed in an aroma reminiscent of home. "Fantastic," she sighed and sliced her knife through tender meat. She ate without speaking until the last bite was gone. "You don't know how much I needed this," she said. "Thank you."

"You're quite welcome." Alistair dropped his napkin next to his empty plate. "The pleasure was all mine."

Alistair insisted on covering the ticket and tip. "A gentleman always pays." He walked her home after midnight under a rare, cloudless sky, his arm around her shoulders as a shield against the occasional cool breeze. Although warm enough, Marisa snuggled against him, her arm resting on the belt woven through his waistband. The comfortable silence settled on them as before. Too soon they stood facing each other at the secured ground level entrance to her building.

"When are you going back to the Highlands?"

"Monday morning." He brushed loose strands of ponytail from her shoulder and softly traced her fine facial features, from eyebrows over flushed cheeks to lips, with his fingertips. "Marisa," he whispered, took her in his arms and gently pressed his lips to hers.

For a few fleeting moments, her world swirled and revolved around sensations more intoxicating than Scottish ale. Her hands on his back between jacket and shirt absorbed the heat and feel of him, yearned for more. Heavy eyelids stayed closed even after he broke the spell.

"Goodnight, beautiful lady."

She opened her eyes when he stepped away. "Tomorrow is Sunday." Embarrassed, she breathed deep to control the tremble and tone. "It's my day off."

He checked his wristwatch and grinned. "Today is Sunday," he corrected her. "I'd be pleased to spend the day showing you around the city."

She smiled. "I'd like that very much."

"I'll come round at ten, if that's not too early."

"That's perfect."

"Until then." He kissed her cheek, turned and walked back to the corner. She slid her key in the lock and glanced back to see him step from the curb and climb in the backseat of a hailed taxi.

Marisa skipped up the steps in rhythm with her heartbeats. She hummed a self-composed tune, unlocked the scuffed wood door to her flat, kicked it closed with her foot, and rummaged to the bottom of her purse for the cell phone. A speed dial tap and four long tone rings connected her with Iowa.

"Rachel!" Her sister's name escaped her throat in a high-pitched, excited squeak. "I had dinner tonight with the most perfect man. I think I'm in love!"

Chapter 19

Marisa dreamed of castles anchored on hilltops and warriors in kilts, the ring of clashing swords melding with the harmonic drone of bagpipes. Wind lifted the hood from her cape and lashed long strands of black over her face damp with rain. The McKenna clan brooch that secured the tartan shawl to her cape snapped, the trio of green eyes in the lions' heads blazed. "Alistair!" she called to summon him. The man mounted on the white steed obeyed. Hooves thundered toward her. The sure and steady strength of his arm lifted her. She straddled the animal's broad back and clung to her rescuer on their full gallop to safety.

The alarm jolted Marisa back to real time. She silenced the cell phone's chime and grinned at the memory of her fading dream. "Now where did that come from?" She swung her legs over the side of the bed and opened the single drawer in the tiny side table. Marisa opened the lid and lifted the brooch from the box. "Are you in my head now, too?" A trio of green eyes glistened at her touch.

The buzzer connection from the building's front door to her flat sounded promptly at ten. Marisa checked for imperfections in her mirrored reflection one last time. She grabbed her purse, locked the door and trotted down the stairs through the door into a glorious sunlit morning.

"Your chariot awaits, m'lady." Alistair held open the taxi's backseat door, his grin as broad as the shoulders beneath his shirt.

"Thank you, kind sir." She slid in beside him to enjoy wherever this journey would take her.

"Cup Tea Room," he told the driver.

Marisa relished the big city ambience of reclaimed brick walls and butcher block top tables with comfortably sleek rounded-back white chairs. She savored Alistair's choice of Scottish smoked salmon and poached eggs in hollandaise with a pot of tea for two and held his hand on their two hour stroll to and through the botanical garden. They hand-fed nuts to squirrels tamed by frequent visitors, glimpsed history through plants grouped according to the century first introduced in British gardens, and sat on a bench surrounded by color and scent from nearby blossoms.

They walked to a campus founded in 1451 where Marisa marveled at the ancient architecture. Arched columns connecting courtyards and doorways both protected from rain and welcomed sunlight.

Marisa sighed. "What a lovely setting for wedding photos," she said.

"Aye," Alistair said, "It is. I have been."

Marisa froze. "You've been what?" she asked him, afraid to hear his answer.

"In wedding photos. I stood in this very spot."

She dropped his hand. He stepped in front of her, read the confusion and hurt rising in her eyes, understood the unintended message. "Ah, no, lassie. It wasn't my wedding."

She looked up at him. "You're not married?"

He smiled. "Never have been but would surely like to be one day." He brushed her lips with his thumb, cradled her face in his hands. "Marisa," he whispered and kissed her, gently at first, then urgently. His arms enfolded her. Mutual passion deepened with his tongue between her lips and hers to his. She melted into him, oblivious to the world around them. She ached for him, longed to give herself to him, shuddered at the power of her first love and the desire for him erupting from deep within.

Breathless and reluctant to end their moment, Alistair kissed her closed eyelids and pressed her against him. "I wish this day would never end."

"So do I," she sighed into his chest.

"I don't know how yet. But I want you with me, Marisa." He lifted her chin with a soft touch of his fingertips and lightly kissed her. "Will you go with me to the train station in the morning? Will you come to the Highlands?"

"Alistair, I can't just leave tomorrow. I've got another job at a fish and chips shop during the day and the pub at night and my flat …"

Alistair smiled and shook his head. "As much as I would love to take you with me, I know you have a life here. I'm asking you to come to me, see where I live. I'll buy your train ticket as insurance."

"Insurance?"

"That we'll be together again soon," he murmured and kissed her again.

Chapter 20

Brenda couldn't put her finger on the change in Alistair's behavior since his return from another wedding weekend in Glasgow. But anxious and restless was not his usual way.

"I'm going into town in the morning," he told her before she and husband Robbie left for the day. "I won't be here for the midday meal."

Brenda closed the creaking passenger's side door on the rusted yet trusty red pickup truck. The old engine rumbled under the dented hood. Robbie steered his aging pride and joy over stones in the driveway toward the paved road leading to home a few clicks north of the west coast seaside town of Mallaig.

"Has McKenzie said anything to you since he got back from Danny's wedding?" Brenda asked her husband.

"What do you mean, said anything."

"Anything about something that might have happened."

He grunted. "You're talking in riddles, woman."

"Don't you and McKenzie ever have a conversation?"

"I talk to the boss about what needs to be done around the farm."

"That's it?"

"The Celtics and Rangers come up during football season."

She rolled her eyes and groaned. "Does he seem different to you these past few days?"

"Different how?"

"I don't know. Preoccupied. Like there's something or maybe someone on his mind."

"I haven't noticed."

"Of course you wouldn't." She crossed her arms over her chest. "Did he tell you he was going into town tomorrow?"

"Aye. He's got business in town to attend to." He shot a warning glance at his pouting wife. "And I still have a bruise on my shin to remind me that his business is none of ours."

"Unless it means we're out of work," she shot back.

"What's put that crazy thought into your head?"

"I think he's tired of being alone. I overheard him on the phone. He was talking in a low voice like a man does when he's courting a woman."

"Oh, for feck sake, Brenny! You've no right, eavesdropping on the boss! If he's got something to tell us, he will when he's ready."

Strained silence rode with them the rest of the way home.

Alistair left for Mallaig before the Murrays reported for work. He drove along the nearly deserted roadway in the silver Land Rover he'd purchased prior to the move. The picturesque coastal town where permanent residents served the seasonal influx of tourists hugged the port dotted with small craft and sails. Alistair parked the car across the street from the quaint hotel and restaurant owned by his father's sister Maeve and his uncle Eliot McGillivray.

The clatter of plates signaled the start of another round of Scottish breakfast ordered by guests occupying nine rooms. Alistair scanned the reservations desk and dining room for a familial face.

"Alistair!" Maeve strode between the tables, her generous arms outstretched in greeting. The top of her head of salt-and-pepper hair controlled by a hairnet fit just below his chin. Her rocking hug nearly knocked him off-balance.

He laughed and returned the motion. "How's my best girl?"

"Always happy to see you!" She stood on tiptoe to kiss his cheek. "Will you be staying for breakfast?"

"Looks like you're full up."

She winked a bright blue eye. "I'll look after you."

He followed her through the swinging doors into a kitchen on high alert. Fry pans and a greased griddle sizzled. Hot ovens gave up scones tinged golden brown. White doughy mounds refilled the shiny metal baking sheets in preparation for afternoon tea. Maeve plopped warm scones on a pair of white china plates and motioned for Alistair to sit at the chef's table. She poured coffee into cups, set a half-full carafe on the table and dropped into the chair across from his. She wiped her damp forehead with a clean side towel pulled from her apron pocket.

"First time I've sat down this morning." She sipped coffee and bit into the scone. "I got up so early it seems like afternoon to me."

Alistair's concern showed in his furrowed forehead. "You could use more help."

She nodded. "Don't I know it. Chef has threatened to quit if I don't hire another sous chef soon."

"That's why I came to see you."

She grinned and patted his hand. "You're a good boy, Ali, but you're no cook."

He laughed. "And I never will be. But I know someone who is."

Maeve leaned over her coffee. "I'm listening."

"I met her in Glasgow last weekend. She's worked at a restaurant in New York."

"New York City?"

"The very same. She'll be visiting next week. I'll bring her round to meet you. Oh, and she'll need a room."

A sly smile smoothed Maeve's middle-age wrinkles. "This lass, is she young and pretty?" Alistair blushed. "You fancy her. She's caught your eye. Maybe your heart?"

"I never could keep a secret from you, Auntie Maeve."

"Aye, and you never will." Maeve popped the last of the scone in her mouth and washed it down with a swallow of coffee. "What's her name?"

"Marisa McKenna."

Maeve nodded approval. "A fine clan. I'll tell your uncle to reserve a room with a view for her and an hour of his time for an interview mid-morning on Monday."

"Thank you, Auntie." Alistair stood, grabbed another scone from a passing tray, and circled the table to kiss Maeve's flushed cheek. "For the hospitality and the scones." Alistair left the busy kitchen to scour the shops of Mallaig for new things to refresh his home for a guest he hoped he could convince to stay.

Marisa walked home between shifts hugging a crystal vase filled with a dozen red roses. She read and re-read the card attached to the bouquet by a thin white ribbon tied to a single stem.

Until we're together again, Alistair

She set the vase on her bedside table and speed dialed Iowa on her cell phone. "Hi, Rach. You awake?"

"Yeah, I'm eating corn flakes at the kitchen table."

"How's Mom?"

"The same."

"Has she left the house at all?"

"Not much. She goes to church on Sunday and to the cemetery. Aunt Sam guilt trips her into having lunch at Hank's or dinner at their house every once in awhile. I take her into town to get groceries once a week or so. She still won't drive Dad's car. I don't know what she's going to do when I go away to college in the fall."

"At least you won't be so far away."

"Yeah, about that. I'm not going to Iowa State."

"What! Why not?"

"I got a scholarship at Texas A&M."

"That's great, Rach! What did Mom say?"

"I haven't told her yet."

"You should. You have to. It's July. You'll be moving out next month."

"I know. I'm going to tell Aunt Sam today when I go in to help out at the vet clinic."

"Maybe Mom could go with you. Tell them both at the same time. Aunt Sam can help with the hysterics. She might give Mom her old office job back. You know, a couple days a week with something to do besides sit around the house and mope."

"That's not a bad idea. You've had worse. So what's up with you?"

Marisa caressed a ruby red petal. "I got a dozen red roses and a train ticket to the Highlands from the perfect man."

"Oooooh," Rachel moaned, "how delightfully romantic! When are you going to visit Mr. Perfect? What's his name again?"

"Alistair. I'm taking the train to Mallaig on Sunday."

"You're not staying with him, are you?"

"No, I'm not staying at his farm. He's booked me a room at the hotel in town."

"Wait a minute. Did you say he lives on a farm?"

"A livestock farm, yes. He has cattle and sheep."

The long distance connection rang with Rachel's laughter. "Now that's rich! The big city girl wannabe falls for a Scot hottie who lives on a farm. I can't wait to tell Aunt Sam. Can I tell Mom?"

"Let's wait and see on that. OK?"

"I gotcha. Have fun. But be careful, big sister! Don't go losing your heart or anything else to this guy until you're sure he's really worth it."

Chapter 21

Alistair parked his car on Station Road near the main entrance to Mallaig Station a half hour before the West Highland Line train from Glasgow was scheduled to arrive. He paced the tile in front of the ticket counter and checked his wristwatch every other anxious minute.

"Laddie," the past middle-age man behind the counter tapped on the glass. His wiry grey eyebrows and mustache moved in unison with his curled index finger. "Walking back and forth won't get the train here any sooner. You'll wear out my floor and the soles of your shoes."

"What?" Alistair stopped in mid-stride. "Oh. Sorry."

The corners of the wild mustache lifted with his grin. "Who ye expecting, if ye don't mind me asking?"

"The woman I hope to marry," Alistair responded.

Wiry eyebrows rippled over wide-open watery blue eyes. "West Highland Line from Glasgow?"

"Aye."

"Well, then," the ticket agent checked the display on his computer screen. "I'm happy to report the next train from Queen Street station is on time." He winked at Alistair. "Might even be a few minutes early."

"Thank you." Alistair quick-stepped toward the platform where his tenuous but determined bid for happiness in love and life would begin.

Marisa rode the early bus to Queen Street and was the first westbound passenger to claim her seat on ScotRail. Nervous anticipation prevented her from enjoying the views along Scotland's majestic hills, mountains, lochs and natural movie sets at Glenfinnan Viaduct and Morar's sandy shores. She comprehended none of the words in the book she tried to read and gave up taking a nap

110

to pass time during the five-and-a-half-hour journey. The image of him rested behind her closed eyes. Sensations of where he had and would soon touch her tingled with longing and delight. She shifted in her seat and counted the clicks of steel spinning on steel that would take her to him.

"Mallaig Station." The faceless voice announced their arrival. Marisa squinted through the window into the sunlight that bathed breath-taking landscape she didn't see. She pressed her forehead against the glass, searching for the extraordinarily handsome man she knew would be waiting for her. She slung her backpack over her shoulder, retrieved the soft-sided overnight bag carryon from under her seat, and apologized to the young boy she'd nearly run over in the aisle on her way to the platform.

"Marisa!" She dropped her bag and backpack and fell into Alistair's strong arms. "Ah, sweetheart." His lips covered and consumed hers, hungry for her taste. Her soft moan and parted lips offered him more. They stood locked together, oblivious to the grins and muttered suggestions from passersby.

With fingers laced and palms pressed, the couple walked to the nearby cozy seaside hotel and restaurant owned and operated by Alistair's aunt and uncle. Marisa marveled at the panoramic splendor of the town surrounding the bay below the restaurant's tall windows and quickly devoured every bite of the chef's dinner menu selection.

Alistair grinned at her over his half-empty plate. "When did you last have something to eat?"

Marisa sat back and transferred her napkin from lap to table. "I think I had a piece of toast before I left my flat this morning."

"Then you'll be wanting dessert." Marisa looked up into round cheeks, bright blue eyes and a contagious smile worn by an older woman in chef whites. "You must be Marisa. Alistair has told his uncle and me so much about you I feel like I already know you." She wiped her hands on the side towel in her apron pocket and stuck out her right hand in welcome. "I'm Maeve McGillivray. Pleased to make your acquaintance."

Marisa smiled and shook Maeve's hand. "Thank you for putting me up on short notice."

Maeve pulled out and sat in the only empty chair at the four-top window table. "You're most welcome." She motioned toward the fourth chair filled with Marisa's backpack and overnight bag. "Have you checked in?"

Marisa shook her head. "Yes, but I haven't been to the room yet."

"Eliot reserved the corner suite with a bay view." Maeve winked at Alistair. "Only the best for a guest of our Alistair. So, Marisa, I'd like your professional opinion. What do you think of our restaurant?"

"My professional opinion?" Marisa felt Alistair's discomfort level spike. "I'm working at a fish and chip shop and a pub in Glasgow."

Maeve looked puzzled. "Alistair told us you'd worked at a restaurant in New York City and you were studying to be a chef."

"That is partly true. I did work as an apprentice in the kitchen at Chez Nous in mid-town Manhattan. I was accepted to culinary arts school. But I decided to move to Scotland instead."

Maeve glanced at Alistair through narrowed eyes. Her lips curved to half-grin. "I see. Well, I'd still be interested in hearing what you have to say as an informed customer. Would you have time in the morning to have a look around our kitchen? Let us know how it measures up to big city standards?"

Marisa smiled. "I'd be happy to."

Alistair carried her bag and backpack to the corner suite. She stopped him at the door, her hand on his broad chest.

He read her action as a barrier protecting privacy and modesty. "Well, goodnight then," he said and brushed her lips lightly with his.

"Did you tell your aunt and uncle that I'm looking for a job here?"

Alistair sucked in air between his teeth. "I might have mentioned that in passing."

"And how much did you exaggerate my qualifications?"

"Maybe a wee bit." He smiled and kissed her forehead. "You can't blame a man for trying. I told you. I want you with me, Marisa."

Her key in the lock let them in.

Marisa sighed. "Oh, my! This is lovely!" Her fingertips sank into the pale yellow eyelet quilt and full-sized featherbed beneath. Plush round throw rugs dotted the polished hardwood floor. Open doors on a large armoire revealed a row of drawers and empty side closet to hang coats, suits and dresses. The full bath with large claw foot tub and shower, fluffy white bath towels and scented soaps invited her indulgence.

Marisa pushed back white lace curtains and gasped at the reality of promised view. "I honestly had no idea that Scotland could be this beautiful."

Alistair set her bags on the floor at the foot of the bed and crossed around to stand behind her. "The west coast and Highlands are a world away from the Lowlands." His hands around her waist gently pulled her against him. He nuzzled and softly kissed the sweet spots on her neck, at the nape, behind and below her ears. "Marisa," he whispered. His fingers brushed the buttons on her blouse, followed the waistband of her jeans to the curve of her hips.

113

"Alistair," she breathed. Soft fingers behind his neck from arms raised over her head accentuated sensual points of arousal beneath her blouse. "Please, Alistair." He did as she asked, cupped her breasts in his palms. His erection at her back strained against the confining zipper.

"I promise I'll stop when you tell me to. But don't tease me, lassie." Strong hands on her shoulders turned her in his arms. The crush of his lips burned with fiery passion on hers. His arms lifted and carried her to the bed. She lay back and let his fingers open the buttons he'd caressed. Skinny straps on her cotton camisole slid over her shoulders and down her arms. Marisa gasped when his lips closed around sensitive nipples and suckled her breasts.

"Alistair!"

Foreplay abruptly ceased. "Too much, too soon." Reluctantly, he covered her with the blouse he'd unbuttoned. "Goodnight, sweetheart." His tender kiss contrasted the hunger and burn of only seconds before.

He slipped off the bed, adjusted himself, crossed to and opened the door. Light from the hallway silhouetted all she'd dreamed of and desired. "I'll see you in the morning, love." The door softly clicked closed behind him.

"Dammit!" Her palms spanked the quilt. She hadn't meant to push him away. She wanted him to make love to her. The urgency of his need to claim her and the intense arousal at his touch had startled her. She undressed, drew a bath and soaked in soothing warmth. The day of travel took its toll in the tub. Marisa willed her drooping eyelids open, patted dry with a fluffy towel and slept naked between crisp sheets warmed by the quilt.

The dream returned that night. She called to him and he came to her, scooped her up and carried her from danger to safety, straddling the back of a brilliant white horse. This time the sleep-induced illusion continued on a bluff above the churning sea. He lay her down in swaying tall grass, parted her legs and entered her, thrusting deep in rhythm with her until they cried out together in shuddering climax.

She woke clutching a pillow, knees bent, heels dug into the feather-bed, moaning his name. A primal urge beyond explanation or control compelled her to search her backpack for the brooch within the box. Sparks snapped from precious metal to the tips of her fingers. The lions' green eyes glowed.

She burrowed into the pillows for a return to sleep that eluded her. She gave up as the pink blush of dawn turned gold and the sun's slanted rays through the windows duplicated lace curtain patterns on the room's white walls. Marisa showered and dressed for breakfast and the promised assessment of the hotel's kitchen.

Dining room tranquility dissolved to chaos on the other side of the swinging doors. A bus boy lost his grip on a tray loaded with dirty plates, cups and glassware, spilling a trail of leftovers littered with sharp shards of broken china and glass across the floor. A line cook shouted over an unintended flambé. Marisa snatched an open box of baking soda from the pastry chef's station and smothered the flames.

"Oh, Marisa! Thank heaven you were here." Alistair's Auntie Maeve wiped a grease-stained side towel across her face damp with sweat. Marisa recognized the frantic buried-in-the-weeds look and offered her help. "Bless you!" Maeve replied. "Chef took a personal day and we're already down a sous chef."

Marisa put on the cleanest apron and chef coat she could find, calmed the rattled cook, soothed the sputtering bus boy, and went to work commanding the chef-less kitchen. Three hours, dozens of eggs and several pounds of sausage and bacon later, Marisa noticed Alistair sitting at the chef's table with Maeve. His smile at her over the rim of a coffee cup weakened her knees and lit up her core.

115

Maeve motioned her over. "Sit down, my dear," the older woman crooned. "You were a godsend this morning." She patted and squeezed her nephew's hand. "Ali, I'm sorry you had to change your plans. I just don't know what we would have done without her."

Marisa sat down and grinned at Alistair. "What plans?"

"Nothing we cannot do tomorrow, love." He leaned forward to lightly kiss her lips. "Or maybe another morning," he whispered.

"There's my love." Maeve reached for the hand of the tall, dark, brooding man standing next to her. "Marisa. Have you met my husband?"

"Eliot McGillivray." He extended his right hand. "Thank you for your help." Marisa shook his hand and nodded. "My wife may have mentioned we have an opening for a sous chef. From what I've heard and seen today, you are more than qualified to do so."

Marisa shook her head. "Well, I don't know about that. I mean, I'm not trained to be a sous chef."

Maeve laughed. "You sure fooled me. You ran the kitchen this morning like it was second nature to you."

Eliot pulled out and sat in the last empty chair at the table. "It is. She's Chef Darien McKenna's daughter. It's in her blood."

Marisa's grey eyes opened wide. "H-how did you know …" she stammered.

Eliot smiled and the heavy mood around him lifted. "I'm an American ex-pat, like you. My parents immigrated from Edinburgh to Brooklyn. Your father was a celebrity. My Mum and sisters never missed his cooking shows on the telly. They wanted to go to his restaurant, swoon over him in person and eat a meal he prepared. But my working class family couldn't afford Chez Nous." He stood, ending the impromptu interview. "The job is yours if you want it."

He grinned at Alistair and slapped his shoulder. "Do what you can to convince her, Ali."

Chapter 22

Alistair waited in the hotel's lobby while Marisa freshened up and changed into a clean pair of jeans and short-sleeved lavender sweater. He envied the fabric that hugged her breasts and body and savored the sensual swing of her hips as she walked ahead of him admiring Mallaig's storefront displays. He treated her to a late lunch in town before heading into the Highlands and home.

He opened the Land Rover's passenger's side door for her, rounded the silver hood and slipped behind the steering wheel on the vehicle's right side.

Marisa sighed. "I'm not sure I'll ever get used to this. It's backward."

He laughed. "Not to us." Kilometers passed in idle conversation over two-lane curves on rural road. The driver in a passing pickup honked and waved. Alistair returned the greeting.

"Who was that?" Marisa asked.

"Robbie and Brenda," he replied. "They're on their way home." He leaned over and kissed her cheek. "We'll have the farm all to ourselves tonight."

Driveway gravel ground under the tires. Alistair parked the car between the barn and the farmhouse front door. Marisa stepped away from the vehicle and around in a 360 degree slow turn. "Oh, Alistair." Her eyes glistened. "You live here?"

"Aye." His arm around her shoulders pulled her to him. "This is my home."

"It's so much like the farm in Iowa where I grew up." She grinned. "Except we had a horse and a dog instead of sheep and cattle." A deep frown erased her grin. "And the apple orchard."

Alistair stared at her in disbelief. "You grew up on a farm?"

She nodded. "I was born in the farmhouse, in my parents' bedroom."

He shook his head. "I had no idea." He turned to her, lifted her chin with his fingertips. "What is it about the apple orchard that makes you sad, love?"

Tears welled and spilled from her eyes. "My Daddy had a heart attack last summer. I was in New York. He died there, under an apple tree."

"Ah, sweetheart." He held her, stroked her hair, kissed her forehead as she cried against his chest.

"I wanted to be a chef like him." The words flowed with her tears. "I worked in the restaurant where he had been the exec, moved into an apartment in the building where he had lived. When he died, I ran away. I quit my job and came to Scotland. I don't really know why. I just knew I had to."

"I'm so glad you did." He cradled her lovely face in his hands and touched his lips to hers. "Come inside with me now." He walked with her up the steps and through the front door to the hallway that led to his sanctuary. He settled her onto the overstuffed sofa. On his knees, he slipped off her shoes. She moaned softly as he massaged her feet.

He noticed her glance at the massive floor-to-ceiling stone fireplace. "I could light a fire, if you'd like," he said.

"Well, it is a little cooler than I'm used to in July." She grinned.

He grinned back. "I'll take that as a yes." He piled fresh wood behind the protective brass screen. Satisfied that he'd stoked the flame to sustained life, he poured a dram of whisky for himself, a half dram for Marisa, and sat beside her. "What is it you Americans say? Cheers." He handed the glass to her.

"Cheers." Marisa raised the liquid gold to her lips, swallowed quick and coughed. Again and twice more.

Alistair patted and rubbed her back between the shoulder blades. "You're meant to sip it, sweetheart. Take it slow. The first time can be a wee bit rough."

She smiled and shrugged. "I'm in Scotland. I'll get used to it." She pointed to her empty glass. "Even enjoy it."

He held the open bottle over her glass, hesitated before pouring her another. "Are you sure?"

"Absolutely."

Alistair re-heated Brenda's doubled batch of mid-day mutton stew and served dinner in front of the fireplace. "Please give my compliments to the chef," she told him. They cuddled on the sofa, watched whatever the BBC televised, and dozed off. Alistair's heavy eyelids snapped open around midnight.

"Marisa?" She slept against him, comfortable and safe in his arms. "Well, you won't be needing that hotel room tonight, sweetheart." He carried her up the stairs to his bed, covered her with the duvet and kissed her cheek. "Sleep well, love," he whispered, lay down beside her and drifted back to sleep.

The sound of water pummeling tile in the bath next door slapped him wide awake. "What the hell," he muttered, then remembered he had a house guest. Invading light leaked into the hallway when the door opened. Marisa stepped through the door to his bedroom wrapped in one of the newly-purchased snow white bath towels.

"I'm sorry. Did I wake you?" She closed the distance between them slowly, deliberately, as though stalking prey. The closer she got to him, the more seductive her purr, the more his erection swelled. She dropped her towel. He groaned and freed his body of clothes.

He dropped to his knees in worship of the beauty that stood before him. "Oh, Marisa," he moaned. He touched, explored, caressed and tasted every inch of her, from the honey that coated her inner

120

thighs to the nipples he'd suckled the previous night. Gently, he sat her down, legs dangling over the side of his bed. His hands slid under her, squeezed her buttocks, lifted her from the mattress, opened her hips and thighs to nibble, tease, lick and mold his lips around her most feminine spot.

She arched her back, clamped her knees around him and tried to push away. "Alistair," she panted, "I can't …"

"Yes, you can, love." He licked her juices and softly pulled at what pulsed with his lips.

The duvet knotted in Marisa's clawing fists. She screamed his name. Tidal waves of sexual euphoria overwhelmed her. Between her cries she heard what sounded like a wrapper being opened. His hands spread her legs wide.

Intense pain unleashed a new and very real scream. She retreated in self defense, hugged her knees, rolled away from him and whimpered.

"Marisa?" His voice trembled, heavy with fear, concern and confusion. "Did I hurt you? I didn't mean to hurt you." Alistair touched her shoulder. She recoiled. "Ah, God, lassie. I'd never hurt you." He fell back into a mound of pillows scattered against the carved wooden headboard. Realization demanded he ask a delicate question. "Marisa, am I your first?" He touched her shoulder again. "Are you … a virgin?"

She nodded yes and fought back a sob.

"Ah, God," Alistair repeated. "I'd guessed you were younger than me. I know you have to be eighteen to work in a pub."

"I'm nineteen!" She bolted from the bed, grabbed the towel she'd dropped on the floor, and threw his discarded clothes at him. "Get dressed! Take me to the hotel! I'll go back to Glasgow and we'll forget that any of this happened!"

121

She stomped down the hall and slammed the bathroom door. Panic seized him. "Marisa!" He ripped the sheet from the bed and wrapped it around his waist. "Marisa, please!" His fist hammered the door between them. "Don't do this! Give me, NO! Give US another chance!"

"You don't want me!" she howled.

"Ah, lassie, nothing could be further from the truth. I've wanted you in my bed since I saw you at the pub." He grimaced, cursed himself. "No, that didn't come out right. That's not what I meant. Well, yes it is, but … oh fuck me!" He slid down the wall, buried his head in his hands. "Let's start over. We'll take it slow. We'll date. Get to know each other better. I'll take you to a movie, a play, a concert, a football match. Whatever you want me to do, I'll do it. I promise." He wiped away tears of desperation with the back of his hand. "Please, Marisa! I want you with me. I'll break down this door if I have to."

The door opened. He looked up. She hadn't dressed. Only the towel covered her.

"It wasn't locked." She held her hand out to him. He clutched it for dear life. "Come back to bed with me, Alistair." He pushed himself up and followed her back into the bedroom. She tossed her towel on the bed, reached around and coaxed the torn sheet from his waist. The barely used condom dropped with it. She took another from his bedside table, unwrapped it. Her smooth palm and long fingers stroked the length of his shaft, teased the sensitive tip.

He moaned her name. "Are you sure?"

"Absolutely." She rolled on the latex protection, lay back on the bed and held her arms out to him. "Go slowly, Alistair." She bent her knees, planted her heels in the mattress, and opened her legs. She drew in breath when the tip of him penetrated.

"Does that hurt?"

"No. It feels good. Keep going, Alistair."

He kissed her, covered her, pushed inside her. A wee bit. Then a wee bit more. Patience required to please without inflicting pain, and the strain of holding back, was agonizing, blissful torture. Beads of sweat drenched him. Finally fully inside, he hissed through gritted teeth. "Lassie, I can't do this much longer. You've got to let me move."

"What can I do?" she gasped.

"Move with me."

She dug her fingernails into his sweaty shoulders, pumped her hips in rhythm with his thrusts, rode with him over their brink of rapture.

He rolled to his back, breathless, satisfied at last. Trembling fingers laced through hers. "Are you OK, sweetheart?" he asked her.

"Yes. I'm fine. More than fine. Wonderful." She squeezed his hand, rolled on her side. Her head on his heaving chest, she snuggled against him. "I could get used to this."

He covered them, lovers entwined beneath the duvet. Though exhausted, he held her until sure she was asleep. "So could I, my love," he whispered, "for a lifetime and beyond." He closed his eyes and drifted off to dream.

Chapter 23

Robbie Murray piloted the aging pickup through early morning mist from his modest home in the Highlands to the McKenzie farm he'd tended for twenty years. Brenda, his Brenny, wife and mother of three grown sons and a lively teen-aged daughter, wiped condensation from the windshield with her handkerchief and squinted through the peephole. "Something's wrong." She mopped more fog from the glass as the truck's tires spit driveway gravel.

Robbie parked the truck behind Alistair's Range Rover and silenced the rumbling engine. His eyes scanned the surroundings. "McKenzie usually leaves the barn door open while he's working." He shrugged. "Maybe he closed it to keep out the rain."

Brenda opened her door. "It's not raining that hard." She swiveled and landed both boots down. "And it's too quiet."

"Don't borrow trouble, woman." Robbie got out of the truck, strode to the barn and opened its massive doors. Three pair of canine eyes greeted him, tails wagging the other end. "What the devil? Why are you lads still in here?" The lead dog nudged Robbie's leg with the empty food bowl clamped in his teeth. "No food or water?" He scratched his head and whistled. Three sets of ears perked up. "Well I'll be damned." He filled the bowls and trotted to the house.

"Brenny?" The screen door slammed behind him. He crossed through the kitchen, found her standing in the hallway at the bottom of the stairs.

"His car is here. He has to be here, Robbie." Worry etched more lines on her face. "Maybe he's not feeling well. Do you think we should go up and check on him?"

Robbie shook his head. "Upstairs has always been the boss' private space."

"We've got to do something."

"McKenzie," Robbie called. "Is everything alright?"

"Alistair! Wake up!" Marisa tried to shake him awake.

Afterglow laden sleep lifted slowly. The grin still stretched his lips. He pulled her to him, arms open, eyes closed.

"Alistair!" Marisa persisted. "There's someone downstairs!"

"What?!" His senses snapped to attention. Bright daylight filled the room. Too bright. He checked the digital time displayed on the clock near the bedside lamp. "Shit!"

Alistair scrambled from under the duvet, squirmed into jeans, threw on a shirt and tried in vain to tame his hair with his fingers. "That would be the Murrays. Get dressed." He groaned when she kicked free of the duvet that covered her naked beauty. "Although I really wish you wouldn't." He leaned over and kissed her lips hard, fast, and sweet. His bare feet slapped hardwood across the bedroom floor, down the hallway and stairs.

"Morning, Robbie. Brenda." He half-tucked an open shirt into his jeans. "Sorry. I slept in."

A knowing half-smile accompanied the mischievous twinkle in Robbie's eyes. "Just you, McKenzie?" The older man laughed at Alistair's red-faced admission.

"I'll, uh, finish upstairs, and …" Alistair winced. Robbie's bawdy laugh echoed up the staircase.

Brenda elbowed her husband in the ribs. "Breakfast will be ready in fifteen minutes."

"Set the table for four this morning, boss?" Robbie wiped watery mirth from his eyes.

"I-I guess … yes. Thank you." Alistair scampered back up the stairs.

"Take your time, McKenzie!" Robbie shouted after him.

Brenda shoved Robbie's muscular overweight self down the hall toward the kitchen. "What's gotten into you?"

"It's more about who McKenzie's gotten into." He hugged his wife before she could push him away and laughed at her wiggle of protest. "Ah, my girl. How could you be married at the tender age of eighteen, bear four children, and not know when a man's had a good shag?"

Eggs and sausage sizzled in the pan under the lid. Brenda kept one eye on breakfast and the other on the kitchen doorway, waiting for the main attraction to appear. Robbie stomped in from sending the dogs off to morning duty. He eased himself into a kitchen chair.

Brenda pulled plates from an upper cupboard. "You could pour the coffee." The lid she lifted from the pan clattered into the sink.

Robbie sighed, grunted, pushed himself up and across to the perked pot on the stove. Black coffee splashed into white china cups lined up like soldiers on the counter. Carefully, he set one beside each of four spoons on round vinyl placements.

"Cream." Brenda pointed at the fridge with the spatula she wielded like a surgical instrument.

Robbie pulled the silver handle, opened the fridge door and grabbed a pint bottle. "Anything else?"

"Sit," she ordered.

"Gladly." He slammed the fridge door, dumped cream into his coffee and set the bottle within the potential reach of all at the table. He plopped into his place at the table, picked up his spoon and glanced toward the doorway. His mouth dropped open in unison with the spoon.

Marisa stood beside Alistair. Long sleek black hair cascaded down her shoulders and over breasts beneath her form-fitting lavender sweater. Make-up free cheeks and lips blushed a light shade of ruby rose. Long black lashes swept smoky grey eyes turned up slightly at the corners. Jeans followed curves of shapely hips and legs Robbie followed with his eyes.

Alistair looped his arm around Marisa. "Robbie. Brenda. This is my, um, guest. Marisa."

Marisa smiled. Robbie shifted in his chair and cleared his throat. Brenda glanced up at Marisa and over to her husband's inappropriate reaction.

"I'm very pleased to meet you both. And thank you so much for the mutton stew, Brenda. It was delicious."

"I always cook double at mid-day for McKenzie's dinner. No big thing. But thank you. I'm glad you liked it." Brenda moved full plates of food to each place at the table. "Let's eat." She sat at her place, spread the napkin across her lap, and kicked her husband's shin with the toe of her boot."

"Ow! Again with the boot!"

She glowered at him. "It's not polite to stare."

Alistair pulled a chair away from the table for Marisa. "Can I get you anything else, love?"

Brenda grunted. "It seems she has all she needs."

Movement around the table stopped except for the eyes that locked on Brenda. She clamped a hand over her open mouth. "I don't know why I said that. How rude of me! I am so sorry, McKenzie."

His blue eyes darkened. "I believe you owe the apology to my guest."

Marisa shook her head. "It's OK, really."

Robbie scowled at his wife. "No, it's not. McKenzie's right. Marisa is a guest at his home where we are lucky enough to have work."

Brenda's lower lip quivered. "I'm sorry, Marisa. Please excuse me." Brenda tossed her napkin on the table and stood. Her boot heels rapped the kitchen floor and down the hardwood hall.

Marisa glanced from Alistair to Robbie. "Excuse me. But what just happened?"

Alistair shook his head. "I'm afraid I have no idea."

"I think I do." Robbie picked up the spoon he'd dropped and pointed the tip of it toward the doorway. "Brenny's got this crazy idea that you're going to sell the farm and move back to Glasgow so you can be with your lassie."

Marisa crossed her arms over her chest. "Well, I wish she would have stayed to hear what I have to say about that."

Alistair's eyebrows arched. "Which is?"

"I'm going to take the job your aunt and uncle offered me at their restaurant. I'm moving to Mallaig."

Robbie beamed. "Well, now, that's right fine news. What do you have to say about that, boss?"

Shock, disbelief, and delight passed in waves of emotion across Alistair's face. He took her in his arms, pressed his body to hers. "Are you sure?"

"Absolutely."

His lips closed on hers. Their kiss carried on for long, luscious moments.

Robbie pushed away from the table. "I'll go get Brenny." He grinned, stood, pivoted and backed through the doorway. "Her breakfast is getting cold."

Chapter 24

The day at Alistair's farm ended much better than it began. Marisa pitched in to help get the daily chores back on timely track. Brenda accepted and began to enjoy Marisa's guidance and companionship in the kitchen. Robbie was impressed with her willingness to throw hay and obvious first-hand knowledge and gentle care handling the animals.

Alistair never stopped smiling.

"I don't know how you did it. But you've found your perfect match, McKenzie." Robbie closed the barn door and grinned at his boss. "When is she going back to Glasgow?"

Alistair's smile disappeared. "Tomorrow morning."

"No worries. It's only a temporary separation."

"You know I'll sweat it until she steps off that train again in two weeks."

"I would, too, if I were in your boots." Robbie opened the driver's side door and climbed in the truck beside his wife.

Brenda leaned over her husband's lap. "Make sure she comes back." She grinned and winked at Alistair. "Ask her to marry you before she gets on that train."

The truck growled to life. Alistair stepped back, waved, and watched red tail lights dissolve in the mist. "I plan to do exactly that," he said.

That Marisa would stay the night with Alistair was an unspoken given. He'd called ahead to open the room for another guest, told Maeve they would retrieve Marisa's belongings that evening, and made a reservation for two for dinner. While Maeve and Eliot were pleased to gain her employment, Chef Bryan Dumont's cool reaction gave Marisa second thoughts.

Even in flats, Chef stood a full head shorter than Marisa. His girth forced him to wear a full apron with bib. A waist apron would not span and tie around his rotundity. "You don't have the experience or credentials I normally require of a sous chef in my kitchen," he told her in his most condescending tone. "But the McGillivrays insist. Family and favors always come first."

Marisa covered her irritation with sarcasm delivered through a tight smile. "My work in this kitchen during your absence has already impressed the owners. I'll do my best to prove myself to you, Chef." Head held high, she turned on her heels, slapped the swinging doors open with her palms, and joined Alistair in the idling Land Rover.

Alistair couldn't wait to get her back in his bed. Marisa was more than ready to oblige. The sweet love they made would have to satiate desire for a fortnight.

"Alistair." Marisa's whisper in his ear and her teasing fingernails up, down and around his arousal fired every nerve in his body at once. "Do you like what I'm doing to you?" she purred. "Does this give you pleasure?"

He moaned through a spreading grin. "It's a good place to start."

"What about this?" She disappeared beneath the sheet, slid down his torso. The tip of her tongue traced from his sternum to the tip of his erection. Her lips closed around it. Her tongue circled it. She flipped the sheet back. The sultry smoke in her steel-grey eyes stoked his fires. "Do you want more?" She blew on his dampness.

He sucked in breath. "Ah, God yes!"

He watched her lips take him, descend the length of him, rise and fall again. And again. Each time, at deepest descent, the low hum vibration from the back of her throat jolted him closer to the brink of release.

His hips jerked when she caressed with her fingers what her lips did not. "Marisa!" The alarm sounded. The fire raged. Only she could ever relieve him. Save him. He pounded the mattress with his fists and flooded the hum. Extinguished the fire.

For now.

She sat back on her heels and watched him recover. He opened his eyes to the smoke that smoldered in hers. She licked her lips and smiled at him like a pleased Cheshire cat. "What would you like to do next?" she asked.

"Give me a minute." He filled his lungs, forced a return to rhythmic breathing. And laughed.

She frowned. "What's so funny?" Her lower lip protruded to pout.

He propped up on his elbows. His love for her overwhelmed him. He stroked her cheek, wound his fingers through her hair, followed the strand to her breast he caressed. "You came to my bed a virgin. You've become a seductress."

"Is that bad?"

"On the contrary." He pulled her down, rolled her over, opened her legs wide with his hands, kissed the sweet spot between them. "That is very, very good."

Chapter 25

Robbie and Brenda had breakfast at home and took care of the early morning chores to give Alistair and Marisa privacy. While they remained aware of time's passage, they tried not to think about the inevitable, although temporary, time apart.

Marisa set her backpack and bag at the front door. "It's only two weeks." She reached for his hand, wove her fingers through his. "Do you think you'll be able to find me a place to live in town by then?"

He checked his wristwatch, kissed her forehead. "Let's talk about that." He led her to the sofa where they'd spent their first evening together in the home that he hoped would soon be theirs. "Why not live here with me."

"Alistair, I don't have a car and I can't drive yours. How would I get to work?"

He squeezed her hand and smiled. "I'll give you driving lessons. In the meantime, I'll take you to work and pick you up."

"Restaurant hours can be very unpredictable. Schedules can change."

"We'll manage."

She shrugged. "I don't know."

"My love, if it's commitment you need, I'll give you that." He reached in his jacket pocket.

"Wait! I have to show you something first." She went to the door and sifted through the contents of her backpack for the box she brought to him. She opened the lid, felt its power surge without touching it. "Grandma Donna gave this to me. She said it would help me find my way."

Alistair low-whistled through his teeth. "The McKenna Clan Crest. May I?"

"Of course."

Mini-lightning bolts of static charge leapt from the lion's green eyes to Alistair's outstretched hand. "My God!" He jerked his hand away. "Does that always happen?"

Marisa laid the brooch in her palm. The metal snapped and sparked. Green eyes glowed. "Only for me. And for you."

"What does it mean?"

"I'm not sure. But I know I've found my way. To you." She put the brooch back in the box, closed the lid. "Now what were you saying about commitment?"

"I have something to show you." He reached back in his pocket for a small blue velvet pouch. "My grandmother wore this ring. My mother gave it to me." Alistair opened the drawstring. A gold band with diamonds half-moon set around a single carat heart-shaped emerald dropped into his hand. "I promised her I would give it to my true and only love." He took her left hand in his and slipped the ring on her third finger. A perfect fit. "I love you, Marisa. Will you marry me? Will you be my wife?"

The tingling sensation under the gold band felt the same as the first time she'd touched the brooch. The dazzling emerald glowed like the lions' eyes. Joyful tears of affirmation flowed. "Oh, yes, Alistair. I love you. I belong here with you." Her arms around his neck held him close. "I will always and forever be yours," she whispered in his ear.

Chapter 26

Text messages and cell phone conversations would have to bridge the distance and time between Marisa's departure and return trip arrival at Mallaig Station. Marisa called Alistair from the grand lobby of Glasgow's Queen Street Station. She flopped on her flat's lonely bed for one and phoned him again, moaned his name after the last I love you, see you soon, and fell asleep.

Rachel answered on the third long tone call to Iowa the next day. "Are you back in Glasgow, big sister?"

"Yes. But not for long. I called my landlord and told him I'm moving out. I gave both my bosses two weeks' notice. I scored a sous chef job at a restaurant in Mallaig. That's the town on the west coast near where Alistair lives."

"Where are you going to live?"

"With Alistair. Rach, he asked me to marry him!" Marisa waited long seconds for Rachel's reaction.

"I'm guessing you said yes."

"Of course I did! I am so in love with him. I don't know how I'm going to get through the next two weeks. I want to be with him so bad!"

"Marisa. Get real," her eighteen-year-old sister scolded her. "You've been with this guy a few days total and you're ready to move again, live with him, sleep with him?"

Marisa laughed. "Yes, yes and already have. You forgot marry him. "

"You are so much like Dad. Jump first and look later."

"That's not fair!"

"Oh, yeah? Did you use contraception?"

135

"That's none of you business but, yes, he did use condoms and no, I'm not pregnant. I got my period last night." Marisa fought the urge to throw the phone across the room. "You know what? Forget it. I thought … I wanted you to be happy for me. I'm happy for me! Maybe you're just jealous! Goodbye, Rach."

"Marisa …"

She hung up and turned off the phone.

Alistair paced the fence line while Robbie whistled the dogs in at another day's end. He checked his cell phone for a text message, voice mail message, words written or spoken by Marisa.

Nothing.

He swore under his breath and paced the fence line again.

"What's wrong, boss?" Robbie closed the barn doors and leaned an elbow on the top fence rail.

"I haven't heard from Marisa since she called me from her flat last night." Deep lines of worry appeared to age him years instead of hours. "Every call I make goes to voice mail. I've left messages, texted her." He checked his phone again. "I'm calling the Glasgow police."

"Hold on, McKenzie." Robbie's large, calloused hands settled on Alistair's shoulders. "Don't you know someone in the city who could check on her? Where is she now?"

"She should be working behind the bar at the pub where I met her. I tried calling there but the fecking line is always busy."

"What about your brothers?"

Alistair shook his head. "They're both living in Edinburgh now."

"Your mother?"

Alistair's blue eyes flashed. "I'm not going to ask my mother to go to a pub and check on my fiancée that she's never met. She doesn't even know about me and Marisa."

"You haven't told your mother?"

"I haven't had time!"

Robbie removed his cap and scratched his head. "Well, what about a friend?"

Alistair's eyes lit up. "A friend! Yes! Dougie! He went with me to the pub." He punched the number and paced. "Dougie. Hey, it's Alistair. I need you to do me a favor."

Dougie waved goodnight to his office mates and pulled car keys from his pocket. "I will if I can."

"Remember that beautiful woman who served us whisky at the pub after Danny's wedding?"

"Aye. That lassie's pretty hard to forget."

"I took her out, she came to visit, and we got engaged."

"Feckin' hell! That's only been, what, a few weeks?"

"I fell fast and hard."

"You certainly did."

Alistair's rapid fire delivery sped up with every word. "She's in Glasgow. She went back to quit work and move out of her flat. She's not answered a text or returned my calls all day. I'm worried."

"More like frantic. Take some deep breaths and calm down. She's probably just been busy."

"Dougie! Listen to me!" Alistair shouted into the phone. "Please go to the pub. See that she's there, that she's," he swallowed hard, "safe."

"Alright, Alistair. I just left the office. I'm only a few blocks away."

"Call me when you get there. Please, Dougie," he pleaded and hung up.

"I will. Alistair!" he frowned at the phone. "Shit!" Dougie hit redial.

 Alistair answered. "There's no way you're there already."

"You didn't give me an important piece of information. What's her name?"

"Marisa."

The after work crowd packed the tables and lined the bar. Dougie pushed his way through, saw the flash of black ponytail, a white tank top dipped and stretched over perfect breasts, and caught the attention of eyes the color of smoke. "Ah, you lucky bastard," he muttered.

"What?" A taller portly man at Dougie's elbow glared down at him.

"Not you. My friend. He's engaged to marry that lovely lass who's about to serve you a pint."

The big man's smile widened in appreciation of the view. "Aye." He nodded. "Lucky bastard."

"What can I get for you?" Marisa set the glass of ale on a coaster in front of her customer and turned to Dougie.

"You're Marisa, right?"

 "Have we met?"

"I'm Dougie MacLeod, a friend of your fiancé. I was here with Alistair the night you two met."

His envy of Alistair ratcheted up with her dazzling smile. "Oh, yes, I remember. You ordered a drink and left before I could pour it. Would you like a dram of Glenlivet or something else?"

"You've a good memory. Well, that's not why I'm here, but sure." He used the time between placing the order and her return with his drink to call Alistair. "I'm here at the pub and so is Marisa. She's fine, my friend. She's pouring me a dram."

Dougie felt the relief in Alistair's audible release of breath. "Thank God."

"You're welcome."

Alistair laughed. "Would you ask her to call me as soon as she can and, Dougie, tell her I love her."

"I'll do the first and as to the second, you've asked her to marry you. I'm pretty sure she knows."

Marisa closed the pub's employee break room door and fished the cell phone from the bottom of her purse. She frowned at the lack of signal then cursed at the reason and turned the phone on. Text and voice mail messages, all from Alistair, filled the screen.

"Alistair, I'm so sorry. I turned off my phone to keep my sister from calling me back and I forgot to turn it back on. Your friend Dougie told me how worried you were."

"I may have overreacted a wee bit. I love you so much, Marisa. I couldn't bear the thought that something might have happened to you. That I wasn't there and couldn't get to you."

"May I remind you that I've been living in Glasgow on my own for six months?"

"I know and you're perfectly capable of taking care of yourself. Can I help it that I want to do that now?" He sighed, changed the subject. "So why don't you want to talk to your sister?"

"When I told her about us, she went all parental on me. She said I was just like Dad, that I don't look before I leap."

"What did she mean by that?"

"To make a long story short, I was born in May and my parents got married two months later."

"So you told her we had …"

"She asked me. I wouldn't lie."

"Of course not. Did you also tell her we're engaged?"

"Of course I did. But she'd stopped listening and so did I." Marisa glanced at the round wall clock. "Break's over. I've got to go."

"Call me when you get back to your flat tonight, sweetheart. I love you."

"I love you."

His cell phone rang as soon as the call from Marisa ended. "Hello?"

"Evening, McKenzie." Robbie's deep voice rumbled through the connection. "Did you hear from Marisa?"

"Yes, she's fine. Her phone was off. I just finished talking to her."

"That's grand news. Mind if I give you a wee bit of advice?"

"I'd be pleased if you did."

"You've got to trust that everything will be alright. You'll drive yourself crazy if you don't. Take it from an old married man and a father of four who's just found out that he's soon to be a grandfather."

"Congratulations to you and yours, Robbie."

"Thank you, boss. Get a good night's sleep. After you call your mother. She needs to know you're getting married."

"All good advice. See you in the morning." Alistair ended one call and speed dialed another. "How are you, Mum? I know. I'm sorry I haven't called in a while. Are you busy? No? Good. I've got something to tell you and someone to tell you about."

Chapter 27

The longest two weeks of their young lives ended at Mallaig Station. Alistair held his future wife in his arms and vowed never to be apart from her again. He filled the back of the Land Rover with all she owned in Scotland and pressed his lips on hers as soon as the car doors closed. Shaking fingers pulled her tank top free from the band of the pencil skirt she wore. His hands sought out bare skin beneath, caressed over and under her bra. His lips left hers to trail kisses down her neck, whisper her name. She guided his hand in hers between her spread legs, moaned when he pushed her panties aside.

"Ah, my love. We need to be home." He kissed her, started the engine, and sped out of the car park. His erection throbbed under her cupped hand caress and his closed zipper. Pressure and pleasure mounted with each stroke of her palm. "Marisa, sweetheart." Breath rasped from his throat. "I love what you're doing. But we'll never make it to the farmhouse."

"Then pull over."

"Here?" The car crested the hill overlooking the bay and ocean beyond.

"This car will go off road, won't it?"

"Yes, but …"

"Then pull off."

He dropped the transmission into low gear and bore left through heather and swaying grass.

"This is it. This is the place. Stop!" she commanded.

Alistair applied the brakes, shifted gears and cut the engine. Marisa jumped from the car and slammed the door.

"Marisa?" He got out, closed his door and chased her as she ran through the grass. In hands held high above her head she clutched the blanket he kept in the car for comfort in case of emergency. The rough cloth billowed in the ocean breeze, fluttered like a cape behind her. She tossed the blanket to the ground and knelt on it. Her long silky black hair flowed around her. Graceful arms slipped the tank top and camisole over her head.

"Marisa!" In his wildest erotic fantasy, Alistair had never imagined a woman more beautiful than his. He knelt behind her, covered her breasts with his hands, brushed fingertips over nipples raised from arousal and the wind. She hiked her skirt to her waist and rocked back into his erection. "Take me here. Now!"

"I don't have anything with me," he protested. "Nothing to protect …"

"That doesn't matter! I love you, Alistair!"

"Are you sure?"

"Absolutely!"

He moaned in relief as he unzipped. Satin and lace panties slid over her hips, down her thighs. He joined her, slid easily into her, joined with her as she bent forward. His palm rubbed her nipple. His thumb circled the hot throbbing spot near where he'd entered her.

"Do you like what I'm doing to you, Marisa?" he breathed into her ear.

"Yes!"

"I want to please you. Tell me. Am I giving you pleasure?"

"Yes, Alistair!"

"Are you ready for me, my love?"

143

Her long moan rose to scream his name over the crash of churning waves on the rocks below. He thrust deep inside her, rocked against her. The tip of him at the entry to her womb flooded her. Locked together, facing the ocean, they writhed as one in passion and completion.

In the box in the backpack pressed against the car window, the brooch trembled and sparked. The lions' watchful green eyes flickered. The emerald set in the ring of betrothal on the third finger of Marisa's clenched left fist shimmered, glowed, and burned cold.

They moved about their home, new to domesticity yet comfortable with the routine. Marisa unpacked her clothes, found shelf space for books and photos and tucked away personal items. She laid out a clean chef coat and pants with her knife kit, ready for her first day on the job as sous chef.

They made love sweetly, softly, tenderly. "Why bother," she told him when he reached for a condom and sighed as he entered her uncovered.

He took her to work the next morning before mid-day, shared a meal with the Murrays as usual, excused himself and made a phone call before afternoon chores.

"Benjamin," he greeted a former colleague and long time friend on the other end of the connection to Glasgow.

"Alistair! How's life treating you?"

"Good and getting better, thank you for asking. I'm getting married and I need a favor."

"You're getting married? To a Highlands lass?"

"No. Marisa just moved here from Glasgow."

"Anyone I might know?"

"I doubt it. She's American. We need to cut through some red tape, if you know what I mean."

"That can be a lot of red tape."

"She has a work visa."

"Well, that helps a wee bit."

"It would be best if we didn't have to wait twenty-nine days."

"Oh." Benjamin clicked his tongue at Alistair. "I see. A bairn on the way, perhaps?"

"Could be." Alistair crossed his fingers at the possible circumstantial evidence. "Her documentation would be on file in Glasgow. She's lived and worked there for six months."

"You want me to push the paperwork through to the registrar."

"Aye, in Broadford."

"The Isle of Skye? Ah, Alistair. Why did you have to go and make this more difficult?"

Alistair laughed. "I have faith in you, Benjamin. If anyone can make it happen, it's you."

He picked her up at the restaurant at the end of her work day and kissed her as though they'd been apart for weeks. "How was your day, sweetheart?"

She shrugged and buckled her seatbelt. "Chef is a jerk. Nothing I can't handle. Besides, eight and maybe ten hour work days with real breaks are a piece of cake."

"You worked longer than that in New York?"

"Twelve or fourteen hours, sometimes longer shifts straight with no break."

"What! That's criminal."

"I agree. This is much better." She squeezed his hand. "In so many ways."

They snuggled on the couch after sharing Brenda's hearty soup and fresh baked bread. "Marisa, my love. We need to talk about getting married."

She sighed and stretched out, her head in his lap. "Alistair, I just got here. What's the rush?"

"Unprotected sex." She laughed. "I'm serious. Making love without anything between us is pure heaven on earth. But I want us to be married before you get pregnant."

"Does this have anything to do with what Rachel said? About me being like Dad and not looking before I leap?"

He nodded. "In part, yes. Say I'm traditional, old-fashioned, whatever. I want to marry you as soon as possible. To that end, I called in a favor from a friend. He can rush through the documents we need to the registrar's office in Broadford on the Isle of Skye. I'll have to make a trip over there tomorrow to sign everything. We can be married at two in the afternoon a week from this coming Wednesday."

Marisa stared at him without blinking. "You're kidding me."

He shook his head. "No. I'm not. It's all arranged."

Conflicting emotions roiled within her. "Alistair, you just went ahead with this without asking me."

"Sweetheart, if we want a formal ceremony in a church later on and a big celebration, we can still do that."

"This is important to you, isn't it?"

"Aye. It is."

"Don't we need witnesses?"

He grinned. "I hadn't thought of that. I'm not sure either of my brothers would be able to take off work and get here from Edinburgh. I know my friend Dougie can't."

"Rachel sure won't be coming from Iowa. We're not even speaking to each other right now."

"Ah, sweetheart. She's your sister. You need to take care of that."

"I will." She smiled up at him. "I'll call her after we're married. I'll have to ask Chef to change next week's schedule." She snorted. "That should be a popular request." She snapped her fingers. "What about your Aunt Maeve and Uncle Eliot?"

He smiled back. "I think they'd like that. We'll ask them tomorrow. For now ..." he lifted her head from his lap, stood, and held out his hand for her to take. "Let's go up to our bed and have unprotected sex."

He held her, caressed the soft supple skin of her side breast and savored the sensation of her fingernails weaving through his chest hair.

"Alistair?"

"Yes, my love?"

"You haven't told me much about your family. Does your mother live in Glasgow?"

147

"Aye, in the house where my brothers and I grew up. She's a lot like you. Feisty. Determined. When I told her about you, she said it was about time I found a lassie to tame me, settle me down."

Marisa laughed. "I'll like her."

"I'm sure you will. She already likes you."

"And your brothers?"

"I'm the oldest. Charlie is two years younger than me. He's the sensible one. Always has to have a plan. He laid out this grid, this matrix of important milestones in his life and so far he's hit every one of them. He graduated from university, got a good job in Edinburgh, married, two children," he grinned, "a boy and a girl, of course. Charlie talked our brother Andrew into moving to Edinburgh and starting a brokerage business together. They're doing quite well, I'm told."

"What about your Dad?"

"Charles senior." Alistair's voice went soft. "My memory of him is fading. He died when I was very young, not long after Drew was born. He worked hard. He was always tired. But never too tired for his family." He grinned. "Or the Rangers. He followed every game either in the stands at the stadium or on the telly. I remember going with him, the sounds, the smells, hanging on to his hand so I wouldn't get lost in the crowd. He put me on his shoulders so I could see."

He turned his head, looked into her eyes, shared the boundless depth, indescribable intensity and virtuous power of his love for her. "He worshipped my mother, as I do you. That's what I waited for, hoped for, was afraid I would never find." He kissed her, stroked her hair, breathed her in. "I love you, Marisa," he whispered. "Truly. Completely. Forever."

Chapter 28

Marisa inspected her reflection in the guest room full length mirror. The white cotton A-line dress with delicate scalloped scoop neckline and cap sleeves displayed in the window of a shop in Mallaig fit as though made for her. The emerald green silk sash she'd chosen to wrap around her waist fell to the hem just below her knees. The strap around her ankles anchored white leather dress shoes on two-inch heels.

Alistair knocked on the guest room's closed door. "Marisa? Are you ready, love?"

After one last look and approving nod, she crossed the oval wool rug over worn planks of wood and opened the door. "You're not supposed to see the bride until the wedding," she said.

Alistair's breath caught in his throat. "You are the most beautiful bride ever." His arms reached for her. She stepped back.

"I want to look like this when I say I do." She clucked her tongue at him. "So don't touch."

He moaned and grinned at her. "The best day of my life is going to be a long day."

"This look suits you," she said. "But I am a little disappointed."

"Why?" He looked puzzled. "I have other suits. But I prefer this blue one. Should I change?"

Marisa smiled. "No, love. The color matches your gorgeous eyes and the suit is super sexy. I just thought you'd wear your kilt."

He rolled his eyes. "When we get married in the church I'll wear my kilt. I promise. Not today." He held out his hand to her. "Are you ready to be Mrs. Alistair McKenzie?"

"Mrs. Marisa McKenzie."

He sighed. "Aye, whatever you say." He clasped her hand and led her to the Land Rover.

Maeve and Eliot were waiting for them in front of the hotel. Maeve's cherubic face and bright smile beamed from under the wide brim of her white straw hat. "What a brilliant day for a wedding!" she crooned. She struggled with the skirt of her dusty pink dress and juggled an odd-shaped box bearing the local florist's stamp. Her dark brown-suited husband took the box from her and opened the vehicle's rear door. "Thank you, love."

She slid in behind Alistair and patted Marisa's shoulder with her white-gloved hand. "Aren't you a bonnie bride!" She leaned forward and kissed her nephew's cheek. "Such a handsome groom!"

Eliot settled in beside his wife with the box across his lap. "Maeve insisted on flowers," he explained.

"A bride must have a bouquet," she said.

Marisa turned and peeked at the box of greenery and white roses tied with blue and white ribbons, the colors of the Scottish flag. "Oh, they're beautiful!"

"There are flowers for your lapels and a corsage for me in there as well," Maeve said.

"We've reservations for dinner at the lodge in Sleat," Eliot said.

Alistair pulled away toward the ferry to Armadale. "How did you manage that on short notice in high season?" he asked.

His uncle grinned. "The owner is an old friend. He'll look after us."

Marisa marveled at the sun-drenched serenity of calm passage and the port and peaks surrounding the isle's rugged Cuillin Mountain range. Traffic on the two-lane road along the eastern coast did not delay the journey. They arrived at Broadford twenty minutes before the scheduled ceremony. Maeve pinned sprigs of roses on suit coat lapels, fluffed Marisa's hair and handed her the bouquet. "Oh, my dears," she clucked. "I am so happy for you!"

"Alistair McKenzie and Marisa McKenna." A tall slender woman with dark-rimmed glasses perched on the bridge of her nose led the bridal party through doors to the registrar's chambers. "I'm Abigail McCluskey." Marisa wondered why the woman seemed so interested in her waistline. "What a lovely dress," she said. "You wear it well."

"Thank you." Marisa laced her fingers through Alistair's.

"Please." The registrar directed each to their place, read the required definition of marriage and recited the legal marriage declarations. Alistair slipped a gold band on his bride's finger. Marisa pledged her love for him and slid a matching ring on the third finger of his left hand. In a matter of moments, the registrar pronounced them husband and wife. The signed marriage schedule finalized a ceremony sealed with a sweet and tender kiss.

"Congratulations." Abigail shook their hands and cast a final look at Marisa's middle before she led them back through the doors.

The celebration continued over dinner prepared by a Michelin star chef. Marisa scanned the menu and ordered a steak dinner.

Alistair smiled at her choice. "Don't you eat anything else?" he said and told his aunt and uncle about their first date in Glasgow.

"Not if I can help it," Marisa said and sliced into the half-pound sirloin.

Maeve declared the cured salmon dish a delicacy. Marisa asked to taste Alistair's roasted lamb that Eliot also chose as his entrée.

"Give us your honest opinion," Eliot requested.

Marisa wrinkled her nose. "It's good. But I would have roasted the lamb in garlic and rosemary rather than thyme."

Maeve and Eliot exchanged a quick glance. "Why?" he asked.

"Garlic and rosemary compliments the flavor of the lamb. It's a richer and more satisfying dining experience, in my opinion," Marisa answered.

Eliot raised his eyebrows and dram of Scotch in salute. "Yes, Chef," he said and winked at his wife.

Alistair pulled the Land Rover's passenger side door parallel with the front porch steps and stilled the engine. "Welcome home, Mrs. McKenzie," he said and kissed his bride. He got out and trotted around the car to open her door, take her hand, help her to her feet, close the door and hand her the keys.

"Why do I need these?" she asked.

"To open the door," he replied. He picked her up, mounted the porch steps, waited for her to turn the key in the lock, carried her across the threshold and up the stairs to their bedroom. "I've been good. I kept my hands to myself all day." He took off his suit jacket and unzipped her dress, lifted the cap sleeves from her shoulders, slid the straps of her silk slip down her arms, unhooked her bra. "Oh, my love, my wife." He suckled her breasts, blew breath on the raised wet nipples, felt her shiver as her wedding dress and everything underneath tumbled to the floor.

He sat her on the bed, removed her shoes, massaged her feet. She loosened and cast aside his tie, unbuttoned and pulled his shirt from the buckled band of his suit pants. She loosened the buckle and belt, opened the zipper, pumped her palm in slow deliberate motions on his shaft. "Do you want me, my husband?" she purred, low and sensual, in his ear.

Alistair growled, disrobed, stood naked and hard before her. She shimmied onto the bed, bent her knees, and peered at him with smoky eyes through her open legs. "Here I am."

He drove into her with the force and intensity of a feral animal. She wrapped her legs around his waist, pushed him deep inside her with her heels on his hips. "Yes, my love," she cried out between thrusts, "my first and only love! Take all of me! Give me all of you!"

"Ah, God, Marisa! You and only you! For the rest of my life!" He thrust full and held, his back arched. His body shook. His head snapped back. Breath rushed from his throat in a roar of surging release. He felt her shudder, clench around him, heard her scream his name as wave after climactic wave washed over her.

He rolled off her, pulled her to him, gradually breathed slower with her. "It's good we're married." He kissed her damp forehead. "If we keep this up, pun definitely intended, we'll be parents much sooner than later."

He cried out when she poked his ribs. "What was that for?"

"Do you have any idea why the registrar was so interested in the way my dress fit? Why she kept looking at my belly?" She poked him again when he didn't answer.

"I may have led my contact in Glasgow to believe that we had reason to expedite our wedding date."

"She thought I was pregnant! Didn't she?"

"That might have been the case."

"Oh, Alistair." She pushed up and away from him. "How many more lies will you tell to get your way?" The steel-grey in her eyes darkened.

"Oh, love, don't be angry," he pleaded.

"Then don't lie."

He sat up, circled her with his arms, lay his head on her shoulder. "I won't. Not ever again. I promise you."

Alistair stirred beside his sleeping bride as the approaching dawn nudged voluminous clouds in the silver sky. He wriggled away from the warmth of her, dressed for chores and padded down the stairs in stocking feet. He sifted through the untouched pile of mail on his desk and grinned at the familiar milky white envelope. Alistair twisted the gold band on his finger. "You don't know it yet. But you're the last unmarried man among us, Dougie. " He tapped out an email message to his friend. My wife and I will be pleased to attend your wedding. Congratulations to you and Molly. Alistair and Marisa McKenzie

He chuckled and hit send.

Alistair tucked his cell phone into the deep pocket of his work jacket, pushed his feet into work boots and stepped into misty daylight. He laughed at the vigorous greeting from his border collie workers eager to eat and begin their day with cattle and sheep. Hay bales seemed lighter. The temperamental latch on the heavy fence gate annoyed him less. He scrolled through the digital phonebook on his cell phone screen and looked up the number of his bothers' Edinburgh office.

"Charles McKenzie." Alistair waited for the voice mail message and beep. "Hello?"

 "Well, what do you know. A real person!"

"Alistair. 'Tis an early hour to be kicking shite on the farm."

 "Too early for your arse to be warming an office chair, Charlie."

"Aye. My clients set the hours. So what message were you going to leave on my voice mail?"

"I'm married."

Charlie slurped and choked on a beverage. "Feck it! I just spit coffee all over my desk. This had better not be your idea of a joke," he sputtered.

"No joke. Marisa and I got married yesterday."

"You phoned before office hours so you wouldn't hear me choke and curse. Am I right?"

Alistair laughed. "You know me too well."

"Does Mum know?"

"Not yet. I'll call her this morning."

Charlie's low whistle traversed the connection to the Highlands. "Mum told Drew and me about her. Said you were serious. I guess you were. I mean, are. Congratulations to you both."

"Thank you."

Background voices interrupted their conversation. "I gotta go. Call me at home tonight."

"I will. Charlie? Tell Drew."

"Right. Give your bride all our best."

Alistair skipped up the porch steps and hummed his happiness through the door and into the kitchen. Marisa sat at the table wrapped in a white cotton robe that brushed her bare ankles, the land line phone pressed to her ear. She smiled at her husband and his heart skipped a beat. "He just came in. I'm looking forward to meeting you, too." Marisa stood and held the phone out to him. "It's your mother."

Alistair scooted a chair away from the table and sat. He took the phone from her in one hand and patted his thigh with the other. She curled into his lap, hugged and nuzzled his neck.

"Good morning, Mum."

"Is there something you're not telling me? I already know you're married. Maeve sent me copies of the photos she took at your wedding."

"That's what I was going to call and tell you. Right after I talked with my wife about bringing her home to meet you."

"I'm happy for you. Truly I am. Marisa seems a sweet lass. It's just this is all so sudden. You haven't known each other long. But I suppose long enough. Alistair, I have to ask. Is there a grandchild on the way?"

Alistair bit his lip to squelch the laughter. "Not that we know of."

"I had to know."

"It's alright, Mum."

"Talk to your wife, then. Let me know when you'll be coming home."

"We will."

"She's lovely."

"That she is."

"You look so happy in these photos of Maeve's. Are you happy, my wee laddie?"

Alistair smiled and held Marisa close. "Ecstatic. Over the moon and back again.

"Ah, that's good. I'll see you soon. I love you."

"I love you too, Mum."

Alistair clicked off the cordless phone, set it on the table, and lightly touched his lips to hers. "When will you ring up your Mum, love?"

"Tonight after dinner. Before bed." She snuggled against him, breathed in the mingled scent of him and the land around him. Felt the fire that coursed through him, between them, and the love that stoked the flame.

Engine rumble and a car door slam broke the mood. Alistair moaned. "Hold that thought." He savored the sight as she left his arms and the room to shower and put on chef whites.

Chapter 29

Sentiments warm and cool greeted Marisa's return to the hotel's kitchen. Maeve beamed and bragged about the beauty of the bride, her handsome groom, and shared every detail of the joyous previous day event. Wait staff and line cooks hugged and congratulated Marisa. The pastry chef presented her with a mini-wedding cake for two topped with rose petal colors of butter cream icing.

Chef scowled in silence until Maeve's mid-afternoon break. "You're on the schedule for Sunday brunch. I trust that you will grace us with your presence. Or will the newlyweds be too inconvenienced?"

Marisa sharpened a knife from her kit and stared him down over a growing mound of fresh-cut produce. "I'll be here." She finished dinner preparations and ignored him through the end of shift.

"How was your day, sweetheart?" Alistair leaned against the Land Rover. A dozen long-stemmed red roses wrapped in cellophane rested in his arm.

"Oh, Alistair, they're beautiful." She cradled the roses and buried her nose in the blooms.

"So are you, my love." He opened the car door for her. "What's this?" He nodded at the small white box tied with a blue bow.

"A wedding cake made by Anna. The pastry chef." She maneuvered into the passenger's seat with the cake and flowers. Alistair slid behind the steering wheel.

"This is getting ridiculous. I've got to start driving myself to work."

"You'll have your first lesson on Sunday."

She wrinkled her nose. "Later in the day, I'm afraid. I'm working brunch."

"I thought Sunday and Monday were your days off."

"Not this week. I took Wednesday off."

"To get married." He started the engine and pulled away toward home. "Sweetheart, you know that you don't have to work."

"Yes, I do. I took this job and I'm not going to quit because Chef is an ass. I've worked with worse."

"I'm sure you have. I'll support you no matter what you decide."

"I know you will, love. But for now I need to do this. For me."

A heart-shaped cake iced pink with a single piped red rose decorated the center of their kitchen table set for two. Marisa opened the envelope wedged under the cake plate and read aloud the Murrays' wishes for a long and happy life together.

Alistair added Anna's cake to the table contents. "We'll cut them both and make a wish." He reached for Marisa and frowned when she resisted.

"I smell like an onion dipped in garlic butter." She stripped off her chef coat and stepped out of the loose-legged pants. "I'm not even going to wear these upstairs."

"Don't stop there." Alistair stood inches away, his blue eyes dark with desire. "Here, let me help." His fingers squeezed, opened and discarded her bra on the pile of chef clothes. His palms pushed her panties past her knees. He offered his hand for balance as she removed what remained and stepped back to admire her.

They walked hand-in-hand through the downstairs hallway and up the stairs to the bath and shower. He adjusted the water temperature for her, offered his hand again to steady her step into the wide cast iron tub and under the shower head flow. He undressed and joined her, lathered his hands and massaged bubbles and foam in sensuous circles on her neck, shoulders, arms, back, belly and breasts. She gasped when his fingers parted her, played with her, penetrated her.

"Sweetheart, making love this way is like nothing you've ever experienced. Do you want me to show you?"

"Yesssss." Her breath escaped between clenched teeth. She closed her eyes and leaned into his wet body, felt his muscled forearms slide under her arms and press against her ribs. With his weight leveraged against the shower tiles, he bent his knees, lifted her, opened her legs with his thighs. The tip of his erection entered her. His hands covered and caressed her breasts.

"Do you want more of me, love?" Slight extensions of his flexed biceps rocked her forward, pushed him deeper into her. "I'm a patient lover. Your pleasure is mine." His muscles flexed, extended. Deeper. "I can wait until you are ready."

Marisa trembled. She mewed like a kitten starved for nourishment.

"Put your hands on my thighs, love."

She did as instructed, pressed her fingertips into wet skin over tense muscle.

"Are you ready for all of me, love?"

She jumped, cried out at his first thrust.

"I have you, love. I won't let you go." He gripped her shoulders, thrust again. "Move with me, Marisa." She locked her thighs around his, ground against him, rode his thrusts, moaned as exquisite rounds of ecstasy overtook and claimed her. His deepest thrust opened her legs wide. His rumbled groan of release vibrated in his chest against her back and up her spine.

He leaned into the lip of the tub and she melted into him, twitching muscles turned flaccid, unable to bear weight. "Relax." The warmth of his breath on her cheek soothed her. "I've got you."

"You do. In every way possible." She exhaled a quavering sigh. "Alistair?"

160

"Yes, love?"

"If I just got pregnant it was so worth it. Remind me of that when I'm giving birth."

Chapter 29

They fed each other wedding cake in bed and shook crumbs from the sheets. Marisa laughed at the mess they'd made. "When I was a kid, Dad's dog Ivory ate anything my sister and I dropped on the floor or gave her if we didn't want it. We need a dog to clean up after us."

Alistair grunted. "We have dogs. They work."

"Yes, the border collies here. But you haven't always lived on the farm. Didn't you or your brothers have pets?"

"No. Mum wouldn't allow it. She said she had enough to do taking care of us and she didn't need another mouth to feed."

"You missed out. I cried so hard when Ivory died, almost as much as when I begged Dad to let us keep Scooter." Sadness clouded her mood. She snuggled under her husband's arm for warmth and comfort. "I don't even know if that little old guy is still around."

Alistair squeezed her shoulder. "Call home." He grinned. "You might also mention you've a husband who loves you more than life."

She kissed him, sat up and reached for the cell phone on the bedside table. "I'll do that." Her thumb punched the long series of numbers necessary for an international connection. Marisa was about to hang up when Rachel answered.

"Hey, Rach."

Long pause. "Hi."

"Are you OK?"

"Fine. Did you move?"

"Yeah. About two weeks ago."

"Do you have an apartment or what?"

Marisa took a deep breath. "I'm living on the farm with Alistair. He's my husband, Rach. We got married yesterday." The second pause stretched painful and long. "Rach? Are you still there?"

"Yeah."

"How's Mom? Can I talk to her? Tell her the news?"

"Mom's asleep. I don't want to wake her up."

"I'm really happy, Rach."

"Good for you. I gotta go." The connection to Iowa ended.

Marisa's lower lip trembled. She threw the phone as hard and far as she could, buried her face in her hands, and bawled.

Alistair hesitated, shocked at the outburst caused by a reason unknown to him. He cradled her, tried to console her, suffered with her as sobs drained her of strength and tears.

Marisa's fists clenched. "She's so damned jealous she won't even talk to me! I hate her!"

"Ah, sweetheart, you don't mean that. She's your sister, your family."

"You're my family!" Her blood-shot eyes blazed fire. Her open palm beneath the sheet fumbled for and found what she needed. "I belong to you." Her lips brushed his. "Take me, Alistair. Fuck me!"

"No, Marisa!" He pushed her hand away. "We make love! We do not fuck!"

Her wail pierced his ears and heart. She rolled to her back, looked away from him, and lay rigid. "What's the difference?"

She'd wounded him. He fought to temper the rising anger, drew in and held his breath, clenched and unclenched his fists, composed his closing argument. When he spoke, the controlled tone cloaked

163

his true hurt. "I don't know what I can say or do to make things right between you and your sister. I can't help what's happened because I don't know the why. I do know that I love you and I will not let anything or anyone sully what we have."

He grabbed and squeezed her hand. "Look at me." Marisa turned her head. "Do you understand?"

Marisa's wide-open stare met raw emotion harnessed to a determined pledge. She blinked, nodded, whispered. "Yes." She clung to him, her tear-stained cheek against his chest. "Oh, my love. I am so, so sorry." She closed her eyes and savored his touch, the reality of him and all he meant to her. "I love you so much."

He tucked the duvet around them, stroked her hair, felt her heart beat with his. "Shhhhh. Hush now." The soft veil of descending twilight drew the curtain on the day's drama and lulled them to sleep.

Chapter 30

Marisa inspected the hotel kitchen's sanitized stations at the end of a routine day. Satisfied, she dropped her soiled apron in the hotel hamper, ignored Chef's grumbled reminder that she was covering Saturday breakfast and Sunday brunch, and trotted to the idling Land Rover.

Alistair kissed her cheek and dropped a paper gift bag in her lap.

"What's this?" She dipped her hand in the bag and pulled out a replacement for the shattered cell phone and a palm-sized orange ball. Marisa squeezed the spongy ball. "What's this for?"

He grinned. "Throw that next time." He laughed at her pretend pout and pulled away from Mallaig toward the promise of a peaceful evening at home.

The persistent cell phone ringtone shattered the peace at three in the morning.

Marisa rubbed her eyes open and squinted at the caller ID display. "Rach? What's up?" Her sister's hysterics crackled through the connection. "What? Slow down and say again."

"Mom! I can't control her! She's broken a bunch of stuff! She's threatening to kill herself! She's torn the place apart looking for Dad's knife kit and the pills I hid from her!"

"Oh my God! Rach! Call 911!"

"I did! I called Aunt Sam and Uncle Trevor. They're on their way."

"Where is Mom now?"

"Outside in the orchard. She's hugging the tree where Dad died and screaming her head off!"

"What happened? What set her off?"

"I told her you got married. Sheriff Ellis is here. I gotta go!"

"Call me back, Rach!" Marisa dropped the cell phone on the duvet and hugged her knees. Dry eyes opened wide. Her hand clapped over a silent scream.

"Marisa?" Alistair switched on the lamp at his bedside table. Concern turned to blind fear of the unfolding calamity that had drained the blood from his wife's face. "Talk to me, sweetheart."

She shook her head. He held her, whispered assurances he did not feel. "I'm here. I love you. Whatever it is, I'll do what I can to help make it right. Just tell me, love."

Marisa's shoulders shook. Pent up tears dampened her lashes. "Mom didn't take it so well when Rachel told her we were married. She threatened to kill herself. My sister called the police. The sheriff is there now."

"I don't understand. Why would our being married cause your mother to want to take her own life?"

"I honestly don't know. She hasn't been herself since my Dad died."

"My Mum had a rough go of it after Dad passed away. But certainly nothing to that extreme."

Marisa stiffened in his arms. Anger flashed through the pain in her eyes. "Did she wake up and he wasn't there? Did she look out the window and see him lying on the ground? My Daddy had never been sick a day in his life! He was dead and she didn't even get to say goodbye!"

Alistair winced, closed his eyes. "Ah, God. The poor woman."

Cheery ring tones mocked her fear. Marisa scooped up the cell phone. "Rach? Oh, Aunt Sam. How's Mom?"

"Not good, honey. We couldn't get her back in the house. Sheriff Ellis subdued her and the medics got her in the ambulance. Doctor Gregson has been called. He's going to meet us at the hospital in Cedar Rapids."

"Is Rachel OK?"

"She's doing as well as can be expected. We all are. I'm sorry this happened so soon after your wedding."

"Why did my getting married make Mom so upset? I feel bad about that."

"Don't. I'll call you from the hospital as soon as we know anything."

Marisa clicked off and stared at the cell phone. "I've got to go home, Alistair."

"Of course you do. We'll go together."

Marisa shook her head again. "This is my problem. Not yours."

He cradled her face in his hands. "Yes, it is. You are my wife. I took a vow to be with you in good times and bad. I take that vow seriously, love."

Alistair dressed while Marisa showered. He flicked on lights to chase away the darkness and put on a pot of coffee to clear out mental cobwebs. Sunday rail schedules from Mallaig to Glasgow popped up on his laptop. Tickets secured, he made a note in his calendar to call his mother and inform her of their sooner than expected overnight stay. Next, he checked Monday morning flights from Glasgow Airport. But to where? He cursed his limited geographic and logistical knowledge of his wife's home country and town.

"Marisa?" She sat on the side of their bed, her lovely body wrapped in a robe, her hands busy towel drying raven black hair. "Where do your mother and sister live in Iowa? Which is the nearest airport?"

"They live in Harmony. Ironic, isn't it? We'll probably have to fly into Chicago and get a connecting flight to Cedar Rapids. That's the closest airport. Harmony is about a forty-five minute drive away. Maybe Aunt Sam or Rachel can pick us up. Otherwise, we'll have to rent a car."

He sat next to her, a physical reaction to an impending long journey. "That's a full day."

"I know. I'm exhausted just thinking about it."

"Well, at least we'll break up the trip a wee bit on the train Sunday. We'll stay overnight at Mum's. I'll book us a flight out of Glasgow the next morning."

"We're leaving that soon?"

"Isn't that what you want, love?"

Marisa sighed. "Chef is not going to be happy about working Sunday brunch. Or another request for more personal time off."

Alistair borrowed a page from Robbie's book of advice. "We've got to trust that everything will be alright." He kissed her and went downstairs to make online reservations and a phone call.

"Auntie Maeve? I'm sorry to call so early."

"You know me. I'm always up before the sun. What do you need, lad?"

"Another favor. Marisa's Mum has taken ill. We're leaving Sunday and we'll be gone two weeks, maybe more. She's fretting about being away so long."

"Tell her not to worry. Her job will be waiting for her when she gets back."

"Thank you, Auntie."

Chapter 31

Travel and absence plans clicked into place on either side of the pond. Robbie and Brenda assured Alistair all would be well until his return. Arrangements were made to pick up Marisa and Alistair on arrival at the Cedar Rapids airport.

Alistair's mother opened her arms and home to her new daughter-in-law.

"There are three Mrs. McKenzies now. Please call me Jeanne." Marisa enjoyed the brief calm before the storm and cried when she hugged the petite older woman at the departure gate.

"There, now." Jeanne dabbed at Marisa's tears and pressed the white handkerchief into her palm. "After these troubles pass, we'll plan a fine party to properly welcome you into our family." Jeanne stood on tiptoe and hugged her son. "Take care of her and yourself, Ali."

"I will. I love you, Mum." He kissed his mother's cheek, took his wife's hand, and boarded the international flight.

They dozed in abbreviated shifts. Disorienting jet lag set in during the three hour layover at O'Hare. The short and bumpy ride on a cramped plane from Chicago to Cedar Rapids landed early evening local time in the middle of the travelers' internal night.

Marisa spotted Samantha Grady at the baggage carousel. "Aunt Sam!" She grabbed her weary husband's hand and dragged him across stained carpet and scuffed linoleum tiles.

"Marisa!" Sam hugged and held her niece at arm's length. "You look as tired as I feel." Sam smiled at Alistair. "And you look like you're going to fall over."

"Aye. It's been a long day."

"How's Mom? And Rachel?"

"Let's get your bags. We'll talk in the car."

Alistair insisted on shouldering most of the burden. He stretched out as best he could in the back of Sam's sedan and fought to stay awake.

"We brought your mother home this morning. She's on some pretty high-powered anti-depressants. She slept for awhile. But she wandered downstairs and was sitting at the kitchen table when I left for the airport."

"Rachel told me Mom went ballistic after she told her I was married."

"That's only the half of it. First Rachel told her that she'd changed her college plans and would be leaving for Texas A&M next week. Then she told her about you and Alistair. Seems she hadn't shared any of that information. Your Mom didn't even know you'd met someone much less married him. Honey, my sister had this idea that you were homesick and you'd come back when Rachel left for school. She repeated that pipe dream so many times that I think Rachel was beginning to believe her. Maybe that's why she waited to tell Mira that she wasn't going to Iowa State. She thought you'd come home."

"So when I told her I was married ..." Marisa's voice trailed off.

"I'm glad you're here, honey. Both of you." She glanced in the back seat, grinned and gestured for Marisa to do the same.

She giggled at Alistair's awkward pose in slumber. "Welcome to America, my love."

Sam delivered them to the doorstep of bed and breakfast proprietor Adele Murphy. "Sweetheart." Marisa brushed stray strands of wavy curls from Alistair's forehead. "Wake up, love."

Alistair blinked glazed over eyes. "I'm awake." He sat up, rubbed the knotted muscle in his neck and swung his legs out the open car door. Concrete and houses cluttered his view. "I thought you said you lived on a farm."

171

"I do and I did. We're staying in town tonight." She got out of the car and followed Sam around the trunk. The women hoisted out bags that Alistair grabbed, carried up the porch steps and into the front hallway.

"Marisa, it's so good to see you, dear!" Adele's eyes sparkled under a mound of grey hair. "Is this handsome man your husband?"

"He is. Alistair, this is Adele. She owns the best and only place to stay in Harmony."

Alistair swayed under the weight of luggage and exhaustion. "We're staying here?"

Marisa lifted her bags from his hands and lightened his load. "I better tuck him in. C'mon, love." Marisa led the way up the winding staircase. "Goodnight, Adele. Thanks, Aunt Sam. We'll see you in the morning." She pushed open the door to the first room on the right and set the bags inside. Dainty crystals in the chandelier centered above the king-sized bed shimmered in the soft glow controlled by the dimmer switch on the wall.

Alistair dropped luggage next to hers, closed the door and kicked off his shoes. "Why are we staying here, love?" He stepped out of his pants and tossed his shirt over the back of a nearby chair.

"To get a good night's sleep." Marisa turned back the bed and used the ensuite bath. "Aunt Sam figured we'd be too tired to deal with Mom and Rachel. She'll be back in the morning to take us out to the house." Marisa turned out the bathroom light. "That was pretty thoughtful of her, don't you think?" She stepped into the bedroom and smiled at the man she'd married.

Alistair lay on his back with one leg under the sheet and comforter and the other stretched out full on top. Feather pillows cradled his head. Arms rested limp across his chest that rose and fell with the deep regular breaths of sleep.

Marisa undressed, dimmed the chandelier and slipped between the sheets beside him. She yawned and closed her eyes. "Goodnight, my love," she whispered.

Windblown tree branches tapped the shingled roof and metal gutters, waking Alistair at daybreak. His eyes scanned the unfamiliar room. "Where the hell am I? Marisa?" He reached across the rumpled sheet, touched her shoulder, relieved that she was there. Then he remembered how and why they'd journeyed from his homeland to hers.

He slipped silently out of bed, into the bath and under the soothing pulse of warm water. Clean jeans and a wrinkled shirt from the bag he'd packed would do for now. He kissed his sleeping wife's forehead, closed the bedroom door and trotted down the polished wood staircase toward the smell of fresh brewed coffee.

"Good morning!" Adele had arranged plates, cups, saucers and an array of silverware on the rectangular dining room table covered in lace and set for six. "You're an early riser. But then you've come from a long ways away."

"I'm used to getting up early to take care of the animals and such. I tend a sheep and cattle farm in the Highlands."

"Do you now." She wiped wrinkled hands on her faded floral apron and pulled out a chair. "Breakfast isn't quite ready yet. But I can offer you coffee."

"That would be grand, thank you." Alistair sat on the ruby red upholstered seat and leaned back against ornately carved wood. The room reminded him of his barrister days calling on clients with Victorian taste. Wallpaper matched red and gold brocade curtains. Crisp white doilies surrounded silver tea sets on the far corners of a massive buffet. Framed photos oval and rectangular dotted the walls. A serene landscape of planted fields and wild flowers caught and held his attention.

"Marisa's mother painted that." Adele poured coffee in his cup and set a silver carafe on the table in front of him. "She was a very talented artist."

"It's stunning." Alistair sipped his coffee. "You said was. Is she not painting anymore?"

Adele pulled out and sat in the chair next to his. "Miranda hasn't been at her studio in town since she lost her husband. It's a shame. Everything is still there just as it was the day before he died. She has a studio at her home. But I haven't seen any new art work."

"I apologize for my rude behavior last night." He stuck out his hand. "Alistair McKenzie. Pleased to make your acquaintance."

"That's quite alright, Mr. McKenzie. Adele Murphy." The strength in her handshake surprised him. "I've lived in Harmony all my life. But I do remember how tired I was when I came home from visiting family in Ireland with my husband so many years ago." She touched her forehead, heart and shoulders in the Christian sign of the cross. "God rest his soul."

"I'm sorry for your loss, Mrs. Murphy. Please call me Alistair."

She smiled. "Only if you call me Adele."

"Fair enough. Forgive me, but I know very little about the town where my wife was born."

"Probably even less about the McCullough and McKenna families you've married into."

He nodded. "Aye. I'm afraid that's true." He finished his cup of coffee. Adele poured him another.

"Marisa's mother Miranda and her sister Samantha, the lady who brought you here last night, lost their mother when they were very young. Doc Sam is Harmony's only veterinarian. Miranda had finished two years at the community college in Cedar Rapids and was about to enroll in the University of Iowa school of fine art when their father died. Sam was still in high school."

"High school?"

Adele's musical laugh filled the room. "Oh, let me think. I believe that would be secondary school in Scotland. Anyway, Miranda went to work to keep a roof over their heads. She helped her sister get through university and made the down payment to open her practice."

"Did Miranda ever go back and finish her education?"

"No. She managed her sister's office in the morning and kept her art studio in town open afternoons and on weekends during tourist season. She lived in a tiny apartment at the rear of the studio and gave Sam the family home. Everything changed when Darien McKenna sat next to Miranda at the counter of Hank's Longhorn Café."

Adele poured herself a cup of coffee and stared into the rising steam. "He was larger than life. Tall, black hair and grey eyes like Marisa, and so handsome. Every woman in Harmony swooned over him." She winked. "As they will over you. They'll be just as jealous of Marisa as they were of her mother. They're so alike in that way."

"How do you mean?"

"Miranda was a beautiful woman. Long red hair, lovely green eyes. Tall and slender like your wife. Every bachelor in the county had asked her out. She refused them all until she met Darien. Marisa didn't date any of the young men who fancied her. I think she did appease her mother and went to her senior prom."

"Senior prom?"

"The last year of high school formal dance. Boys in tuxedos. Girls in frilly dresses." Adele smiled at his raised eyebrows and incredu-

175

lous expression. "No one was surprised when Marisa moved away to New York City. She had always been Daddy's girl, soaking up everything he taught her about cooking like a sponge." Adele sighed. "She wanted to follow in his footsteps. But those were big shoes to fill. So she left for Scotland after her father passed away. She's always been impetuous and headstrong. You'll have your hands full with her."

Alistair laughed. "I already do."

Adele settled back in her chair and shook her head. "I don't understand why her family was surprised when they found out Marisa had married. She looks like her father. But her interest in men is just like her mother. Marisa would never settle for second best or anyone less than the greatest love of her life." She patted his hand. "That must be you."

Alistair climbed the stairs with a tray of toast, juice, and coffee prepared by Adele. The brass knob on the unlocked door turned easily in his hand. He pushed the door open with his shoulder, closed it behind him, and smiled at his good fortune in love.

Marisa labored over an ironing board. Her hands spread a bright yellow cotton shirt over the cushioned pad tied to the flat angular surface and unfolded metal legs. The upright iron spit steam from holes in its steel face. She flipped damp hair over thin bra straps on her otherwise bare shoulders. Black jeans clung to long shapely legs and ankles over bare feet.

Alistair set the tray on the bedside table and crossed the area rug between them. His hands around her caressed bare skin and cupped breasts barely covered by her bra. Her nipples responded to his fingertip touch. "Ah, my love." His lips brushed her neck. He felt her shiver.

"You're certainly livelier this morning than you were last night. Take off your shirt."

"With pleasure." He unbuckled his jeans and unbuttoned his shirt. She caught it as he tossed it toward the bed. "It's wrinkled." The iron hissed against the yellow shirt's collar. She righted the iron, whipped the yellow shirt from the ironing board and slipped her arms through the sleeves. Her hands spread his shirt across the cushioned cover. "Aunt Sam will be here to pick us up in less than an hour. Have you had breakfast?"

"I was hoping for breakfast in bed." His fingers beneath her open shirt unhooked her bra and resumed the caress. "I come bearing toast. Juice. Coffee." He wrapped his arm around her waist and pressed the hard heat of him against her. "Me."

"Oh, Alistair. You are impossible."

"No. I'm insatiable." He loosened her jeans, burrowed his fingers into her panties, and caressed the spot that made her quiver.

"We don't have much time," she moaned.

"Then we'll be brief." He unzipped his jeans, pushed hers down her hips to the floor. He turned her around, lowered her to the bed, stepped out of his jeans and opened her legs. He teased her with his tongue, pushed the loose cups of her bra aside with his fingers.

She groaned, gripped and tugged at his shoulders. "We don't have much time," she repeated.

"As you wish." He covered her, slid into her, thrust deep in rhythm with the roll of her hips. She gripped his with her thighs and refused to let him go until the last clench of climax faded.

Spent and satisfied, he flopped on the bed beside her. In afterglow they lay, fingers laced, eyes closed.

"Your shirt still needs ironing. I'm sure mine needs touched up."

"The toast is probably cold."

They looked at each other and laughed, a light moment shared between lovers for life.

Chapter 32

The farmstead loomed large yet curiously small. Alistair held Marisa's hand, whispered their mantra in her ear. "Trust that everything will be alright."

Sam rounded the curve off the two-lane highway from town and turned left onto the concrete driveway. Marisa gasped at the forlorn appearance of the overgrown lawn and ornamental shrubs her father had so meticulously pruned and maintained. "My boys are coming out this afternoon to cut the lawn and keep my sister occupied. With any luck, we can sneak the two of you and Rachel out of the house and back into town for a family pow-wow."

"What does she mean by a family pow-wow?" Alistair whispered in Marisa's ear.

"We're getting together at Aunt Sam and Uncle Trevor's to talk about what to do for Mom," she whispered back.

"Oh." He got out of the car and followed the women up the sidewalk and porch steps.

Rachel opened the farmhouse front door. "Well, look whose here." She stepped back to let them in.

Sam glanced past her niece and through the open archway into the kitchen. "How's she doing today?"

Rachel shrugged. "The same."

"Did she sleep at all last night?"

"Three, maybe four hours." From the tips of his polished black leather shoes to the fallen auburn curl on his forehead, Rachel's eyes scanned every inch of man who held her sister's hand. "You're Alistair?"

He smiled, nodded. "Hello, Rachel."

Marisa touched her sister's arm. "Rach, I …"

Rachel jerked her arm away. "Save it for Mom. I'm going upstairs to pack." She turned and took the stairs two at a time.

"Mira." Sam pulled out the chair next to her sister at the kitchen table. "Marisa is here." She motioned for Marisa and Alistair to join her.

Alistair held his breath and forced down the shock that rippled through him. Adele's description of Miranda in no way matched the woman who sat and stared at a ghost only she could see. Tangled knots of copper-colored strands dulled by streaks of grey trailed down her back. Glassy green eyes held no spark. A faded black tunic hung from thin shoulders. Fisted hands tapped knuckles on the tabletop. Legs crossed at the knees twitched beneath dingy white slacks. A flip-flop slipper slapped against her bare heel.

Marisa swallowed hard and forced a smile. "Mom?" She sat in the empty chair and touched her mother's hand. The tapping stopped.

"Marisa?" Her empty stare turned to her daughter. "Is it really you?"

A tear slid from the corner of Marisa's eye. She wiped it away. "Yes, Mom."

Miranda smiled. "I knew you'd come home. I told them you would. They didn't believe me. They even lied to me. They told me you were married. That you wouldn't be coming back." Miranda kissed her daughter's hand and rubbed her sallow cheek against it. "I knew they were wrong. Everything will be alright now."

Alistair stepped forward to comfort his wife in obvious distress. He rested his hands on her trembling shoulders.

Miranda looked up at him. "Who are you?"

"Alistair McKenzie, ma'am. Marisa's husband."

"You are not!" Miranda recoiled as though shot.

Sam hugged her sister, both to soothe and restrain her. "Yes, he is, Mira. He's come all the way from Scotland to meet you."

Miranda stared at Marisa in wide-eyed disbelief. "Is this true?"

"Yes, Mom."

Miranda let go of her daughter's hand. "I want to lie down. I'm tired. Take me upstairs."

"OK, Mira." Sam guided her stricken sister from the chair to the second floor master bedroom.

Marisa collapsed in Alistair's arms and cried. "I had no idea she'd gotten this bad. Poor Rachel. She's had to deal with this all by herself. I should have come home and helped her."

"Then we may never have met and certainly not married. Tell me, my love. If you could, would you turn back time and change what is?"

She looked up into his dazzling blue eyes. "Of course not. I love you. I want to spend the rest of my life with you."

He kissed her, wiped away her tears, and held her in the certain strength of forever. "So you will."

The great room's flickering fireplace flame calmed the couple that nestled on the sofa. Marisa rested under her husband's arm, her legs curled on the cushion. Her hand patted the grizzled grey head of the senior Schnauzer asleep behind her knees. "I'm glad you're still here, Scooter," she said. The old dog grumbled in slumber.

"Marisa?" Sam stood behind the sectional that divided the great room. She touched her niece's shoulder. "Your mother wants to talk to you."

Alistair kissed her forehead. "Go on, love." She squeezed his hand, crossed the room and climbed the stairs.

Sam sat next to Alistair. Scooter grunted. "Sorry, old boy," she said and rubbed his ears. "Alistair, I need for you to know that our family has not always been like this. We are … were … very close." She grinned. "Almost normal."

He grinned back. "Who really knows what normal is."

"Thank you for understanding and being here for Marisa."

"She's my wife. No matter the circumstance, my place is with her."

"The bags are still in the car. You've seen what it's like here. I can take you and Marisa back to the bed and breakfast. It's your choice."

He shook his head. "That would be the coward's way out and that has never been the path I choose."

Sam smiled. "You're a good man, Alistair."

"I try to be." He slapped his knees and got to his feet. "Let's get those bags."

Chapter 33

Marisa's feet dragged up the once comforting stairway to her childhood haven for adolescent dreams. She knocked on the closed door at the top of the stairs. "Mom?"

"Come in, Marisa."

She filled her lungs with calming breath, counted to three and opened the door to what had been her parents' bedroom. Miranda sat propped on pillows in the bed she'd shared with Darien, where she'd given birth to their daughters. Her hand patted the mattress. "Sit with me." Marisa walked across the throw rug dotted hardwood and sat where her mother requested.

Her mother's unsteady hand reached out. "Give me your hand." Marisa lifted her right hand. "No. Your left hand. I want to see your wedding ring."

Marisa laid her left hand in her mother's palm. A simple gold band anchored the brilliant heart-shaped emerald embraced by a half-moon crescent of sparkling diamonds.

"Oh my." Miranda's left hand flattened on her chest above her heart. "Your husband must be a man of considerable means."

"Not really. The ring is a family heirloom."

"It's exquisite." Miranda's fingers curled around her daughter's hand. "Were you married by a minister in a church?"

Marisa shook her head. "No. We were married in a registrar's office."

"By a justice of the peace?"

"I guess so. Something like that. We are going to have a church wedding either in Mallaig near Alistair's farm in the Highlands or in Glasgow where his mother lives."

"When?"

"We're not sure. Maybe at Christmas or next spring."

Miranda sat up straight, away from the mound of pillows. "Go to the closet in my studio. There's a long white box on the top shelf. Bring it to me."

Marisa stepped into and down the hallway. She glanced toward the bedroom of her youth and smiled at the pile of luggage inside the open door. She would sleep with her husband in the bed where she'd envisioned a future very different from her cherished reality.

The next hallway door on the left opened into her mother's home studio. Her smile disappeared. Undisturbed dust covered every surface. Marisa shook off the gathering gloom of melancholy. She retrieved and brought the box to her mother.

Miranda caressed the lid and whispered words too faint for her daughter to hear. "Open it for me, please."

Marisa gasped at the revealed carefully folded bridal gown the color of ripe peaches. Delicate peaches and cream fabric flower petals adorned a woven circle crown of flowing ribbons.

"I wore this dress when I married your father. It should fit you. Take it back to Scotland. Wear it when you marry in the church." The light in Miranda's eyes flickered. Emerald green returned for a few shining moments. "I thought that would be the happiest day of my life. But every day with Darien was my happiest day." A smile curved her lips. "I hope and pray you are as happy with Alistair and always will be." She leaned into the pillows and closed her eyes. "I need to rest now."

Marisa put the lid back on the box that held her mother's treasured keepsake and carried it away to a bedroom and bed that was once hers alone.

Deafening silence settled over the farmhouse after Sam left to pick up and return with her ground crew sons. Alistair paced the great room floor from the fireplace to the bottom of the staircase. He tip-toed up four steps to the first floor landing and listened for voices, footsteps or any hint of movement in the rooms above.

"Feck it." He scaled the staircase and turned left around the banis-ter. Marisa stood before a full length mirror in the room where he'd stashed the bags they'd brought from home. Her arms hugged the bodice and waist of a long dress. Thin peach and ivory satin ribbons cascaded down shiny black hair from a circle of matching flower petals.

"You're beautiful." Alistair admired her from the bedroom doorway.

"It's my mother's wedding dress." The skirt moved with Marisa's swaying hips. "She wants me to wear it when we're married in the church." She turned to her husband. Her sadness raised tears in his eyes. "I wish you could have seen the look on her face when I opened the lid." Marisa draped the dress over the box that had protected it for nineteen years. "She was happy again. Just like I remembered." She took off the flower crown and put it back with the dress where it belonged. "I wish she could be there to see me wearing it and you in your kilt. Hear the two of us say I do again."

"Maybe she can."

She sighed. "She'd never be able to make the trip."

"Doesn't she attend church here?"

"Yes. Rachel said she goes to services almost every Sunday at Our Savior Lutheran Church."

He grinned. "Well, at least it's a Protestant church so they'll let me in the door."

"That's not such a big deal here. Are you suggesting that we get married at the church in Harmony?"

"Sweetheart, if that will make your mother happy, I'm all for it."

"But what about your mother? She's ready to plan a party around our church wedding in Scotland."

"We're legally husband and wife. A church wedding is just a formality no matter where it is." Alistair kissed his bride. "I love you, Mrs. McKenzie. I'll marry you again anytime. Here, there, or anywhere."

Chapter 34

Sam emptied cubes from the fridge ice maker into a pair of glass pitchers. "Trevor? Did you get more ice tea mix?"

"I'm brewing the real thing." Sam's husband dropped tea bags into a steel carafe filled with boiling water. "There's lemonade mix in the pantry."

Sam popped the plastic lid and spooned yellow granules over the ice. "Can you finish up in here? I'd better get back in the living room and referee."

"How did you get everyone out of the house under Miranda's nose?"

"She was asleep when we left. I managed to hustle Rachel out without too much protest."

"She's probably saved it for here."

Sam rolled her eyes. "No doubt." She kissed Trevor's cheek. "Thanks, honey."

"You're welcome, babe."

Sam walked into a scene of quiet tension. Marisa and Alistair sat close together, huddled on the sofa facing the McCullough family home fireplace. Rachel occupied the chair in the far corner of the front room near the window. Arms crossed, she stared out at nothing.

Sam sat in the loveseat that served as a mini-divider between the living and dining rooms. A long low table, cleared of the usual magazines and homework in various stages of completion, stood within reach of all who might want or need refreshments.

Trevor set the tray with pitchers of iced tea, lemonade and five glass tumblers on the table. He wiped his hands dry on khakis that covered long, muscular legs. "Alistair, I don't believe we've met. I'm Trevor Grady." The men shook hands and exchanged greetings.

Trevor settled on the loveseat beside his wife. "Help yourself to a beverage. Would anyone like anything else?"

Rachel snorted. "Yeah. Outta here."

Sam launched the first verbal volley. "Rachel! Adjust the attitude. What we have to talk about isn't going to be easy for any of us."

"Easier for some than others," Rachel grumbled.

Marisa tried to ignore her sister. "Aunt Sam, what does Doctor Gregson say we should do for Mom?"

Sam sighed. "Given the threats she made, he doesn't recommend that she live alone. We can hire a nurse practitioner for the short term. I'll stay with her at night until we can find a reliable live-in caregiver."

"How long will that take?"

Sam shrugged. "That's anybody's guess."

"It's not fair to Uncle Trevor or the boys for you to be gone that much. What if you get called out in the middle of the night?" Marisa asked.

Alistair nodded. "Farm animals don't keep office hours. What other options are being considered for Miranda's care?"

Sam rubbed at the worry lines etched in her forehead. "The only other option that's been discussed is the worst case scenario. Forced admission to a psychiatric hospital."

Marisa gasped. "No! We can't do that to her!"

Rachel frowned. "You got any other ideas?"

"Has Miranda been evaluated by a psychiatrist?" Alistair asked.

188

Sam nodded. "A psychiatrist, psychologist, therapist, counselor. You name it, we've been there. We tried a grief recovery support group. She wouldn't go."

Alistair snapped his fingers. "Rachel told Marisa their mother attends church services. Maybe her minister could offer some guidance."

"There's a great idea. Maybe we can get one of the Sunday school teachers to babysit Mom," Rachel muttered.

"Rachel!" Trevor launched the second verbal volley. "Your sarcasm is not helpful."

Rachel stood, arms straight at her sides and hands clenched into fists. "None of this is helpful!" She jabbed her finger in Alistair's direction. "What's with all his questions? We're not on trial. Who does he think he is? An attorney?"

Marisa shifted to the edge of the sofa cushion, spine rigid, face flushed. "Actually, he is!"

Rachel snorted. "He's a sheep farmer!"

"My husband was a barrister in Glasgow," Marisa retorted.

"Well, we're not in Glasgow and he has no say in what happens to our mother!"

"Tone it down, Rachel," Trevor warned. "Alistair is family as much as I am."

"Yeah, you were all so there for me." Rachel crossed her arms and turned her back on her family.

Marisa stood, went to her sister, reached out to embrace her. "Rach. I'm sorry that you had to take this on. I wish I had known."

"Would it have made any difference?" Rachel spun around. Rage flared in her blue eyes. "Would you have given up your romance

189

novel life to come back here so I could try out for the all school play? Coach softball? Go to senior prom? Oh, yeah, I had a date. I'd bought a dress. I had to cancel because Mom had a manic attack that night. I sat in my pajamas and bawled my eyes out while Mom ripped up their wedding pictures and cussed Dad out for dying! That was a big time! Meanwhile you're in Scotland getting laid by the perfect man!"

"That's enough!" Alistair bellowed, bolted from the couch and wrapped his arms around Marisa. Rachel withered under the icy blue glare in his eyes and take-charge set of his jaw. "I will not let you insult my wife or our marriage."

Rachel dropped into the chair, eyes downcast, knees together, hands clasped in her lap.

Sam groaned.

Trevor pushed back damp blonde strands from the sweat on his forehead and cleared his throat. "I think we'd better take a break."

 "Not necessary." His arm around her waist, Alistair guided Marisa back to the sofa. "If Rachel chooses not to constructively participate, that is her right." His years of litigation experience clicked in. Questions came. Procedure took precedence. "Now, then. We all agree institutionalization is our last resort. Psychiatric intervention and counseling have been tried and failed. The most immediate concern is Miranda's need for twenty-four hour supervision and care."

Trevor leaned forward, elbows on his knees, his pale blue eyes downcast. "She's not leaving that house. We told her she could move in with us when Rachel leaves for college. That just set her off again. The hospital has us on the twenty-four-seven caregiver list."

Alistair directed his questions and search for answers at Trevor and Sam. "Is there anyone in Harmony who could stay with Miranda?

Give you some relief? For compensation, of course."

Sam tugged on her husband's short shirt sleeve. "Jacob could go over after school when he doesn't have softball practice. Maybe even stay with her a night or two a week."

"He's our oldest," Trevor told Alistair. He looked at his wristwatch. "Which reminds me, I've gotta go pick up the grounds crew. I know they'll be hungry. I sure am." Trevor grinned. "How about we treat Alistair to a real down home Iowa meal?"

Marisa's strained expression brightened. "Is it still meatloaf Monday at Hank's?"

Trevor winked. "It sure is, darlin'. Why don't the four of you walk over and get us a table? I'll collect our boys and see if I can coax Miranda out of the house to join us."

"I want to go back home." Rachel grumbled. She followed Trevor out the door to the car Sam had parked at the curb.

Marisa sighed. "I don't know what to do about her."

"There's nothing you can do, honey." Sam toted the unused tray of drinks and glasses to the kitchen and returned with her purse and keys. "She has to deal with her demons."

Marisa and Alistair stepped out on the front porch ahead of Sam, who closed and locked the front door. "I hope she'll get over herself so I can ask her to be my maid of honor," Marisa said.

Sam's eyebrows disappeared beneath her blonde bangs. "But you're already married. Aren't you?"

"We are." Alistair took his wife's hand as they descended the porch steps and walked the green lawn and white picket fence-lined side-walk to Harmony's main street. "It's Miranda's wish and ours that we be married in the church."

191

"Mom gave me her wedding dress to take back to Scotland. That's what she wanted to talk to me about this morning. Alistair and I talked it over and we've decided to have the ceremony here so that Mom can be there. We thought maybe helping plan the wedding and seeing me wearing her dress could be good for Mom. What do you think, Aunt Sam?"

Sam smiled and nodded agreement. "Something to celebrate may be just what the doctor hasn't ordered."

"Then it's settled. We'll call on the minister tomorrow." Alistair held the door open to Hank's Longhorn Café.

"Or you can meet him right now." Sam nodded toward a booth along the restaurant's wall. "I'll introduce you." Sam led them to a round-faced, clean-shaven, forty-something man seated in a booth and hunched over the last of his dinner. A slice of white bread in his hand mopped up golden gravy from his plate. Brown eyes glanced up then opened wide in recognition and greeting.

"Doc Sam!" He wiped his fingers on a clean napkin.

"Evening, Pastor. How's Jenny doing?"

"Oh, she's just fine. She wolfed up her kibble this morning and took me for a walk. Thanks for asking and for taking such good care of my girl."

"Pastor, this is my niece Marisa and her husband Alistair. They'd like to talk to you about setting a wedding date." Sam backed away and dodged islands of four-top tables toward the café's co-owner and head waitress Shayla Malone working her station behind the counter.

"Pastor Pete Maloney." The man of the cloth stretched out his hand. "Please, have a seat. I'm curious to know why a married couple wants to set a wedding date."

"My wife and I were married in the registrar's office on the Isle of Skye near our home in the Highlands," Alistair explained.

"I've been there. Beautiful place. You're Miranda's daughter?" the pastor asked Marisa.

"Yes."

Pastor Pete sighed and shook his head. "Such a sweet soul. She's sat in the second row nearly every Sunday since I came to Our Savior Lutheran Church last September. She takes a hymnal out to the cemetery, rain, snow or shine, and leaves it in the back of the church about an hour later." He reached over and patted Marisa's hand. "I'm so sorry for your loss."

Marisa blinked back tears. "Thank you."

Alistair swallowed and cleared the lump in his throat. "We're only visiting Harmony for a short time."

"How short?" Pastor Pete asked.

"Two weeks," Alistair answered.

Pastor Pete scratched his head. "You're already married so there's no need for legal documentation. I can bless your marriage anytime. But I'll have to check the schedule. Saturdays could be a problem."

"It doesn't have to be a Saturday," Marisa said. "We'll just need a few days to tell my Mom and take care of some details."

"Like planning a party." Shayla had circled around the dining room from the eight top she'd set up with Sam to accommodate her family. "Didn't mean to eavesdrop, Pastor. Doc Sam gave me a tip about a catering job." She winked at Marisa and her grin got wider. Only the lines and skin sags of advancing middle age dated her. Bright brown eyes swept over Alistair in obvious admiration. "You and your Mama sure can pick the handsome men to marry."

193

Alistair blushed.

Shayla laughed. "Modest to boot." She tapped Marisa's shoulder with the pencil she plucked from behind her ear. "You just let us know when and where, hon. Buck and I will drag out the grills and the chafing dishes." She pulled the pad of food order slips from her apron pocket and turned to take another order from a nearby table.

Pastor Pete smiled. "Shayla and Buck are salt of the earth. That's what I love about Harmony, the down home charm and the people." He unfolded bills from the wallet removed from his pocket. "Give me a call in the morning. We'll get your wedding on the schedule. Let me know if I can help with anything else."

Alistair leaned over the table. "Does Marisa's mother come to church only for Sunday service?"

Pastor Pete scratched his head again. "She's stayed behind to help Adele tidy up the church. Polish the silver, change out the hymnals, that sort of thing."

"The owner of the bed and breakfast?"

Pastor Pete nodded. "Same lady. She used to volunteer in the church hall but I'm pretty sure other ladies have taken over helping Shayla and Buck cater the bridal and baby showers, receptions, and funeral luncheons."

"Mom used to teach art class at Sunday school when Rachel and I were kids." Marisa smiled. "It was kinda cool having her as our teacher."

Pastor Pete perked up. "I've gotten a lot of requests from parents for after school activities. Do you think your Mom would be interested in teaching art classes a couple afternoons a week?"

Marisa shrugged. "I don't know. My sister says she doesn't leave the house much. She probably won't have dinner with us, especially since Rachel went home."

The café door opened. Two balls of red-headed energy bounced into the restaurant followed by their frazzled older brother. Jacob dragged out a chair from the eight-top table and folded his long legs underneath. "Don't ever make me do that again," Jacob muttered to his mother and glared at the twin sources of his disgust.

"Keith! Kevin! Sit!" Trevor commanded. The whirling dervishes sat on either side of Sam and snickered behind menus.

Trevor held the door open. Marisa gasped. "Mom."

Miranda walked into the café. Freshly washed and combed hair streamed down the back of her clean white blouse that had been pressed to wrinkle-free perfection. Dark denim jeans fit legs made longer by the heels of her black leather ankle boots. Gold hoops dangled from her pierced ears. Makeup blushed her cheeks. Shiny gloss accented smiling lips.

Alistair's jaw dropped. "Well, I'll be damned. Pardon me, Pastor," he apologized.

Chapter 35

Questions, answers, stories and smiles were shared over meatloaf dinners, grilled cheese and fries for the twins, and dessert bowls overflowing with generous portions of Shayla's apple crumble. Everyone marveled at the change in Miranda. She ate everything Shayla served, complimented her on the crumble, praised Jacob's shrub pruning skills and laughed at Keith and Kevin's knock-knock jokes. During the drive home, she chatted with Trevor about preserving the fall crop of apples from the orchard. Miranda grinned while pretending to scold a noticeably stunned Rachel for missing a pleasant evening with family.

"I'm going up to bed, love." Marisa got up from the sofa.

"Go on ahead, sweetheart. I'll be up shortly."

Marisa followed her mother to the bottom of the staircase where Miranda paused, her hand on the banister. She smiled and nodded toward her son-in-law seated on the sofa, his back to them. "It's nice to have a man in the house again." She ascended with her daughter and kissed her cheek before retiring behind her closed bedroom door.

Alistair waited until the women had settled in upstairs before joining his wife in her childhood bedroom and bed. He closed the door behind him and stripped down to his boxers. The sheet covered his wife from a fraction below the mid-thigh hem of her lemon yellow cotton nightgown.

He grinned. "You look cute." He folded back the sheet on his side of the queen-sized bed, settled in and nuzzled her neck.

"Alistair, I'm worried."

"About what, love?"

"I can't get over the sudden change in Mom."

"At least it's a change for the better."

"But for how long?" She reached over and turned off the bedside lamp. Light from a full moon filtered through curtains on the window and cast patterned shadows across the floor and walls. "She mentioned how nice it is to have a man here again. I hope she's not still thinking I'm back home and brought you with me."

Alistair sighed. "Don't borrow trouble. Just enjoy the moment."

"I guess you're right." Marisa snuggled against his chest.

He stroked her arm with his fingertips. "So you told your sister that I'm the perfect man."

"I did because you are. But don't let it go to your head." She touched her lips to his. "Goodnight, my love."

He grinned and closed his eyes. "Good night, sweetheart," he whispered.

Marisa knew where she was without opening her eyes. The familiar feel of the farmhouse where she'd grown up surrounded and soothed her. She smiled, stretched, opened her eyes and saw the unmistakable look of mischief brewing behind Alistair's brilliant blue eyes.

"I know what I'd like for breakfast." He lifted her thin cotton nightgown and caressed her.

"Alistair," she protested, "this is my parents' house."

"You're such a bad girl, sneaking a boy into your bed," he growled.

"Don't be ridiculous. I didn't sneak you in and you're my husband."

"Ah, love, a little role play can do a marriage good." He kicked off his boxers and plucked at her nightgown. "Take off your jim-jams. I want to play with what's underneath."

Marisa pulled the nightgown over her head. She sucked in breath as Alistair's lips suckled her, moaned when his thumb rubbed the sweet spot between her legs. "That's my girl." He parted her thighs with his knee and stroked his heat against her.

Marisa played along. "We've got to be quiet." She fisted his hair, lifted her head from the pillow, sealed their lips, and parted his with her tongue. He groaned and matched her urgency. Taut muscles trembled with the visceral pain of promised pleasure. "Does the bed squeak?" he rasped between kisses and ragged breaths.

"Let's find out." She palmed and guided him into her. Her heels on his hips drove him deep. Their locked kiss of passion muffled mutual cries of desire, longing and release.

He collapsed on top of her, unable to move or remove himself from her. "For a bad girl you are so very good," he wheezed.

Her wicked laugh stopped with a sniff. "Alistair. Do you smell bacon?"

Only his eyelids moved. "What?" He blinked. "Do I what?"

"Smell bacon." She pushed him off and sprang out of bed. "Rachel must be making breakfast."

Marisa wriggled back into the nightgown and grabbed a robe she'd left on a hook in her bedroom closet. She opened the door, stepped through to the hallway, turned back and flashed him a seductive grin. "I'm the best you'll ever have, naughty boy," she purred. Marisa closed the door and grinned when she heard him laugh.

Her bare feet slapped the hardwood steps in rapid descent. "Rach?" She turned the corner at the bottom of the stairs and stared in disbelief. Her mother wielded a spatula over bacon sizzling in a pan on the stove.

"She's been up and gone an hour or more ago." Miranda nodded at produce piled on the butcher block countertop Darien had chosen for his renovated kitchen. "I couldn't seem to find any sharp knives. So I had to use this one to cut up the potatoes." She opened a drawer and retrieved a small paring knife. "I looked up traditional Scottish breakfast on the internet. We had almost all the ingredients. Could you slice the tomatoes and mushrooms, please?"

"Sure." Marisa moved close to her mother, took the knife and silently slid the blade through firm mushrooms, ripe red skins of tomatoes and soft inner pulp.

"I don't think we ever did this. Prepare a meal. You always cooked with your Dad."

Realized regret tugged at Marisa's heart. "You're right. We never did."

"We are now." Miranda turned down the burner's blue flame, put a lid on the pan, rested the spatula close to hand on the counter and turned to face her daughter. "I was so worried about you. Rachel told me you left New York. I knew you were in Scotland. But I didn't know why you went there, where you were living or what you were doing. All Rachel would tell me was that you were OK. Maybe she thought she was protecting me. She didn't want to upset me. But not knowing just made it worse."

Marisa whimpered and tumbled into her mother's open arms. Miranda rocked her as she had so many, yet so few, years ago.

"I fell apart when Rachel told me you were married to a man I hadn't even met. You're so young and I was so afraid that you'd made a horrible mistake. But now I know that you didn't. I saw the way he cares for you. The way he looks at you. Alistair loves you. He's a good husband and if it's what you both want, when the time comes, he'll be a good father."

Marisa wiped her nose and tears on the sleeve of her robe. "I love him so much, Mom. I want to have children with him, as many as we can."

"Oh, my baby." Miranda wept with and for her firstborn.

Showered, shaved and dressed in khakis topped with a sky blue golf shirt, Alistair walked down the stairs and in on an intimate scene. "Excuse me." The smiling tear-streaked faces of his wife and mother-in-law sent mixed signals. He hesitated, shifted weight between the shoes on his feet. "Is everything alright?"

"Everything is fine, Alistair." Miranda released her daughter, took the lid from the pan, and stirred mushrooms and tomatoes into cooking oil. "I didn't have sausage. But I did have everything else to make you feel more at home. Marisa, will you get down plates for me?" She filled three dinner plates with fried eggs and bacon, sliced potatoes, mushrooms and tomatoes. A stack of toast joined glasses of orange juice, cups and a carafe of coffee, silverware and napkins on the kitchen table.

Miranda served full plates at each place set. Alistair pulled out chairs from the table for his wife and her mother before seating himself. "This is more than I expected and very much appreciated. Thank you."

"You're most welcome." Miranda spread the napkin across her lap and lifted her fork. "It's been a long time since I've cooked anything." She winked at Marisa. "I rather enjoyed it."

"So did I, Mom."

"What do you two have planned for today?" Miranda asked.

The couple exchanged looks. Marisa took a deep breath. "We have decided to hold our church wedding here in Harmony. We're going to meet with Pastor Pete to set a date and make the arrangements."

Miranda dropped her fork. Her lower lip quivered.

Marisa rushed into her explanation. "We want you to be there, Mom. See me in your wedding dress. We thought it would make you happy."

Miranda's shocked expression shifted from her daughter to her son-in-law. "You'd do that? For me?"

Alistair reached for Marisa's hand. "It was important to me that I marry Marisa before she changed her mind." He smiled and brought her hand to his lips. "It's important to you that we be married in the church and for us to share that blessing with you."

Miranda covered trembling lips with her hand and wiped her eyes with the napkin. "I'd like to go with you to meet with the pastor, if I may."

Marisa smiled and squeezed her husband's hand. "We'd like that. Wouldn't we Alistair?"

"Aye, we would. Very much indeed."

The paper avalanche in Pastor Pete's office flowed from stacks in corners and on every horizontal surface. Pete darted around the piles in a valiant attempt to clear enough chairs of unfiled debris.

"Don't trouble yourself, Pastor." Alistair stood behind Marisa, his hands on her shoulders.

"My apologies. I just can't seem to find the time to tidy up." Pete shuffled folders on his desk and muttered through pursed lips. "Now where is the church calendar? Ah, ha! Found it!" He flipped through pages of dates, names and notes. "The church and the church hall are open a week from this Friday."

"That's perfect!" Marisa said. "We'll have time to plan the wedding and still have a couple days before our flight back home."

"Good! We'll schedule the wedding at six with reception immediately following." Pete noted the details with his pen on paper. "You're all set."

Miranda clasped her daughter's hand and kissed her cheek. "I can't believe this is happening." She looked up at Alistair and smiled. "Thank you." She turned to Pastor Pete. "Thank you for your help, Pastor. Now I'd like to offer mine." Her gaze swept over the room's clutter. "I managed my sister's veterinary office. I'd be pleased to lend my assistance in organizing yours."

Relief and a broad smile spread across Pete's round face. "You're hired!" He stood and reached over a dark computer monitor to shake Miranda's hand. "Are you computer savvy? I am not. I know if I were it would make my life a whole lot easier."

Miranda laughed. "I am and I'll teach you."

"Fantastic! We'll get started as soon as the dust settles after the wedding."

Alistair glanced at his wristwatch. "I might be able to catch Robbie and Brenda before they leave for the day." He punched the Murray's number into his cell phone. "Brenda. Hello. Everything alright? Good. I have a favor to ask. Go into my closet and get my kilt. Pack it up and ship it express to the address Marisa is about to give you."

He handed the phone to his wife, who relayed the information Brenda needed. "Alistair needs his kilt for our wedding here next week. He promised me he'd wear it when we got married in the church. We'll tell you all about it when we get home. We miss you too. Take care. See you soon."

Alistair tuned out most of the excited chatter between Marisa and her mother during the drive back to the farmhouse and over lunch. He spent the afternoon making minor repairs around the farmstead. Unaccustomed to Iowa's summer heat, Alistair put down the hammer he'd used to nail a loose board and gulped a tall glass of ice cold lemonade Marisa brought to the barn.

"You didn't have to do any of this," she said.

He wiped his lips and cleared the sweat from his eyes. "I need to feel needed, just like your Mum."

"What do you mean?"

"Ah, love, don't you see? Your Dad is gone. You've gone away and married. Rachel is leaving. She didn't feel needed anymore. Helping Pastor Pete gives her life purpose again."

"I never thought about that." Marisa kissed her husband. "You're so smart."

He laughed. "Wisdom earned by experience."

"So what can I do to patch things up with my sister?"

Alistair sighed. "I haven't a clue there. But maybe your Mum does."

"Good idea. I'll ask her."

Chapter 36

Miranda stirred fresh ground pepper into a bubbling pot of pasta sauce. She blew on the tip of the wooden spoon, tasted her creation, and smiled. "I've done you proud, Darien." She turned down the stovetop's blue flame and put a lid on the rising steam.

"Smells wonderful." Marisa got a clean spoon from the utensil drawer, lifted the lid and dipped the spoon into the sauce. Savored memories mingled with the flavor. "Just like Dad's." She dropped the spoon in the sink. "Mom, I want to ask Rachel to be my maid of honor. But I don't think she will."

"Why not?" Miranda sat at the kitchen table and nudged a chair with her foot. Her daughter caught the signal, pulled out the chair and joined her mother at the table.

"I thought she was just jealous. But it's more than that. She blames me for messing up her senior year. Missing tryouts and prom, that sort of thing."

"You weren't here to help take care of me." Miranda shook her head. "I was so steeped in my own pain that I didn't notice hers. Do you want me to talk to her?"

"Maybe. I wish I knew what to say. I tried to apologize. That didn't work."

"You could try talking about something else first. What she's packing to take to college. What you miss and she might miss about Iowa." Miranda's green eyes opened wide. "Yes. That's it! Pasta sauce."

Marisa blinked. "The sauce is perfect. I don't understand."

"The sauce reminds us of your father. It brings back good memories. Think of good memories with Rachel. Remind her of a memory you share."

"But which memory? There's so many."

"I can't help you there, honey. That's up to you. But try to tie in the memory and what you want to ask her with why she's angry."

Marisa shook her head. "I still don't understand."

Miranda pursed her lips and tapped the table top. "Let me think." Her green eyes shone and her fingers snapped. "She's never worn her prom dress."

Marisa's frown flipped to a wide smile. "She could wear the dress in the wedding."

Miranda smiled. "I think she'd like that."

Rachel ate her plate of pasta without looking up or joining in the dinner conversation. She loaded the dishwasher and fled up the stairs to her room on the tired excuse that she needed to pack.

Marisa explained her reconciliation plan to Alistair. "Wish me luck," she said.

She gathered strength with every step down the hallway, let out a deep breath, and knocked on Rachel's bedroom door.

"Door's open."

Marisa nudged the door and stepped into her sister's domain. Clothes, books and memorabilia lay scattered on the bed and floor. Pictures removed from hooks sat propped at forlorn angles against the wall and along the floor. "It doesn't look like you've made much progress. Do you want some help?"

Rachel didn't look at her. "No, thank you."

Marisa deflected the clipped, icy comment. "I didn't either when I was getting ready to leave for New York. It's tough deciding what to take. It's hard to believe that was only a little over a year ago. Remember that last night in the apartment before you went back home with Mom and Dad and left me in Brooklyn?"

Rachel tried to zip close a bulging soft-sided suitcase on wheels. "We slept in the same bed and cried ourselves to sleep."

"I'd already started missing you and home. So much has happened since then."

"Yeah. All good for you."

Marisa winced at the verbal gut punch. "That's not fair, Rach. I lost my Dad, too."

"And got a husband."

"Getting married was not part of the plan. Neither was being sous chef on the west coast of Scotland."

"Yeah, about that." Rachel stood at the end of her bed and glared at her sister. "You just started that job. How did you get so much time off so soon?"

"Alistair's aunt and uncle own the hotel and restaurant where I work."

Rachel's eyes narrowed. "Oh, I see. He got you the job so you'd move in with him."

"He loves me, Rach. He wanted to marry me. I could have said no and stayed in Glasgow. The truth is I wanted to be with him as much as he wanted to be with me."

Rachel kicked the bloated suitcase. "He's a jerk." She glared at her sister, challenging her to respond.

Marisa shrugged. "He can be. We all can."

Rachel sat on the bed and turned away. "I guess I've been a jerk," she muttered.

"Yes, you have. We all make choices. You accused me of running away to Scotland. Maybe I did. I could accuse you of running away to Texas. Well, here's another truth." Marisa stood in front of Rachel and put her hands on her sister's shoulders. "I'm proud of you. You got a scholarship to one of the best engineering schools in the country if not the world. That's a big deal."

Rachel sniffed, wiped her nose and caught tears in her sleeve. "I didn't think anybody gave a shit."

"I do." Marisa crossed to her sister's nearly empty closet. A simple strapless floor-length gown of filmy buttercup yellow chiffon hung under a dry cleaner's clear wrapper. "Is this your prom dress?" Marisa brought the dress out into the dim evening light. "It's beautiful."

"Yeah. I spent a chunk of my savings on it and couldn't take it back."

"Will you wear it in my wedding?"

Rachel rolled her eyes. "You're already married, remember?"

"Pastor Pete is going to bless our marriage next Friday at Our Savior Lutheran Church. I'm going to wear Mom's wedding dress and I'm asking you to be my maid of honor. Will you do it?"

Rachel took the dress from her sister, held it under her chin and stood in front of her full-length mirror. "It is a shame to waste a nice dress. So sure, I'll do it." Rachel returned the dress to her closet and resumed packing.

"Thanks." Marisa stepped through and pulled closed her sister's bedroom door. Alistair was waiting for her in the bedroom at the other end of the hall.

"Well?" he asked. "How did it go?"

"She's still pissed off. But she is going to be in our wedding."

Chapter 37

Sam and Trevor arrived with their family and a very special guest just after noon on the day of the wedding.

"Big brother!" Marisa bounded down the stairs and into Nathan McKenna's outstretched arms.

"Hey, little sister!" Nathan whirled her around the great room until she giggled. He stopped their spin, hugged her close and laughed with her. "It's great to hear you laugh again."

"It's so much better than crying. Thanks for standing in for Dad."

"I'm flattered and honored that you asked me to." He kissed her flushed cheek. "When do I meet the groom?"

"Now would be a good time." Alistair leaned against the banister, arms crossed over his chest, a bemused grin on his lips. "Alistair McKenzie." He stuck out his hand. "Marisa never mentioned her brother."

Nathan laughed. "That's because I'm really her cousin. Darien was my uncle." He shook Alistair's hand. "Nathan McKenna."

Marisa mocked a punch to his ribs. "Doctor Nathan McKenna, Ph.D., best-selling author and professor of English at the University of Iowa."

Alistair's eyebrows arched. "You're an author?" he asked. "I think I've read one of your books."

"I've published several titles in a variety of genres. Was it fiction or non-fiction?"

"Fiction, I hope. International espionage set in Scotland at Faslane nuclear submarine base."

Nathan grinned. "That was mine."

"No kidding! I really enjoyed it. Couldn't put it down. I did have one problem with your novel, though. Scotch whisky is meant to be sipped not slurped."

Nathan laughed. "I'll remember that next time."

Sam poked her head through the open front door. "I hate to break this up. But the women in the bridal party have appointments to get our hair and nails done. Your mom and sister are already in the car, honey."

"OK." Marisa hugged her cousin, kissed her husband and followed her aunt across the porch and down the driveway.

Nathan sighed. "I can't believe little Marisa is all grown up. She was just starting to walk when I moved to Iowa. Rachel was a newborn, only a couple weeks old."

The men walked together and sat across from each other at the kitchen table. "It's been over a year since their world was turned upside down." Nathan shook his head in disbelief. "Time passes so fast."

"Why does Marisa call you her big brother?" Alistair asked.

Nathan ran his fingers through thick brown hair and grinned. "I'd always been close to my Uncle Darien. I spent a lot of time here at the farmhouse while Marisa was growing up. She was the cutest little girl. Inquisitive. Ambitious. Loving. My big sister Hannah moved to Australia with her husband while I was still in high school. I'd never had a little sister. So I adopted Marisa. I took her on campus, showed her off to my friends. Brought her books and read to her." His grin turned to a wide smile. "I'll never forget the day we spent at the Iowa State Fair in Des Moines. She was five, maybe six years old. I threw baseballs at bowling pins until I knocked enough of them down to win her a big stuffed teddy bear. I filled her full of cotton candy, snow cones, hot dogs, anything

209

she wanted. I brought her home filthy dirty and sound asleep in my arms. Uncle Darien laughed and carried her up to bed. Aunt Miranda was not so amused."

The story ended when the back screen door slammed. "Keith! Kevin!" Trevor corralled his rambunctious twins on their second poke and shove pass from the back porch through the kitchen. "Park it!" He plopped them on the sofa in Darien's designated sanctuary, punched the remote and loaded an action film into the home theater. He retraced his steps to where his oldest son had settled with Alistair and Nathan around the kitchen table. "Jacob!" Trevor's thumb gestured in the direction of the film's opening fanfare. "Keep them in there."

Jacob's slump in the chair broadcast deep disappointment. "Aw, c'mon, Dad."

"That's not a request."

Jacob punctuated his frown of disgust with the scrape of chair legs on hardwood. His foot dragging could be heard from the kitchen to the undesired destination.

Trevor dropped in the chair his son had vacated. "If either of you ever have boys, take my advice. You have got to get and keep the upper hand or they'll run you ragged."

"You look like you could use a drink," Nathan said.

Alistair grinned. "I've got just what you need." He climbed the stairs, rummaged in his suitcase, and brought a bottle of single malt to the table. The cupboard nearest the table stored clear juice glasses. "These will have to do." He returned to his chair, poured a dram for each of them and raised his glass.

"Sip, not slurp," Nathan joked.

Trevor choked on his first sip. "That's the real deal."

"Aye. Duty free at the Glasgow Airport."

"Hits the spot." Nathan swirled the golden liquid, sipped and set his half-empty glass on the table. "I think I'll brew a pot of coffee for insurance."

"Insurance?" Alistair asked.

"That we'll still be relatively sober when the women get back." Trevor tapped his empty glass. "Like Nathan said, hits the spot."

Alistair laughed and poured another dram all around.

Muffled female voices filtered through the closed door to the room where Miranda helped her daughter dress for the blessing. Behind the bedroom door down the hallway, Alistair unpacked his kilt from the box marked for international delivery. He looked up when the closed door opened.

Breath caught in his throat. His heart beat fast. "Marisa." He walked toward her without feeling his body move. Peaches and cream glow surrounded her, from the floral crown on her head to the hem of the swirling skirt at her ankles. Styled black waves and soft curls framed china doll delicate curves and lines from forehead past shoulders. Her smoky grey eyes sparkled like stars winking through wispy clouds on a clear night.

"Ah, my love." He resisted the near uncontrollable urge to reach for her, confirm with his touch that she was real. "There has never been and will never be a woman more beautiful than you."

She closed the door, stepped into his embrace, whispered in his ear. "Put on your kilt." She backed away from him, her eyes on the vibrant green and blue, bright white and blood red of the McKenzie tartan colors.

"As you wish, m'lady." He undressed to his boxers, slipped his arms into the long sleeves of the white dress shirt, buttoned to cover his chiseled chest and abs, and threaded the black bow tie under the collar.

"Let me help." Marisa tied and straightened the bow. She lifted the lid from the square box he handed her. "What are these?"

"Cuff links."

"I can see that. What are these?" Miniature banners on elastic garters displayed the same colors as the kilt.

"They're called flashes. They hold up my socks."

"Hold out your arms." Marisa closed the cuffs around his wrists with the silver posts. She watched him wrap the kilt around his waist and giggled when he fastened the second buckle. "I thought men were naked under the kilt."

He nodded. "Some are. I have been. But not today." He looped his black leather belt and the silver chain of his sporran around the kilt, hooked the silver crest belt buckle and clipped the ornate silver and rabbit fur-faced pouch to hang beneath it. She watched him sit on the side of the bed, roll thick creamy kilt hose and the flashes to his knees and pin the symbol of his clan on the outer apron of his kilt. He tied the laces of his black brogue oxford dress shoes and stood to put on the black vest and jacket seeded with square silver buttons.

Marisa's eyes widened at the last accessory. "Is that a knife?" she asked.

"Of a sort. It's a sgian-dubh."

"A what?"

"A skee-an-DOO," he pronounced. "My ancestors used it to cut food and eat as well as for protection." He tucked it to the hilt into the top of the kilt hose on his right leg. "Well? Does my attire meet with your approval?"

Marisa sighed. "You look as you did when I met you and fell in lust at first sight."

He laughed. "Not in love?"

"That happened later over a steak dinner." She reached for his hand. "Why were you wearing your kilt the night you came into the pub?"

"I'd been to the wedding of another friend who'd found his lassie before I did." He laced his fingers through hers. "I thought I would never find you. I'd call into the wind 'where are you lassie?' and hope that you would hear me."

"I did. From the other side of the ocean." Her eyes met the question in his. "I was still in Brooklyn trying to decide what to do, where to go. I heard you call and I answered."

His fingers caressed her cheek. "I'm here." His thumb brushed her lips.

She took his hand in hers. "I'll find you." She pressed his palm over her heart. "I did."

A loud knock on the bedroom door broke the spell. "Hey there, bride and groom." Trevor's knuckles rapped the wood again. "Are you about ready?"

"Aye, we'll be right down." Alistair kissed his wife. "I love you, Mrs. McKenzie."

"I'll love you forever, my husband."

The ceremony proceeded as rehearsed the night before. Sam's twins sat on either side of her in the front pew where usher Jacob seated the mother of the bride. Best man Trevor stood in the only vested suit he owned alongside the kilted groom and appropriately robed Pastor Pete. Rachel walked the aisle ahead of the bride on Nathan's arm. Hankies dabbed at free-flowing tears when Darien's nephew gave Marisa's hand to Alistair.

Memories of her own wedding day replayed behind the tears in Miranda's eyes. The infant she'd held in her arms for the first family portrait after she and Darien had exchanged rings and vows now wore her gown. The child Miranda had nursed would have children of her own with the man she promised to love, honor, comfort and keep all the days of her life.

"I wish you could be here, Darien," she whispered.

The softening shadows of approaching evening bent refracted sunlight through the church windows. A shimmering golden globe of otherworld radiance backlit the bridal couple and the minister blessing their union. A presence in the globe formed to shape features familiar and beloved. Tall, strong and indescribably handsome as the day she married him. Darien kissed his daughter's cheek. His glowing hand touched Alistair's shoulder. His nod of approval and broad smile lifted Miranda's soul-crushing burden of goodbye. Her lips formed the words I love you. She blew a kiss at the fading vision.

Pastor Pete pronounced Alistair and Marisa husband and wife for life. The groom kissed his bride.

Trevor looped his arms across the second time newlyweds' shoulders after the cake cutting and bouquet tossing traditions had been carried out and the photographer had framed the final required pose. "Are you two about ready to get out of here?"

Alistair smiled and thanked another couple in the evening's endless stream of arriving and retreating well-wishers. "I'd like nothing better," he said to his best man.

Marisa bent to accept a kiss on the cheek from the wrinkled lips of another elderly Harmony matron. "Trevor, I swear, if one more sweet little old lady tells me what a beautiful baby I was at my parents' wedding I am going to scream."

"Keep smiling and walk with me." Trevor steered them out the side door of the church reception hall toward his parked sedan. White crepe paper streamers, bright yellow, orange, blue and green balloons fluttered and bobbed from the trunk, bumpers and side mirrors. A white shoe polish heart pierced by an arrow smeared the back window. "I am going to kick the ass of whoever did this and I've got a pretty good idea who won't be sitting down for awhile." He opened the back door for the laughing bride and groom. "Get in before anyone notices we're gone."

He drove the back roads around Harmony and circled back into town.

"We're not going back to the farmhouse?" Marisa asked.

Trevor winked in the rearview mirror. "Not on your wedding night." He pulled the violated sedan into a parking spot behind Adele's bed and breakfast and handed them the key. "That'll get you in the front door and into the bridal suite upstairs. Oh, yeah, one more thing. Sleep in."

Alistair turned the key in the lock that opened the suite's double French doors. And whistled. "Would you look at this!"

A king-sized canopy bed draped in rose velvet faced bay windows overlooking Harmony's municipal park. Identical velvet framed the windows and covered cushions on the window's seat. Frosted glass

French doors opened into a four-piece white tiled spa bath with jetted tub and separate glass surround shower. His and her white terry robes and full-body bath towels hung on hooks outside the shower doors. A large gift basket filled with pastries, chocolate, and cheese sat next to a coffee maker on a bar fridge stocked with wine, craft beer and bottled water. A pair of chairs with velvet upholstered seats and a round cherry wood table occupied an intimate corner of the room. White lace covered the table set with delicate bone china and silverware for two.

Marisa kicked off her shoes and sank her toes into the plush carpet. "This has got to be one of Harmony's best kept secrets." She unpinned the crown of fabric flowers and ribbons and shook her hair free. "What do we do first?" She peeked in the fridge. "Open a bottle of wine?" She peeled back the gift basket cellophane, popped a chocolate in her mouth and stepped through the French doors onto the smooth, cool tiles. "Take a shower? Or fill up this awesome hot tub." She reached behind her head to unzip the wedding dress.

She turned around at the cork pop. Alistair had shed his kilt. He set the open bottle of chardonnay and two fluted glasses on the granite counter between double sinks. "Let me help you, love." He opened the zipper from neckline past waistline. "That's what husbands are for."

He held her hand to steady her as she stepped out of the dress. Love and desire mingled in his eyes. "Hold that thought," she said. She grabbed the robe marked Hers from its hook, handed His to him, and hung the dress in the suite's armoire next to his kilt. She slipped into the robe and looked out over her hometown from the comfort of a velvet cushion.

"What are you thinking, sweetheart?" Alistair sat with her and handed his wife a glass of the wine he'd poured.

"I thought you didn't drink wine."

"I don't. But you do." Touched rims of fluted glass chimed. "I can tolerate the occasional glass of anything as long as it's not champagne."

She giggled. "So that's why you faked it during the wedding toasts."

He nodded. "I just can't get that bubbly stuff past my tongue."

She sipped her wine and smiled at him. "Thank you for today."

He shrugged. "I didn't do much but show up."

"You did so much more. You helped my mother be happy. She smiled. Really smiled and laughed. I was so afraid I'd never see or hear her do that again."

Alistair set his wine glass on the window sill. Anxiety brewed beneath his calm. "What about you, love? Can you leave your family here? Will you come home with me and be happy?"

Marisa set her glass next to his. "I love you, Alistair. You are my family. I'm happy when I'm with you. Wherever you are I am home."

The sincere totality of her love overwhelmed him. The power of his love for her consumed him. She returned his gentle kiss, responded to his soft touch, sighed at his whispered words of eternal endearment. They made love without and throughout the joining and slept entwined as one.

The sweet sensual scent and contours of the love of his life spooned with him soothed Alistair awake the next morning. He breathed her in, nuzzled her neck, caressed the curve where his hand had rested.

Marisa purred, smiled, felt his desire rising. "Ready for more, my love?"

"What better way to start the day." His fingers dipped into dewy warmth.

"Absolutely." She turned in his arms, pressed her lips to his, and rolled him on his back. "Good morning, husband." She opened her legs, bent her knees at his hips, and straddled him. Her fingertips and nails teased him. She rose up and knelt above his erection, the tip of him touching her slippery entrance.

He pumped, she pulled away. "Go slowly, Alistair."

He groaned. "I don't think I can."

"Yes, you can, love. We can." She lowered herself onto him. Deliberate. Gradual. Methodical. Her thighs trembled with the effort. Held breath escaped in a long relieved sigh with the full length of him inside her.

He hissed out pleasure between clenched teeth. "You feel fantastic!"

"So do you." She circled her hips. He moaned with the motion. "Move with me, love." Strokes, thrusts, caresses and cries peaked with loving collapse in each other's arms. The trill of the telephone at Alistair's bedside almost went unanswered.

His fumbling hand brought the receiver to his ear. "Aye."

"So you slept in."

Alistair's chuckle blossomed to full throated laughter.

"OK. Spare me the details. I'll get to the point. There's a suitcase with a change of clothes for both of you outside your door. Give me a call when you're ready to go back to the farmhouse and I'll pick you up."

"Thanks, my friend."

"Alistair, I gotta warn you, man. The women in this family are very fertile."

He grinned. "I'll keep that in mind."

Chapter 38

The weekend and their remaining time in Iowa passed toward Monday morning departure. Marisa packed her mother's wedding dress with Alistair's kilt and promised Miranda she'd wear it again at a future ceremony in her husband's homeland. Late afternoon sunlight filtered through curtains in the bedroom where Marisa had grown from a baby in a crib to a young woman launching a life neither mother or daughter could have imagined.

The women sat on the bed surrounded by luggage ready for overseas return. "Honey, I have to know." Miranda's green eyes locked on the grey of her daughter's. "Why did you leave New York? And why did you go to Scotland?"

"I couldn't stay in New York after Dad died. I didn't want to be a chef anymore." Marisa stared out the window at the winding road to town that divided acres of corn and soybean fields. "I didn't know where to go or what to do." She unzipped the carryon bag at her feet and retrieved the jewelry box from its protective pocket inside. "Did I ever show you this?" She opened the lid. The lions' green eyes gleamed.

"Oh! No, you didn't." Miranda lifted the brooch from the box. "Where did you get it?"

"Grandma Donna gave it to me. She told me to use it whenever I needed to find my way."

"What is it?"

"The McKenna family crest. Alistair recognized it immediately. It does this whenever he or I touch it." Static charges snapped and sparked in Marisa's hand.

"Oh my goodness, Marisa! Does that hurt?"

Marisa shook her head. "Mostly it feels like a cold burn. Like when your bare hand touches an icicle."

"What does it mean?"

"I'm not totally sure. The brooch is why I went to Scotland. That and …" her voice trailed off.

"And what, honey?"

"Well, I heard a man's voice calling to me, asking where I was." She smiled. "He called me lassie. That's how I knew he was in Scotland. So I went to find him." She zipped the brooch in its box back in her carry-on. "Crazy, right?"

"No, not crazy." Miranda closed her eyes. "Your father was at your wedding. He kissed your cheek. Put his hand on Alistair's shoulder. Smiled at me. He looked just like he did the day we got married." She opened her eyes, fearful of her daughter's reaction, relieved at her calm expression.

"I believe you, Mom. Nobody told Grandma Donna that Dad had died. But she knew. She said he came to her in her room at the nursing home and told her I needed help." Marisa squeezed her mother's hand. "The Highlands are amazing. We live on a farm less than an hour drive away from the ocean. I can't even describe the lochs and the mountains to you. They're that beautiful." She nestled her head on her mother's shoulder. "I know it's a long ways away from Iowa. But I really wish you'd come see us in Scotland."

Miranda hugged her daughter's shoulders. "I tell you what. I'll come when you and Alistair have my first grandchild."

"Promise?"

"I promise."

They sat in comforting silence as twilight fell on Sunday evening in the heartland.

Miranda insisted on driving to the Cedar Rapids airport the next morning. "I'm going to be working for Pastor Pete," she said. "Besides, it's about time I got back behind the wheel."

220

Rachel insisted on riding along "to keep an eye on Mom," she told Marisa at the baggage check-in counter for international flights.

"I think she's going to be OK, Rach."

Rachel shrugged. "She has to be. I'm leaving on Friday." Rachel's chewed fingernail began to bleed.

"Just say it before you get down to the first knuckle."

Emotion and words pent up too long rained from Rachel with her tears. "I'm not going to apologize for whatever I did that got you here. I was a jealous pissed off jerk. I zombie walked through my last year in high school and I was scared that I'd have to skip college and stay here."

"I would not have let you do that, Rach. You worked hard to keep your grades up through all of this. You earned that scholarship to Texas A&M." Marisa hugged her sister tight without resistance. "Go be the best damned engineer ever. I know you can do it. Make us proud."

Rachel wrapped her arms around her sister and held on. "I will. Be happy, big sister."

"I am, little sister."

Rachel released Marisa and turned to Alistair at the last boarding call. "I'm sorry that we got off to such a rough start." She stood on tip-toe, hugged him, and whispered in his ear. "Take care of her."

"Always," he assured her and kissed her cheeks.

Chapter 39

Alistair's brothers Charlie and Drew greeted the tired travelers at Glasgow Airport. The couple dozed in the backseat of Charlie's car from the lowlands through the highlands to the farmhouse front door.

Alistair carried Marisa up the stairs and settled her in their bed. "Home at last, my love," he whispered, and covered her with the duvet. He drank a dram with his brothers at the kitchen table and exchanged news of recent events with the Murrays. By late afternoon, Alistair sent his brothers off to Edinburgh with thanks for the lift and the promise of longer visits, climbed the stairs and into bed beside his sleeping wife.

The comfort of daily routine returned soon after they'd unpacked. Maeve and Eliot kept their word and Marisa's job open. Everyone but Chef Bryan welcomed her return. The kitchen and wait staff breathed a collective sigh of relief when Chef left three days later for a two week Mediterranean vacation.

Morale noticeably improved with Marisa in charge. The maitre d' reported no customer complaints. Eliot's steadier hands signed fewer checks to suppliers and his mood lightened with the improved bottom line.

The late arrival of tour buses twice in one week kept Marisa in the hotel's kitchen and Alistair waiting for over an hour in the lobby.

"This is officially getting ridiculous," she said as her seatbelt clicked for the ride home. "I have got to start driving myself to work."

"Alright." Alistair got out of the driver's seat and opened the passenger's side door.

"Right now?"

"Why not?"

"OK." Marisa unbuckled and stepped around the Land Rover. She got in and belted behind the steering wheel on the right. "Here we go."

"Remember to drive on the left and you'll do just fine, sweetheart." Alistair fastened his seat belt and crossed his fingers for luck.

"I saw that," she said and shifted gears to drive toward home.

Alistair breathed a silent sigh of relief at the last curve in the two-lane winding road and anticipated safe turn onto the gravel driveway. "See? I knew you could do it, love."

"This is easier than I thought." Marisa's relaxed grin suddenly turned upside down. Her shoulders stiffened. "Did you see that?" She twisted the wheel to the left.

The tires on Alistair's side of the car dropped off the pavement. His hands on the dashboard braced for impact. "What are you doing, lassie!"

Marisa hit the brakes and shoved the idling vehicle's transmission into park gear.

"There's something down in the ditch. I think it's a dog." Her seatbelt snapped back against the frame of the driver's side door she slammed.

"For feck's sake, Marisa!" Alistair swore as he watched her cross the lanes and disappear into the roadside darkness.

Irritation replaced his panicked expression and warning tone. "Impetuous and headstrong indeed!" Alistair pressed the dashboard emergency flashers into service, grabbed a flashlight from the glove compartment and followed his wife on foot across and off the roadway.

Marisa had dropped to her knees next to a heap of white fur. Blue eyes fluttered open. A matted tail thumped in mud and mangled grass. "You poor darling!" she cooed to comfort the wounded dog.

"Be careful!" Alistair warned. "Mind the teeth. Injured animals bite."

223

The flashlight beam caught the glisten of tears in Marisa's eyes. "I don't think this one can."

Alistair knelt beside the stricken dog. "Aye. The jaw looks broken. Most likely the front leg, too."

Marisa checked for other injuries. The tail thumped again. "Let's get her in the car."

"Marisa," Alistair protested.

"We can't just leave her here!"

He sighed. "No, I don't suppose we can. I'll get the blanket." Alistair climbed the embankment's slippery grass and returned with the rough cloth. The dog whimpered but didn't resist the carry and transport rescue.

Marisa drove the short distance to the farm while Alistair discussed their canine patient's condition with the veterinarian on call for rural clients with livestock. "No, it's not one of my working dogs," he spoke into the cell phone. "We picked her up from the side of the road. I didn't see any tags. I can appreciate the inconvenience and the late hour. But she's got to be in pain. Alright, we'll meet you there. Thank you."

Marisa circled the car past the farmhouse and barn and pointed the hood toward the highway. "Are we going back into town?"

"We are." He grinned. "But I'll drive."

Marisa phoned Alistair at every break in the kitchen ebb and flow of service the next day. "I promise you I'll let you know as soon as I hear anything," he told her. The update she'd been waiting for came at afternoon tea.

"What did the vet say?" she asked him.

"Her injuries aren't severe but they will be expensive."

"I'll pay for it."

"Hold on, love. She's comfortable for now. They're trying to find an owner."

Marisa drove home that night a determined advocate for the life she'd saved, prepared for any rebuttal her former barrister husband might have against her case.

Lights glowed in the farmhouse front windows. She parked the car, trotted up the front porch steps, unlocked, opened and stepped through the front door.

"How was your day, love?" he called to her from the study.

"Busy." She hung her coat near the door and walked into his arms. "Any more news?"

"No word on who she belongs to, if that's what you mean."

"That's because she doesn't belong to anybody. She's a stray that got hit by a car."

"Then we'll pay for her care and the animal shelter will put her up for adoption when she's healed."

Marisa argued for the defense. "If I hadn't seen her, she would have died in that ditch. She's my dog now and I'm going to bring her home."

Alistair countered with the facts. "Marisa, we have dogs. They work."

"Priya is my dog."

"Priya?"

"It means beloved. Yara is my sous chef while Chef is away. She told me it's a traditional Indian name given to girls born in August. I found her on the last day of August. So that's her name." Marisa stood firm. The defense rested.

Alistair accepted the verdict. "Well, that's it, then. There's nothing I can say to change your mind." He held her close, breathed her in, let his love for her conquer him. "Will I ever be able to say no to you?"

"Maybe." She kissed him, smiled, and touched her forehead to his. "But not today."

Chapter 40

Henri Leveque couldn't decide whether to smile or frown at the young sous chef controlling the kitchen in Chef Bryan Dumont's absence.

The McGillivray's had recruited the maitre d' from his post at a Michelin star restaurant in Provence on the advice of a fellow restaurateur and friend. Henri tapped the dinner menu with the pen from his suit coat pocket. Respect for Marisa's ability had replaced his concern for her lack of experience by the end of service her second day. Efficiency, teamwork and the supportive feel of family diminished by Chef Bryan's iron fisted rule gradually returned to the kitchen. Henri didn't miss the dreaded blood boil when Chef called him Henry, an intended demeaning mispronounce of his name.

But Marisa's defiance tempted reprimand and Chef's wrath. Henri tapped the menu again. "Chef is not going to be pleased. He gave explicit orders that his menu not be changed."

Marisa looked up from squares of dough rolled flat for ravioli. "I've got fresh root vegetables to use up on the tasters and a boatload of salt pork to go with the hill of beans I soaked overnight. Cassoulet is the perfect comfort food on a cold rainy day." She shoved a sample plate of each taster and a bowl of Toulouse-style Cassoulet across the pass counter and handed him a fork and a spoon.

Henri's wiry black eyebrows arched closer to his receding hairline. Poached salmon flaked in protest at the tine-stabs of his fork. Ground lamb flavored by a subtle hint of garlic and the fresh floral taste of rosemary broke free of ravioli finished al dente in a boiling pot. Highland beef sous vide and seared aroused every taste bud on his tongue. Roasted blood red beets, yellow turnips and harvest orange carrots held on to the undeniable attributes of extra virgin olive oil. Henri closed his eyes, dipped the spoon in the rich cassoulet broth, and let the memory of his mother's French kitchen overtake his senses as the stew of his childhood warmed him.

"If Chef complains, I can take the heat." Marisa glanced at the clock. "Station!"

"Yes, Chef!" her ready staff responded.

"Yes, Chef," Henri echoed. He turned on the heels of his polished black leather dress shoes, straightened the tie that matched his charcoal grey suit, and prepared to greet the evening's guests.

"Two Cassoulet. Smoked salmon. One Cassoulet. Two tasters. Two Cassoulet." Marisa called out incoming orders at the pass counter.

"That's the way it's been all night, Chef." Sous chef Yara Singh, promoted from line cook for the duration of Chef Bryan's holiday, presented bowls of stew thick with pork, duck confit, French garlic sausage, beans and vegetables. "Every other order is Cassoulet."

"Service!" Marisa alerted wait staff. "I'm sure glad I prepped enough for a monster batch."

Henri circulated among the tables on the other side of the kitchen's swinging doors. His practiced eye observed a well-dressed, middle-aged couple arrive 30 minutes apart and abandon unfinished drinks at the bar. He intercepted the waitress on her way from their table to the kitchen.

"What did table eight order?" he asked her.

"A half bottle of French Malbec, a taster, one Cassoulet a la carte and two glasses of tap water." She held up a clean fork. "I picked this up from the floor. It must have fallen off their table."

Henri breathed deep and surveyed the couple. "Give them exactly what they ordered as expediently as possible." He took the ticket from her hand. "I'll place the order." His heart beat faster with every step toward the kitchen and Marisa at the pass.

Chef looked up at the second swing of the doors. "What's up, Henri? You look like you've seen a ghost."

He fought to control the tremble in his voice. "Table eight. Half bottle of wine, two glasses of tap water, a taster, Cassoulet a la carte, fork on the floor."

She took the order from his shaky hand. "So?"

His serious level gaze stared into her eyes. "Michelin."

Marisa's insides quivered and contracted. She swallowed hard against the rising bile and filled her lungs with a gulp of air. "Yara to the pass!"

"Yes, Chef?"

"Michelin table eight."

Yara gasped. Her brown doe-eyes opened wide. "What do we do?"

Marisa's steel-grey stare mirrored the confident set of her jaw. "We serve them dinner. You've got the Cassoulet. I'll plate the taster."

The news and nervous tension spread fast through the kitchen. Stunned staff buzzed through clean up with the possible reward and repercussion of earning a Michelin star without Chef Bryan. Marisa praised their performance and skipped the family meal she couldn't eat.

Henri pulled out the chair she collapsed into and sat with her in the silent after hours dining room. "I've been there before. What is it you Americans say? This ain't my first barbeque?'"

Marisa laughed at the colloquialism delivered in a French accent. "Well, it was mine."

He tapped the pen on the table. "Ah, but you knew."

Marisa nodded. "My Dad had a Michelin star."

Henri grinned. "Eliot told me it was in your blood. You proved that tonight." He shifted in his chair and leaned forward. "I watched them. Discreetly, of course. From what I saw, I think you got that star." He stood up. "Good night, Chef."

"Good night, Henri." Marisa stared out the restaurant windows overlooking the dark bay. She closed her eyes and imagined packs of pedestrians dodging and breaking trails of headlight beams and red taillights eternally chasing around Columbus Circle. She pulled the cell phone from her chef coat pocket. "I'll be leaving soon, love. I just need some time with my staff. It was an eventful day to say the least. Everything is OK. I'll tell you all about it when I get home. I love you."

Chef Bryan Dumont shuffled through fourteen days of paperwork dumped on his desk. A quick scan of a printed menu from three days prior raised his blood pressure to a red-faced burn. The phone at his ear played back an irritating stream of voice mail messages. The forwarded message from Paris blew the lid off his internal boil.

"What the fuck!" He stormed into his kitchen and threw the wad of paper from his fist onto the chopped celery, carrots and onions of Marisa's mirepoix. "How dare you change my menu!"

All kitchen activity stopped. Marisa flicked the crinkled ball away with the tip of her knife. "How dare you ruin my soup."

His menacing bulk invaded her space. "Your peasant food desecrated my kitchen!"

"My peasant food pushed two hundred covers out of this kitchen in one night and may have earned this restaurant a Michelin star." Her sharp-focused steel stare learned by unyielding example sliced through him. "Tell me, Chef. Which fact is pissing you off the most?"

His face twisted in ugly rage. "Get the fuck out of my kitchen, you snot-nosed mouthy bitch!"

Marisa snickered. "I've taken worse than that from a line cook in Manhattan. You are nothing. I don't recognize your authority to fire me. I was hired by Maeve and Eliot. I'm not going anywhere until they tell me to leave." Her knife pushed the contaminated vegetables into the trash. She set the dirty knife aside, pulled a clean one from her knife kit, and resumed cutting carrots.

Chef's bellowed frustration echoed off the walls and down the hall to the closed door of Eliot's office. His fist hammered the wood. The knob turned in his beefy hand.

Eliot looked up and over the rims of his eyeglasses. "What can I do for you, Chef?"

"I want her gone!" Chef Bryan blasted.

Eliot pushed away from his desk and Chef's contempt. "Who?"

He stomped to the center of the room. "You know very well who. The sous chef. Your nephew's wife."

"On what grounds?"

"Insubordination! She ignored a direct order and changed my menu while I was gone!"

"I know she did. She had product to use up and a reasonable solution that I approved."

Chef glared at Eliot. "Then you have another decision to make. Either she goes or I do."

Eliot planted his palms on the arms of his chair. He stood rigid behind his desk and decision. "I consider this ultimatum your resignation. Effective immediately."

Eliot walked ahead of his fuming former chef as far as the dining room. "Henri," he summoned his maitre d'.

"Yes, sir?"

"Chef has resigned. Send Marisa to my office."

Henri smiled. "With pleasure."

The kitchen staff froze at the simultaneous slam of Chef's office door behind him and Henri's appearance in the kitchen. "I guess I really stepped in it this time," Marisa muttered and followed Henri to Eliot's office.

The owner sat behind his uncluttered desk. "Come in, Marisa. Thank you, Henri." The maitre d' nodded and closed the office door. "Please, sit down," he invited her.

She perched on the edge of the chair opposite Eliot and folded her hands in her lap. "Before you say anything, I want you and Maeve to know that I appreciated the opportunity and I hope that we can put this behind us and still be family."

Eliot looked up. "We'll always be family. This is business." He got up, crossed around and sat on the edge of the desk. "It seems I have an opening in my kitchen for an exec. I'd prefer to hire a chef who has earned a Michelin star." He smiled. "Are you interested?"

She blinked, froze, and felt the room begin to spin. She white-knuckle gripped the arms of the chair in a vain attempt to steady herself. "A Michelin star?"

He nodded. "I got the call from Paris this morning. Congratulations."

"What about Chef Bryan?" she sputtered.

"It was your menu changes the inspectors ordered. You are the chef of record. Chef Bryan has resigned. It's your kitchen now if you want it." He circled back behind his desk and lifted a raincoat from a hook on the nearby coat tree. "I've got some errands to run. Take your time. Think it over." He patted her shoulder on his way out and closed the office door.

The dam broke. Tears fell. Marisa rocked forward, dropped her head in her hands and sobbed. "Oh, Daddy, can you believe it? I'm a chef with a Michelin star."

News of Marisa's stellar accomplishment spread far beyond phone calls to her mother in Iowa and Rachel in Texas. Culinary magazines with international circulation clamored to interview the young American-born kitchen phenom on the west coast of Scotland. Newspapers from the Cedar Rapids Gazette to the New York Times featured stories on the talented daughter of legendary Chef Darien McKenna.

Alistair teased his wife about being the spouse of a celebrity. "What illustrious publication called to print your words of culinary wisdom today?"

"I'm fresh out of quotes," she groaned and kicked off chef clogs under her own kitchen table. "I sure hope this whole thing has run its course." She rubbed Priya's erect white ears and smiled at her husband. "Thanks for bringing my dog in from the porch."

Alistair set glasses of tap water in front of their plates and transferred Brenda's extra dish of creamy warmed chicken and noodles from oven to table. "It's all good as long as she stays in the kitchen." He spooned out generous portions and sat down to dig in. "You got a package today from your Mum."

"I did? What was in it?"

"I wouldn't open anything addressed to you, love."

She scooted her chair back. "Where is it?"

"On my desk." He handed her a fork. "Eat first. Open later."

Marisa downed her dinner, stacked dirty dishes in the sink, and dashed down the hall to Alistair's study. Scissors severed twine on the long, narrow package marked by the distinctive loops of her mother's handwriting. She ripped off heavy paper and snipped at wide tape that held the box beneath together. A note fluttered to the floor. Marisa picked it up, read the note, cradled the contents, and cried.

"What is it, love?" Alistair's face contorted in concern.

She handed him the note and hugged a black leather case to her chest. Alistair read the note out loud. "These are yours now, Chef. Love, Dad."

Marisa's trembling fingers swiped at fresh tears. "This is his knife kit. That's his handwriting."

Alistair sat beside her, held her against him, stroked her hair. "Wherever he is, I'm sure he's proud of you, sweetheart." He kissed her forehead. "And so am I," he whispered.

Chapter 41

Rain soaked September slogged into blustery October. Marisa blamed her mood swings on the weather and dismissed other nagging random physical discomforts as symptoms of stress.

"Are you OK, Chef?" Yara asked after her third call to the pass on a slow afternoon of service.

Marisa soaked a side towel in cold water and pressed it to her forehead, neck and lips. "I'm fine."

"You don't look fine." Concern narrowed her sous chef's normally wide and bright brown eyes. "You're as white as that side towel." Yara reached as tall as her five-foot-two height allowed and pulled down the last two orders. "I checked the dinner reservations list. It's pretty light. With this storm coming in, we'll probably have cancellations. Why don't you go home, take the night off? We can handle it."

Marisa sighed. "You know what? I'm going to take you up on that." She untied her apron. "Thanks. I owe you one."

"See you in the morning, Chef."

Marisa retrieved her raincoat, closed the door to her office, and gave her staff a quick thumbs up on the way out of the kitchen. She shivered, wrapped her coat around her, and ventured out into chilly gusts of wind and a steady cold drizzle.

The Land Rover's tires gripped wet pavement in a determined fight to remain on the road. Marisa fought the need to exceed the speed limit and her stomach's insistent urge to purge what little she'd kept down. She sighed in relief when the farmhouse, barn and paddock at the end of the gravel driveway came into view.

The open barn door signaled the approaching end to the work day for Alistair and the Murrays. Marisa parked the car near the paddock. Priya trotted from her designated daytime place on the back porch and nudged Marisa's hand.

"Hey, pretty girl." Marisa patted her pet between erect ears and closed the car door. The loud slam of the paddock's gate against the fence startled them both.

Swirling gusts swung the gate half closed and back again. The faulty metal latch gouged a deep notch in the fence on the next violent contact with wood. Priya circled Marisa as though trying to herd her toward the safety of sturdy walls and the warmth of the farm-house kitchen.

Marisa hesitated, glanced toward the barn, turned and bent into the wind, determined to close the swinging gate. Each step drained her waning energy. She braced her shoulder near the latch, dug in her heels, and pushed. Nature's gusty blast pushed back and won. Gale forces dragged her with the fence rail she'd grabbed and failed to hold onto. The sharp metal latch gouged a bloody trench through the skin above her left eye. She somersaulted to an unconscious heap in the spongy ground cover of mud, hay and grass.

Priya circled, whined, and pawed at her unmoving mistress. She licked at the seeping wound. A mournful howl of canine distress scattered in the relentless wind. She paced at first, tried again to revive Marisa, sniffed to confirm the direction and presence of humans, and ran to the barn toward their scent.

The border collies stopped eating and bared their teeth in warning. Priya dropped her tail, flattened her ears and dipped her head in acknowledged deference.

"What are you doing in here, girl?" Robbie stepped between the white dog and his workers. Priya whined and nipped at Robbie's pant leg. "Hey now!"

"What's the problem?" Alistair dropped a hay bale and came to Robbie's aid. Priya's barks escalated to hysteria. She ran to the barn door, then back to Alistair, barked and backed away toward the open door.

Robbie took off his cap and scratched his head. "I think she's trying to tell us something. What is it, girl?" Priya repeated her desperate pattern of moves in a plea for help. She ran out the barn door, turned back and howled.

"I'll go see what she wants." Alistair picked up the pace of his long strides to chase the running dog. Wind-driven rain pelted his face. Driveway gravel kept his work boots from sinking deeper into mud. He heard the slam of metal against wood, wiped coat sleeves over his eyes to clear his vision, squinted at where the dog led him and screamed in disbelieving terror.

"Ah God, no, No, NO!"

He ran the distance between them, knelt beside her, used his body as a shield to protect her from the raging storm. Her blood stained the heavy canvas of his tan work coat sickly red. He lifted her in his arms, fought external forces and internal panic to carry her to and through the barn door. "Robbie! Help me!" he pleaded and sank to his knees.

"Dear God!" Robbie's stomach lurched at the gash in Marisa's forehead and the blood staining Alistair's coat. "We've got to get her to hospital!" He ran into the wind as fast as his burly body and gait would allow. "Brenny!" he panted and pushed through the farmhouse kitchen door. "The missus is hurt!"

Brenda stopped stirring the stew and turned off the burner's flame. "At the restaurant?"

"No! She's in the barn! Bleeding pretty bad!"

Brenda grabbed a handful of clean dish towels from the laundry basket at her feet and her coat from the hook near the back door. She slammed the door closed behind them and ran ahead of her husband to where Alistair cradled Marisa in his arms. She muttered a silent prayer and pressed a towel to Marisa's forehead. "Robbie, you and McKenzie get her in the car."

"We're not calling an ambulance?" Alistair objected.

"It's a good forty minute drive to Belford," Robbie told him. "We can get her there in half the time."

Robbie linked arms with Alistair to form a sling under Marisa. Brenda kept pressure on the wound and used her free hand to open the Land Rover's rear door. Alistair scrambled in beside his prone wife.

"Cover her with this." Brenda tossed the rough cloth blanket to Alistair. "Keep her warm as best you can." Brenda closed them in and buckled herself into the passenger's seat. The dogs obeyed Robbie's whistled command and huddled with the white dog behind the protection of the barn door Robbie closed and latched.

Robbie wrestled with the steering wheel along the winding rural Highlands road and cursed the downpour through the full speed slap of the windshield wipers.

"Keep that cloth on her head," Brenda instructed Alistair. Marisa moaned under the pressure. Her eyes fluttered.

"She's coming around!" Alistair cried out. "Marisa! Sweetheart, talk to me."

His voice echoed in the shifting shadows behind her eyes. Pain flowed in waves from the base of her skull to a steady excruciating beat at the pressure point. "Alistair?" Her parched throat prevented anything above a whisper.

"I'm here, love."

"Keep her talking!" Brenda punched 999 into her cell phone to alert hospital staff of the nature of the emergency and their estimated time of arrival.

"Sweetheart, tell me what happened. Why were you home early?"

She tried to touch her forehead but was too weak to bend her elbow. "I got sick at work. Yara took over the kitchen. I should have called and told you I was coming home. I should have got you to shut that damn gate." The shifting shadows beckoned her back to dark relief.

Alistair felt her drifting away. "Marisa! Don't leave me now! Tell me what's on the menu tonight."

"That's good, McKenzie," Brenda coached.

Marisa winced and rode the crest of another painful wave. "Poached salmon and glass noodles in fish broth. Apple pie and honey lavender ice cream. I need to order mussels for tomorrow night's soup." The throbbing wound would not relent. She held her breath, relaxed and tumbled.

"Marisa!" Alistair rocked her in his arms, willing her back to him.

Robbie mopped condensation from the windshield with his coat sleeve. "We're almost there, boss!"

"Don't leave me, love!" Alistair's desperate plea forced the stifled sob from Brenda's throat. Robbie's lips moved in silent prayer. "Ah God, I'll do anything," Alistair moaned. "Please don't take her from me."

The Land Rover's tires screeched to a stop at the entrance marked for emergencies. Choreographed motions of medical team care swirled around them in urgent response. Medics on either side of the gurney lifted and escorted Marisa inside. The intake nurse spied the blood stains on Alistair's coat and asked if he was injured. He shook his head.

"No, that's all from his missus," Robbie answered for him.

Seconds slowed to agonizing minutes seated on a bench under tubes of bright lights in a long hallway. Staff in scrubs and lab coats scurried past and disappeared behind doors. A frantic man jogged behind a heavily pregnant woman in a wheelchair, her arms wrapped around her unborn child. A siren wail announced the arrival of another patient in need of life-saving action.

Alistair pushed damp curls from his forehead, rubbed at the ache that thrummed behind his eyes and groaned. "What's taking so long? Why haven't we heard anything?"

"McKenzie." Robbie settled his arm across the younger man's shoulders. "Do you remember what I said to you when you couldn't reach Marisa in Glasgow?"

Alistair nodded. "You told me I had to trust that everything would be alright."

"Aye. That's right. You were going to call the police. Then you found out she'd turned her phone off. Wouldn't you have felt foolish if you'd made that call?" His big calloused hand squeezed Alistair's shoulder. "These people know what they're doing. You've got to trust because sometimes that's all you've got."

"Mr. McKenzie?"

Alistair looked up. A young blonde woman with a clipboard and file folder tucked under her arm held out her hand. Baggy scrubs matched her pale green eyes. "I'm Doctor Broderson. I've been looking after your wife."

His hand closed over hers. "Is she?" His throat closed over the words.

"She has a concussion and seven sutures in her forehead. We're going to keep her overnight for observation." She smiled. "You should be able to take her home tomorrow."

Robbie beamed. "There, you see, McKenzie!"

"I did order an ultrasound to make sure the baby was fine as well," the doctor continued. "I'm happy to report no problem there at all."

Silence and stares greeted the unexpected glad tidings.

"Baby?" Alistair managed to ask.

The doctor nodded. "Blood work confirmed the pregnancy. Nine weeks along is a wee bit too soon to tell gender." Dr. Broderson opened the folder with Marisa's name on it. "Here's your baby's first picture."

The white image stood out in sharp contrast with the darkness of the womb. Tiny fingers scrunched into fists. Toes spread from little feet. A puffy chest and belly connected short arms and legs and a head that promised features not yet fully formed.

"How precious!" Brenda cooed.

Robbie slapped Alistair's back. "Congratulations, McKenzie!"

Alistair wrestled with a myriad of conflicted thoughts and emotions. Surprise, joy and confusion coursed through him. He stared at the confirming evidence of new life. His son or daughter. The child their love had made. "Why didn't she tell me?"

"She may not know," Brenda surmised, "what with all the troubles with her Mum and sister and this business with her job. Her mind may not have been on her monthlies."

"Mr. McKenzie?" The intake nurse reappeared. "Your wife is settled in her room. She's asking for you."

Robbie winked at him. "Go tell her. Dad."

Alistair followed the nurse down the hallway, around a corner and behind the first pulled drape on the left inside the open door on the right. Marisa's eyes were closed. Her bandaged head lay propped on pillows at the elevated head of the hospital bed. Crisp white sheets, a cotton blanket and a thin floral hospital gown covered her. Alistair sat in the straight back chair alongside her bed and slipped his hand into the palm of her hand not tethered to an IV drip.

"I feel so stupid," she muttered in a weak yet steady voice.

"How do you mean, love?" He scooted forward in the chair to hear her.

"I let that fecking gate get away from me and hit me in the head."

He grinned at her use of the common Scottish swear. "That's my fault. I should have fixed the latch." He gently squeezed her hand. "Sweetheart, is there something you want tell me?"

She half-opened her eyes. "Like what?"

"Like anything else I should know?"

"I don't think so."

His grin widened to a delighted full smile. "You really don't know. Do you?"

"Know what?"

Relief washed away the tension in tight muscles and relaxed edgy nerves. He laughed, leaned over her and kissed her lips.

"Honestly, you're making my headache worse," she grumbled.

"Marisa, my wife. Love of my life. You're pregnant."

Her now fully opened eyes searched his. She frowned at his obvious mirth. "If this is a joke, it's not very funny."

242

"No joke. We're having a baby. The doctor showed me the ultrasound. She says you're nine weeks along."

"Did you say nine weeks?"

"Aye."

A slow smile of realization spread across her face. "I should have known."

"Known what, love?"

"The day I moved here. On the way home. The bluff over the ocean. Remember?"

He'd chased her through swaying grass, covered her exposed breasts with his hands and entered her with nothing between them for the first time. "How could I forget?"

"My engagement ring felt icy hot on my finger. Just like when I hold the brooch. That's when we conceived this child." The sparkle of pure joy danced in her eyes. "Oh, my love! Don't you see? Our love is magic!"

Doctor Broderson sent her patient home the day after the accident with instructions for bed rest and a scheduled appointment with an obstetrician the following week. Brenda fussed over everything she could to comfort and care for Marisa, from plumping the bed pillows to baking a hearty pot pie. Priya wriggled in delight from nose to curved tail and whimpered at the kitchen threshold when denied access to Marisa in the upstairs bedroom.

Brenda stroked the white dog's thick fur. "I'll talk to him. Don't you fret." She sliced and lifted a generous portion of the pie onto a plate for Marisa and set the rest in the center of the table readied for mid-day meal.

Robbie's whistle preceded his heavy footsteps on the porch. "Take those filthy boots off and wash your hands!" she told her husband as she did every day at noon.

"Yes, ma'am!" She jumped at the sound of Alistair's unexpected reply from the hallway door. "Sorry. I came in the front door. I went upstairs to check on Marisa." He stepped to her side and kissed her cheek. "I don't think I thanked you properly for all you did yesterday."

Brenda blushed. "You can thank me by letting that poor dog go upstairs and be with your wife."

Alistair sighed and shook his head. "I don't know. I've never had an animal in the house."

"She's not just an animal. She's earned the right to be much more to Marisa and to you. I hate to think what might have happened if she hadn't come to you for help."

Alistair's gaze shifted from Brenda's scold to the hope in Priya's blue eyes. He glanced at the slice of pot pie on the plate. "Is that for Marisa?"

Brenda nodded. "Aye."

Alistair picked up the plate and a fork from the table. "C'mon dog."

Brenda smiled at the happy yelp and scamper of canine paws alongside Alistair down the hallway and up the flight of stairs.

Chapter 42

Autumn eventually surrendered to winter's grasp. Christmas came in a flurry of family eager to travel to the Highlands and celebrate the impending blessing of an April birth. Marisa remained at the helm of her restaurant kitchen through the eighth month of pregnancy when no chef coat would cover her and the doctor insisted she stop. Yara accepted the ceremonial whisk on Marisa's last day before maternity leave and promised to do her best until Chef's return.

Miranda made good on her promise to leave Iowa and travel to Scotland for the birth of her first grandchild. Robbie helped Alistair settle Marisa's mother into the guest room under conversion to a nursery.

Robbie grunted, shoved the guest bed against the wall, removed his cap and scratched his head. "You know, boss, this wee farmhouse is going to get crowded real quick. You may need to think about adding on a room or two. I know a couple of lads who are top notch builders."

Alistair laughed. "Why do I need to build on? Miranda is only staying for a month. We're not having twins." He stopped, blinked, and pursed his lips. "At least, I don't think so."

Robbie chuckled. "Even so, once a woman has a baby, she wants more. My Brenny wasn't going to stop until we had a daughter." He rolled his eyes. "Thank the good Lord our fourth bairn was a girl."

Marisa's water broke on the morning of her due date. The midwife arrived less than an hour later. Miranda soothed her daughter throughout the replay of her experience with at-home childbirth and assured Alistair all was proceeding as planned. He ignored his wife's threats to his manhood during labor as Robbie had advised and wept when handed his newborn son at two minutes to midnight.

Alistair sat on the bed beside Marisa, stroked her hair, and kissed her damp forehead as she cuddled their firstborn. "Ah, lassie, look what our love has given to us."

A tiny fist closed over his father's finger. Long lashes fluttered. Translucent lids opened, revealing brilliant blue. Miranda patted her son-in-law's shoulder. "He looks like his daddy," she said. "He'll break hearts one day with those beautiful eyes."

Alistair smoothed strands of auburn curls from his son's full head of fine hair. "I thought all babies are born with blue eyes."

"Marisa's had flecks of grey, like her father. This little one's eyes are clearly blue to stay."

The midwife asked a final question to complete her duties. "Do you have a name for this child?"

Marisa reached for and squeezed her husband's hand. "His father and I name him to honor his grandfathers." She kissed the roses in her son's chubby cheeks. "Welcome to the world, Darien Charles McKenzie."

Miranda glanced toward heaven and smiled through tears of joy.

The McGillivrays reserved every room in their Mallaig hotel and closed the restaurant to all but family and friends who'd travelled to celebrate the christening of six-week-old baby Darien.

Marisa's Aunt Sam came to cuddle her great nephew, unload packaged gifts friends and neighbors in Harmony had wrapped and tied with blue ribbons, and accompany her sister on the long flight back to Iowa. Well wishes and bundles for the newborn arrived from the McKenna clan living on two continents, from Jack and Beth in New Jersey, their son Nathan in Iowa and daughter Hannah and her family in Sydney. Rachel called to send love, congratulations and her regrets due to finals week at Texas A&M. She promised to visit Scotland over summer break.

Alistair's brothers Charlie and Drew lifted a dram in toast and added a blessing for good fortune, happiness and siblings for the youngest McKenzie lad. Grandmother Jeanne laughed, cried and marveled at the remarkable resemblance between her firstborn son and he and Marisa's handsome baby boy.

Revelers and long distance visitors dispersed a day later. Routine and relative calm quickly returned to the McKenzie home in the Highlands. Robbie and Brenda's teen-aged daughter Tammy hired on to help her mother care for the baby after Chef Marisa returned to work in her restaurant kitchen. Alistair, Robbie, and the border collies managed the growing flock and herd. Priya tended her sentinel post from the rug on the floor beside the crib, her tail curled over her nose in repose when the baby slept.

Alistair fingered the business card Robbie had given him at the end of the work day. He read the recommended contractor's name and phone number and tossed the card next to the untouched pile of mail on his desk. He grinned at the milky white envelope on top, reached for his letter opener, and ripped a clean line. "Congratulations, Dougie and Molly." He snickered at his son's full-throated wail from the nursery overhead. "Welcome to the joys of parenthood."

He dropped the birth announcement back on the pile and climbed the stairs to help Marisa coax their child to sleep.

"I'm in here, love."

Alistair stopped halfway down the hall at their open bedroom door. Marisa's smoky grey eyes beckoned to him from their bed. Her long black hair cascaded across pillows and duvet.

He answered her siren call, entranced as always by her beauty. She lifted the duvet, revealing all that he would ever desire.

He moaned, smiled a crooked grin, unbuttoned his shirt, and unzipped his jeans. "I'm calling that contractor first thing in the morning."

"A contractor?" she asked. "What for?"

"To add on more nurseries."

She laughed. "What is the Scottish word for children? Barns?" she mispronounced.

He laughed. "Bairns," he corrected her.

She took his hands in hers and pulled him to her. "We have so much love between us. I want to share that love with all the bairns we can."

He covered her body with his. "As do I, my love."

THE END

New Life in Love bonus!
Four sweet short stories …

Tales from Heartland

Kevin Carstens, the shy tractor salesman who wins the heart of the woman he loves.

Bradley Jenkins, the town mechanic chained to his past falls in love at first sight with a beautiful stranded traveler.

Jocelyn Ellis struggles to save the life of her 15-year-old son and begin again with a widowed drama teacher and his autistic daughter.

Adele Murphy rekindles feelings for a high school sweetheart that never was.

… and a steamy novella!
Love Unlikely

Rachel McKenna is guarded and not easy to get to know or get along with. Drew McKenzie is convinced that he has to have her and will stop at nothing to persuade her that they are meant to be together.

New Life in Love Trilogy
Reservations Heartland Belonging

Tales from Heartland
Four Short Stories and Love Unlikely novella

"I read the entire trilogy, becoming impatient waiting for the 2nd and then 3rd books to come out! The author doesn't follow a formula, but rather the characters' lives unfold in some pre-dictable and very unpredictable ways. I love LaBella's style and will continue to follow her works."

Teresa LaBella has been fascinated with fiction since she learned to read. Professional years invested learning the craft of writing and the art of storytelling as a journalist, grant writer and consultant pushed the author past the fiction writing stage of idea to 'I did' in the New Life in Love contemporary romance series.

Teresa and her Canadian filmmaker husband John LaBella are at home with their rescue husky fur babies Rosie and Ellis in rural Nova Scotia.

www.ingramcontent.com/pod-product-compliance
Lightning Source LLC
Chambersburg PA
CBHW060416180626
46817CB00007B/2597